ONE FOR SORROW

ONE FOR SORROW

CHRISTOPHER BARZAK

BANTAM BOOKS

ONE FOR SORROW
A Bantam Book / September 2007

Published by
Bantam Dell
A Division of Random House, Inc.
New York, New York

The chapter "Dead Boy Found" originally appeared in *Trampoline* (ed. Kelly Link, Small Beer Press) in slightly different form.

Book design by Steven Kennedy

Bantam Books and the rooster colophon are registered trademarks of Random House, Inc.

Library of Congress Cataloging-in-Publication Data

Barzak, Christopher.
One for sorrow / Christopher Barzak.
p. cm.
"A Bantam Book."
ISBN 978-0-553-38436-9 (trade pbk.)
1. Teenage boys—Fiction. 2. Self-perception—Fiction.
3. Domestic fiction. I. Title.

PS3602.A844O54 2007
813'.6—dc22
2007015871

Printed in the United States of America
Published simultaneously in Canada

www.bantamdell.com

10 9 8 7 6 5 4 3 2

BVG

For my mom and dad

And for Regina and Ron

The facts of death, like the facts of life, are required learning.
— THOMAS LYNCH

Anything dead coming back to life hurts.
— TONI MORRISON

Death is the chalk-line towards which all things race.
— ROBERT PINSKY

That's the whole trouble. You can't ever find a place that's nice and peaceful, because there isn't any. You may think *there is, but once you get there, when you're not looking, somebody'll sneak up and write, "Fuck you," right under your nose. Try it sometime. I think, even, if I ever die, and they stick me in a cemetery, and I have a tombstone and all, it'll say "Holden Caulfield" on it, and then what year I was born and what year I died, and then right under that it'll say "Fuck you." I'm positive, in fact.*
— J. D. SALINGER, *The Catcher in the Rye*

ONE FOR SORROW

ON YOUR MARKS . . .

GET SET . . .

Go!

In the Beginning

THERE WAS THIS KID I USED TO KNOW WHO ALWAYS sat in class with his head propped up in one hand. He always looked tired or mad about something, or sometimes just sad.

His name was Jamie Marks. But everyone called him Moony.

I'm not sure when or where or why he got the name, but I think it had something to do with him being fifteen years old and still a Boy Scout. It wasn't a good nickname or anything, and I sometimes wondered why, when guys in the eleventh and twelfth grades would sometimes shout in the hallways, "Hey, Moony! Moony Marks!" and laugh like idiots, Jamie didn't do anything to stop them. He'd just pretend like he hadn't heard. Sometimes there'd be a scuffle. One of the jerks wouldn't be satisfied with his silence, so they'd push him into a locker and say stupid shit like, "Speak when you're spoken to, Moony!" But he must have been a Boy Scout through and through, because he never did anything in retaliation. He just slid further down into the bottom of his existence, far away where they couldn't reach him.

When we were freshmen we started sitting next to each

other in our computer classes. I didn't understand computers much beyond playing games on them, so he sometimes helped me. I never asked. Whenever he saw me stuck, he'd just offer his services. His voice was soft, not hard like I'd imagined it would be after everything. He was a good kid, really. I wished I knew how to be friends with him.

That summer I turned fifteen, and when fall came around again, I was put on the varsity cross-country team. I was a good runner. I did a mile in under four and a half minutes. My mother always called me her bolt of lightning. Then she'd tell the same old story again, the one about how I was born after forty hours of labor and how my lungs were undersized and there was a murmur in my heart. "The doctors didn't think you'd live," she'd tell me, or whoever happened to be around to listen. "But you were a fighter, my brave boy. You always fought to live."

I suppose I should probably say a word or two about my mother and the rest of my family.

We live in a white, one-story ranch house on a back road of a small town in Ohio. My father built the house right after he and my mom married, with some help from a few of his friends. He was a construction worker, proud of the buildings his hands brought into existence. When we drove around the countryside or through one of the nearby towns, he'd point out places he'd had a hand in making. He'd say things like, "Did the closets in that one," and would point out my window, his finger drifting in front of my face. I never knew what he was trying to tell me, so I'd just nod, considering the fine black hairs that curled along his arm. It didn't matter how I responded. Most of the time, my dad never had much to say.

My mom, on the other hand, is a talker. She could

outtalk anyone, except maybe my grandma. Mostly she has a good bit of advice or a word of encouragement for everyone. Usually she's in good spirits, unless she and my dad have fought, and when that happens she can be black for days and everyone knows to stay away. I remember in one of her worst moments she stopped me on my way to my room and said, "Don't ever put your happiness in someone else's hands. They'll drop it. They'll drop it every time." She'll always come around eventually, her smile settled back on her face like an advertisement for happiness, but I never believed in that smile except when I was a little kid and didn't know better. I learned early that smiles lie.

Along with my parents is my brother, Andy. He's two years older than me. He was a senior when I started running on the varsity track team. Sometimes teachers called me his name and, after realizing their mistake, said, "I'm sorry. *Adam*. Adam McCormick. Let's hope you're a bit more serious than your brother."

I'm a bit more serious, I guess. All of my teachers realized that quickly. Soon after their initial worry over me being like Andy, who was known for being a part of what you might call the burnout heavy metal crowd that cut class and always smelled like pot, they started making remarks on essays I wrote or on tests I'd taken that said, "Very good, Adam! You're on the right track! Keep it up!"

This was before all of the bad stuff started to happen. Or I should say this was before all of the bad stuff started to happen that had been coming into existence for years beforehand. It's just that none of us recognized it at first. Or I should say it's just that none of us recognized it except my grandma, who died in the spring when I was still fourteen and a freshman in high school. She'd come to live with us after my grandpa died of lung cancer and she'd been with us for a year when I went into her bedroom one morning to wake her for breakfast and found her dead.

Before she died, we'd gotten used to my grandma predicting a great misfortune coming. She always had odd sayings and rhymes to explain anything out of the ordinary. My parents said she was from the old country and never gave up that kind of thinking, but I always thought what she said made a sort of sense. And what she'd been saying for several months before she died was, "God's finger is coming. I see it in the sky. If you people aren't careful, he's going to pick you out for sadness."

To me she said, "If you see his finger coming, boy, run. Run as fast and as far away as you can. Understand?"

I nodded and she smiled, the wrinkles in her face folding. She patted my hand. The skin on her palms was soft and felt like it would slide right off her bones. I sat on the edge of her bed and said, "I'll run as fast and as far away as possible. I'll keep my eyes out for God's finger. I promise."

But I guess I wasn't paying enough attention. Maybe it was because my grandma had been gone half a year by the time the signs began appearing, and by then I'd forgotten. "Bad things come in threes," she always said. But I understand now that sometimes you don't recognize a string of bad things until they're right on top of you.

The first bad thing that happened was that Jamie Marks disappeared in late September. One day he sat next to me in the computer lab, and the next day his seat was empty.

The last time I saw him, I was running home from cross-country practice. The Marks house was on my way back. It sat down from the road in a hollow, gray and ashy, surrounded by maple trees and weeping willows. Red and orange leaves littered the front yard, and a small gray shed stood off to the side of the house with the nose of a tractor poking out. Four dog coops sat in the yard, one at each corner: two under the trees near the road, two under the trees near the house, and the dogs themselves ran back and forth on chains tied to the trees, patrolling. A long drive curled down the hill from the road, back to the shed. The drive was really just tire ruts from where Mr. Marks drove an eighteen-wheeler up and down the lawn from the road. He drove for a company in Youngstown, an hour away from here, and hardly anyone in town ever saw him.

Whenever I ran past the Marks house, I couldn't help but look at the window over the kitchen to see if Jamie was there. I'd seen him there the previous spring on a day soon after my grandma died, watching me run. So after that, whenever I ran past, I'd look to see if he was watching.

The dogs barked angrily as I passed, but Jamie wasn't in the window on the last day I saw him. He came walking up the rutted drive in his Boy Scout uniform to get the mail instead. I waved and he waved back like we were friends, and I guess we were sort of, but not really. Not yet. I thought about asking why he was a Boy Scout, but I kept running instead. Then he suddenly shouted, "Looking good, McCormick!" and stopped me in my tracks.

I kept lifting my knees up, going nowhere, while he came to the mailbox, flipped the lid up and pulled out the usual stack of grocery store coupons and Have You Seen Me? postcards with pictures of missing kids on them. He looked up then and—I'll always remember this—said, "Nothing ever comes that's worth anything anyway."

He said this as if he'd been expecting better, as if something that would change the world as soon as he opened the envelope was supposed to arrive that day. I didn't say anything. I was satisfied watching him sort mail. Looking at his uniform and the round glasses sliding down his nose, I wondered if maybe the glasses didn't have something to do with his nickname. I never did ask, though. Sometimes you regret things like that. Sometimes you regret not asking simple questions.

The uniform looked strange on him, but maybe only because I'd never joined the Boy Scouts. I tried picturing him wearing my clothes instead, but when I opened my mouth I said, "That's a cool uniform."

He was as surprised by the compliment as I was, but he managed to say thanks, even though it was obvious he didn't believe me.

He asked what I thought about the program we learned in computer lab that day and I said, "It's okay, but I wouldn't have understood without your help." He shrugged like it was just this thing he did without any trouble and I suddenly found myself asking if he was going to the Homecoming dance in October.

"No way," he said. "That's for cheerleaders and jocks." As soon as he said it, he looked down at his feet to hide his embarrassment, but I could still see him grinning. "Sorry," he said. "I didn't mean you."

I shrugged like he'd shrugged off my compliment and told him not to include me with the rest of them. "I run," I said. "But I run for myself."

"I can respect that," said Jamie. Then he looked up and down the road as if he expected someone, and the last thing he said before he took the mail in was "I have to go to a Boy Scout meeting in a while, but give me a call sometime."

The next day his seat was empty, and two days later the

whole town started looking for him. I joined in on the search, hoping I'd find him somewhere safe and sound, just hiding maybe, for whatever reason, but it was Gracie Highsmith, a girl in my class, who found his body two weeks later.

It was on that day, the day Gracie Highsmith found Jamie's body, that God's finger descended on my family. It was October. The reaping season, my grandma called it. For days the sky was black with storms, but no rain had fallen.

When I look back now, I don't know why I hadn't seen it coming. I saw things the same way as my grandma, and having that should have been enough to know what was coming. I could count crows, I knew the difference between dreaming and seeing the future, and I always took a different route than the one I'd been on if for some reason I had to turn around and go home. I knew that when a sparrow sang, a spirit was coming down from heaven. And I knew that ghosts always surround us, whether we're able to see them or not. "Don't talk to them too much," my grandma always warned me. "They can be nice, but in the end they're always jealous creatures."

So when all of this started—when my family was picked for sadness—I was sitting in my bedroom, playing a video game called *Nevermorrow*. I played a character who was a knight with a sword and shield. He was trapped in the nine layers of hell and had to kill all sorts of undead monsters to find his way out to the land of the living. While I hacked skeletons to pieces, my parents were out in the living room, yelling at each other.

It didn't really mean anything to me then—my parents had been fighting about one thing or another since I could remember. Usually it was about money or who did more or who was smarter. Sometimes my dad would lose his job and when that happened my mom and he would scream their fool heads off. His excuse was that construction work was seasonal, but there were other men my mother could name without pausing who never got laid off.

My dad was a drinking man, and sometimes my mom was a drinker too. Usually my dad drank when he lost work, then he and my mom would fight, and then *she'd* start drinking and they'd fight even worse. They'd eventually give up after a while, and things would return to normal, or as close to normal as we could get. My brother and I never got into the arguments. We figured it was grown-up stuff and that it'd all be fine in the end. But that day, my father told my mother she was a waste. And that's when the second bad thing began to come into being.

My dad said, "You are such a waste, Linda."

And my mom said, "Oh yeah? You think so? Well, we'll just see about that."

Then she got into her car and pulled out of our driveway, throwing gravel in every direction as she pushed down on the gas. She was going to Abel's, or so she said, where she would have a beer and find herself a real man.

When I look back on it now, I can see the holes they were making. I can see how, with each nasty thing they said, they were attracting misfortune, making doorways for darkness to come into our lives. So when the second bad thing arrived, it shouldn't have been a surprise, but at the time I didn't understand how it could have happened.

When my mother was halfway to Abel's, she got in a head-on collision with a drunk woman named Lucy, who was on her way home from Abel's just then. They were both driving around that blind curve on Highway 88, Lucy swerving a little, my mother smoking her cigarette, not even caring where the ashes fell. When they leaned their cars into the curve, Lucy crossed into my mother's lane and—*bam!*—just like that, they collided. My mother's car rolled three times into the ditch and Lucy's car careened into a guardrail. It was Lucy who called the ambulance on her cellular phone, saying over and over, "My God, I think I've killed Linda McCormick! Oh my God, I've killed that poor girl!"

At that same moment, Gracie Highsmith was becoming famous. While my mother and Lucy Hall were on their way to crashing into one another, Gracie was walking the old defunct railroad tracks that ran through town, through the woods and through the covered bridge that spanned Sugar Creek. She was a rock collector and had gone out that day after school to find something special: some quartz or a strangely shaped piece of coal or nickel, an arrowhead, or one of the blue glass insulators that sometimes fell off power lines. What she found when she lifted a rock from the rail bed, though, was a blue eye staring back at her.

At that very moment, two screams filled the air.

One was the scream of Gracie Highsmith. Her scream erupted somewhere deep in her chest in a place she never knew existed. The scream grew big before it could make its way out. It spread through her heart and lungs until it filled up her throat and poured from her mouth like a fountain of horror.

The second scream was my mother's. While the car spun in the air, while it turned over and over, throwing her unbelted body against the steering wheel, cracking her head against the window, her scream pierced the evening quiet along with Gracie's, shattering the windshield, spattering it

with blood. Her scream filled the air until the car came to a
rest on the passenger side. Then everything went dark and
the only thing she heard was a ticking noise and the sound
of footsteps coming toward her. The last thing she saw was
Lucy Hall walking around outside the wreckage, peering
through the windshield between cupped hands, shouting,
"I'm so sorry! My God, please forgive me!"

And beneath the layers of dirt and gravel, beneath the
rusty rails and rotten ties, Jamie Marks slipped out of his
body. He was found now. And having been found, he could
begin to live again.

DEAD BOY FOUND

AN EYE. A BLUE EYE SURROUNDED BY GRAVEL. THE lid opening slowly, staring. Gracie Highsmith's mouth dropping open. For a moment, nothing comes out of her. She simply gasps and stares at the dead boy's eye. It's when she sees it flicker with blue sparks that she begins her screaming.

I could imagine Gracie Highsmith—a fifteen-year-old loner who collected rocks and got A's in all of her classes, a girl who walked the hallways of our school listening to music on her iPod—finding that dead body, seeing Jamie's ghost slip out of its sack of flesh for the first time, taking on a new way of being, solid as the flesh he'd left behind, visible only to those who knew how to see him. I could imagine her scream, the life it took on, the way it rang and rang over the town for days, for weeks afterward. But what I couldn't imagine, even when confronted with it, was my mother's new way of being.

My mother lay in a hospital bed with tubes coming out of her nose. One of her eyes had swelled shut and was already black and shining. The other fluttered nervously while she slept. She breathed with her mouth open, a wheezing noise like snoring, and when I stood over her and looked inside her mouth, I could see blood had stained her teeth a pinkish color and that several were missing: one in the front and one of her canines. *She's not going to be able to eat,* I thought, *is she?*

We stood around watching while she breathed really loud and the heart monitor next to her bleeped out the proof that she was still alive. When she woke several hours later, blinking her good eye, she saw me first and said, "Baby, come here and give me a hug."

I wasn't a baby, but I didn't correct her. I figured she'd been through enough. A doctor came in a minute later to ask how she felt, and my mother told him she couldn't feel her legs. He said that might be a problem, the not feeling, but that it would work itself out over time. "How much time?" my dad asked from where he stood in a corner, looking at the floor. When we looked back at him, he didn't look up.

"No worries, mate," the doctor said, like he thought he was Australian or something. "It's just swelling around the spinal cord, Mr. McCormick. It'll be fine after a few weeks."

As soon as the doctor left, my father looked up and started talking. "We all have to pull together now," he said. "We'll get through this. Don't worry." He put his arms around me and Andy as if this was our regular pose and we both looked up at him, wondering what he wanted. It was one of his tricks, being friendly, to get us to do things for him. This time his fast-talking and family feeling added up to mean we'd bring my mother home together and put her in my bed so she could rest properly, and that I'd bunk with Andy. And for the next three weeks, my father would keep saying things like, "Don't you worry, honey. It's time the men took over," as he ripped up carpeting and varnished the floors so the house would be wheelchair friendly. I did the dishes and Andy washed clothes. My father brought home pizza or fried chicken for dinner and we started eating in the living room, watching TV, instead of at the dining room table.

My mother rested in my bed with the legs she couldn't feel any longer. They stretched out under her blanket like they were extra people sleeping with her. I brought soup in on a tray for her, and sometimes I'd rub her feet. "Now?" I'd ask, hopeful. "Can you feel them now?" But she'd just shake her head and smile weakly.

"I'm sorry, honey," she'd say. "I'm so sorry."

I didn't know how to feel about anything, but I decided right away I wouldn't be angry. That's how my father acted whenever something didn't go his way. I told myself that stupid stuff like this just happens. It happens all the time. One day you're an average fifteen-year-old with parents who constantly argue and a brother who takes out his problems on you because he thinks it's cool to belittle you in public and then suddenly something happens to make things worse. Believe me, morbidity is not my specialty. Sometimes bad things just happen all at once.

My grandma had said bad things came in threes, and if there was any truth to that, I figured now was the time to start counting. Because two bad things had happened in less than a month: my mother had been paralyzed and Jamie Marks had been found murdered. If my grandma was still alive, she'd have been trying to guess what would happen next.

I mentioned this to my mother while I spooned soup up to her trembling lips one evening. A few weeks had passed since she'd come home and she could feed herself all right, but she seemed to like the attention. "Bad things come in threes," I told her. "Remember Grandma always said that?"

"Your grandma was uneducated," said my mother.

"What's that supposed to mean?" I asked.

"It means she didn't even get past the eighth grade, Adam."

"I knew that already," I said, holding the spoon near her mouth.

"Well, I'm just reminding you."

"Okay," I said, and she took another spoonful of chicken broth. I decided I should keep my thoughts to myself after that.

At school, though, everyone was talking. "Did you hear about Jamie Marks?" they all said. "Did you hear about Gracie Highsmith?"

I pretended like I knew nothing. I wanted to hear what everyone else would say. Rumors filled the air. Our school being so small made that easy. Seventh through twelfth grade all crammed into the same building, elbow to elbow, breathing each other's breath.

"Did you hear about it?" a girl in first period asked. She looked around the room, apparently asking all of us. "Gracie Highsmith saw one of his fingers poking out of the gravel," she said, "like a zombie trying to crawl out of its grave."

"So she pushed away a few stones and there it was," said a kid getting dressed next to me in the locker room during second period. He stepped into his sweatpants and said, "His eye was still open, and it stared right up at her."

"So she screamed and threw the gravel back at his eye and ran home," said a kid who washed his hands beside me in the restroom between classes. "And sure enough, when the police finally got there, they found the railroad ties loose and the bolts broken off."

"So they removed the ties," said Marty Chapman during lunch, mimicking the removal of the ties with his French fries. "Then they dug up the gravel and found the body."

"It was so disgusting," said the boy who took Jamie's seat beside me in the computer lab. "I guess one of the cops had to walk away and puke."

I sat through Algebra and Biology and History, thinking about cops puking, thinking about Jamie's body. I couldn't stop thinking about those two things. I sort of liked the idea of cops puking out their guts, holding their stomachs, shocked into remembering they were human like the rest of us. But I wasn't so sure what I thought about Jamie's body, rotting beneath railroad ties.

At the start of each class, the teachers all had the same spiel for us, as if they'd gotten together to make sure they had the same story: "I understand if any of you are disturbed or anxious, so we'll spend this period getting out all of those feelings, but if you're not comfortable talking, the guidance counselor can recommend a good psychologist to your parents."

The only teacher who left us alone was Mrs. Motes. She taught English. We were reading early American writers of short stories that autumn and, even though they'd found Jamie's body, she kept teaching without making a fuss. Elizabeth Moore, who always had some smart-ass thing to say in class, asked, "Aren't we going to talk about what's happened, Mrs. Motes?" and Mrs. Motes said we could do that, sure, but weren't we talking about it all the time already?

Mrs. Motes scanned the room as if she were looking for someone who was a big talker about this tragedy. Her gaze finally came to rest on me. I wanted to tell her she had got the wrong kid. I was just a listener. But she kept staring at me and finally said, "I think this is all terrible, I do. And if someone wants to talk about how terrible this all is, I think they should do that. I think they should stay after class and talk to me if they like. But otherwise, I think we should talk some more about Nathaniel Hawthorne."

I sat at my desk with my chin propped in my hand, imagining Jamie under those rails staring at the undersides of trains as they rumbled over him. Those tracks hadn't been used since the steel mills in Youngstown closed back in the eighties, but I imagined trains riding them anyway. Jamie inhaled each time a glimpse of sky appeared between boxcars and exhaled when they covered him over. When no trains passed over him, when no metal screamed on the rails, he could finally sleep. But in his dreams he'd see the trains again, blue sparks flying off the iron railing. A ceiling of trains covered him. He almost suffocated, there were so many.

A few days after the cops were done with the crime scene, my brother said, as he drove us home from school, "We're going to the place, a bunch of us. Do you want to come?" He didn't have to explain. I knew immediately where he was going. But Andy's friends were seniors and liked to harass me, so I shook my head and said no. I told him I had to collect money from a friend who owed me. He probably knew I was lying, but he dropped me off at home anyway.

After he drove away, I let the front window curtain fall away from my hand and started going through my school yearbook, flipping pages until I found Jamie smiling in his square on page fifty-two. I cut his photo out with my father's X-acto knife and stared at it for a while, trying to understand him through the shape of his face, through his round glasses. Cut away from the yearbook, though, enough light shined through the paper to make the face on the other side blur with Jamie's and, when I turned the square over, I found my own face on the other side.

I wasn't smiling. I never really was a smiler. I remember the photographer that day couldn't make me. He tried and tried, but finally gave up. So this was the face that looked back at me now, black and white, hard as a rock, on the opposite side of the missing boy's picture.

I swallowed and swallowed. "I didn't like that picture of me anyway," I whispered. I had baby fat when it was taken, and looked more like a little kid. Still I flipped the photo over and over like a coin, wondering, if it had been me, would I have escaped? I decided it must have been too difficult to get away from them—I couldn't help thinking there had to be more than one murderer—and probably I would have died just the same.

I took the picture outside and buried it in my mother's garden, between the rows of sticks that had, just weeks before, marked off the sections of vegetables, keeping carrots carrots and radishes radishes. I patted the dirt softly, inhaled its crisp dirt smell, and whispered, "Don't you worry. Everything will be all right."

When my mother got out of bed and started using her wheelchair, she was hopeful. She said one day soon she'd walk again. But when her legs didn't start getting better and the doctors said she'd need physical therapy, she just shook her head. "The damage has been done," she said, looking up at my father, who looked away. She told us it was no big deal, she enjoyed not always having to be on her feet anyway. Even so, I started to sometimes find her wheeled into dark corners, her head in her hands, saying, "No, no, no." Sobbing.

Lucy Hall, the woman who paralyzed her, kept calling our house and asking for forgiveness but my mom told us to say she wasn't home. "Tell her I'm out contacting lawyers this very moment," she told us. "Tell her they're going to have her so broke within seconds, they'll make her pay real good."

So I'd tell Lucy, "She isn't home, lady."

And Lucy would say, "My God, tell that poor woman I'm sorry. Ask her to please forgive me. Tell her I'll do whatever she wants."

After each call I told my mother Lucy said she was sorry, and eventually my mother decided to hear the woman out. Their conversation sounded like when my mom talks to her sister, my aunt Beth, who lives in California near the ocean, a place I could hardly imagine, a place I'd never been. My mother kept shouting, "No way! You too?! I can't believe it! Can you believe it?! Oh, Lucy, this is too much." She smiled and laughed like a real person for the first time in weeks. I didn't like her talking to Lucy Hall, who had taken everything away from her, but I liked hearing her laugh again.

Two hours later, Lucy pulled into our driveway, blaring her horn over and over, as if once wasn't enough. My mother wheeled herself outside, down the ramp my father had made for her, still smiling and laughing, even though she and Lucy hadn't exchanged a word in person yet.

Lucy was like her horn-blowing: way too much. She was tall and wore red lipstick, and her hair was permed real tight. She wore huge plastic bracelets, hoop earrings and stretchy hot pink pants. She bent down to hug my mother right away, then helped her into the car. They drove off together still laughing, and when they came home several hours later, I could smell smoke and whiskey on their breath.

"What's most remarkable," my mother slurred, "is that I was on my way to the bar sober, and Lucy was driving home drunk." She used her fingers to illustrate the directions their cars had taken, as if I didn't know how the accident happened. They'd both had arguments with their husbands that day, she said. And they'd both gone out to make their husbands jealous. Learning all this, my mother and Lucy felt destiny had brought them together. "A virtual Big Bang," said my mother.

Lucy said, "A collision of souls."

The only thing to regret was that their meeting had been so painful. "But great things are born out of pain," my mother said, nodding in a knowing way as she refilled her glass. She patted the hand Lucy had placed on her wheel. "If I had to have an accident with someone," she said, "I'm glad that someone was Lucy."

I thought about the picture of Jamie and me that I'd

buried. I'd been walking around bumping into things ever since. Walls, lockers, people. It didn't matter what, I walked into it. Even though we were in the same class, I hadn't known him as well as I wanted, and when I tried asking people about him, all they'd do was stare as if I'd stepped out of a spaceship. I stared at my mother and Lucy now and wondered, if he had lived would we have found a way to be friends? Would we be like them? Maybe he'd be a bit messed up in the head from everything, but still here, still breathing. Still possible.

After my brother and his friends went back to where Jamie had been hidden, everyone thought they were crazy but somehow brave. Suddenly they were popular, which was a huge crossover for a bunch of burnouts. Girls asked Andy to take them there, to be their protector, and he'd pick out the pretty ones who wore makeup and tight little skirts. "You should go, Adam," he said one day after we came home from school. "You could appreciate it."

"It's too much of a spectacle," I said, not wanting to talk about Jamie with him. But all of a sudden he grabbed the back of my shirt as I walked past and jerked me to a stop.

When I looked up, he stared at me as if I'd turned into an ant. Something so tiny you had to squint to see it. "You don't have a fucking clue what you're talking about, you little ass," he said. "People are just curious." He asked if I was implying that going to the place was sick and twisted. "Is that what you mean?" he said. "Cause if that's what you're implying, Adam, you are dead wrong."

"No," I said. "That's not what I'm implying. I'm not implying anything at all."

I didn't want to hear his story. There were too many stories filling my head as it was. At any moment he could burst into the monologue of detail he'd been rehearsing since seeing the place where they'd hidden Jamie, so I turned to go to my room and, as I turned the corner, Andy said, "Hey! I didn't get to tell you what it was like!"

I sat at my computer and stared at my reflection in the blank screen. I was starting to think no one really knew Jamie Marks. But even so, it had taken only a few weeks for people to start claiming they'd seen him. He waited at the railroad crossing on Sodom-Hutchings Road, pointing down the tracks toward where he'd been hidden. He walked in tight worried circles outside Gracie Highsmith's house with his hands clasped behind his back and his head hanging low and serious. In these stories he was always transparent. Things passed through him. Rain was one example. Another was leaves falling off trees, drifting through his body. Kids in school said, "I saw him!" the same eager way they did when they went to Hatchet Man Road in Bristol to see the ghost of the killer from the seventies, a man who lived in the woods around the road, who actually never used hatchets, but a hunting knife. Gracie Highsmith hadn't returned to school since she found him, so no one could verify the story of Jamie standing under the maple tree outside her house. The story still grew, though, without her approval, which somehow seemed wrong. I thought if Jamie's ghost was outside her house, no one should tell that story but Gracie. It was hers, and anyone else who told it was a thief.

The stories didn't matter, I told myself. Most of those

kids didn't know how to see themselves yet, let alone a
ghost. After listening to them every day for a week, though,
I decided it was time to see for myself.

Instead of going to cross-country practice the next day,
I went to the cemetery. I'd wanted to go to the funeral, to
stand in back where no one would notice, but the newspaper had said it was for family only. If I was angry about anything, it was that. How could they just shut everyone out?
The whole town had helped look for him, had taken food
over to Jamie's mother during the time he was missing. And
then no one but family was allowed to be at the funeral? It
was just a little bit selfish, I thought.

The cemetery looked desolate at the end of October, as
if it were going to be filmed for a Halloween movie.
Headstones leaned toward one another. Moss greened over
the walls of family mausoleums. I walked down the drive,
gravel crunching beneath my shoes, and looked from side
to side at the stone angels and carved pillars and plain white
slabs that marked the lots. I knew a lot of the names, or had
heard of them. Whether they're relatives or friends, friends
of relatives, or ancestral family enemies, when you live in a
town where everyone fits into three churches, you know
everyone. Even the dead.

I searched the headstones until I found his. The grave
was still freshly turned earth. No grass had had time to grow
yet. But people had left trinkets, tokens and reminders,
pieces of themselves. A handprint. A piece of rose-colored
glass. Two cigarettes standing up like fence posts. A baby
rattle. And at the bottom edge of the grave, someone had
even scrawled their name.

I bent down and, tracing the curve of the letters with my fingertip, whispered the name. And it was as if reading it aloud had been some kind of spell, because suddenly I heard footsteps, and there she was, Gracie Highsmith, walking the path toward me.

I was shocked. Besides his family, I'd thought I'd be the only one to come. But here she was, this girl who'd drawn her name in the dirt with her finger. Her letters looked soft and gentle; they curled into each other with little flourishes for decoration. Did she think it mattered if she spelled her name pretty?

"What are you doing here?"

Gracie blinked as if she'd never seen me in her life. I could tell she wanted to ask who the hell I was to question her, but instead she said, "I'm visiting. What are *you* doing here?"

The wind picked up and blew hair across her face. She tucked it back behind her ears real neatly. She wore black Doc Martens and green Army pants, a white T-shirt with a black vest speckled with buttons of music groups. She looked kind of punk, but I could never tell what her style was. She didn't dress like other girls. Not like the cheerleaders with long hair and made-up faces, and not like the smart girls in sweaters and pleated pants. She once shaved her head in junior high and everyone said she was a witch. I sort of liked her head like that, the skin shining, but couldn't make myself tell her. And after a while it was like with Jamie. The moment passed, her hair grew in, and I was late as usual.

I nudged the ground with my shoe, not knowing how to answer. The way she said *you* made me think she didn't like me. But I had never talked to her—I didn't talk in general—so how could she not like me? She got tired of

waiting for my answer, though, and turned to look at
Jamie's grave.

"Visiting," I said, after she turned. I was annoyed I
couldn't come up with anything but the same answer she'd
given, and crossed my arms over my chest.

Gracie didn't look back. She kept her eyes on Jamie's
grave. I started to think maybe she was going to steal it. The
headstone, that is. I mean, the girl was a known rock collector and a headstone would complete any collection. I wondered if I should call the police and tell them. I imagined
them taking her out in cuffs, making her duck her head as
they tucked her into the back of the car. I imagined her staring angrily at me through the back window as they drove
away. After a while I made myself stop daydreaming and
when I did, I found her on her knees sobbing.

I didn't know how long she'd been like that, but she was
going full force. I mean, the girl didn't care if anyone was
around. She cried like a baby, like a total mess. I thought
maybe I should say something, but I didn't know what. So I
just shouted, "Hey! Don't do that!"

That didn't work, though. She kept on crying. She even
growled a little and beat her fist in the dirt.

"Hey!" I said again. "Didn't you hear me? I said, 'Don't
do that!'"

But she still didn't listen.

So I started to dance.

I kicked my heels in the air and did a two-step. I
hummed a tune to keep time. I clasped my hands behind
my back and did a jig my grandfather once showed me, and
when my idiocy failed to distract her, I started to sing the
"Hokey Pokey."

I belted it out and kept on dancing. I sung each line like

it was poetry. "You put your left foot in/You take your left foot out/You put your left foot in/And you shake it all about/You do the Hokey Pokey and you turn yourself around/That's what it's all about! Yeehaw!"

As I sang and danced, I moved toward a freshly dug grave, just a few plots down from Jamie's. The headstone was already up, but there hadn't been a funeral yet. The grave was waiting for Lola Peterson, but instead, as I shouted out the next verse, I stumbled in.

I fell in the grave singing, "You put your whole self in!" and about choked on my own tongue when I landed. Even though it was still light out, it was dark in the grave, and muddy. My shoes sank and when I tried to pull them out, they made sucking noises. The air was stiff and leafy. A worm wriggled half in and half out of the muddy wall in front of me. When I tried climbing out and couldn't get a grip, I started to worry I'd be stuck in Lola Peterson's grave all night, but finally Gracie's head appeared over the lip.

"Are you okay?" she asked.

Her hair fell down toward me like coils of rope.

She found a ladder leaning against the cemetery tool-shed and lowered it down for me. As I climbed toward her she called me a fool, but she laughed. Her eyes were red from crying, her cheeks wind-chapped. When I thanked her for helping, she said, "No problem. I liked your little dance."

After that we sat down on the path between the graves and she talked about finding Jamie. It was mostly what I'd heard, but the words coming from her mouth felt different. "I'm not interested in it any longer," she said. "It's boring, really. It's the most banal thing in the world."

"What's banal?" I asked. I knew, but I wanted to hear her talk.

"You don't know what banal means?" She laughed. "It was a vocabulary word like four weeks ago, idiot."

"How do you remember that kind of stuff?"

"It was on the last vocabulary test I studied for," she said. "The one right before I found him." She looked down and slipped her hands in her pockets. When she looked back up, she said, "Do you know where I can find any quartz around here?"

"So you really do collect rocks?" I said, and she bobbed her head, smiling.

"Rocks are the best things in the world. No one can do anything to them. You could come over to my place tomorrow and see them. Come around five. My parents will be at marriage counseling."

"Sure," I said. "That'd be great."

Gracie dipped her head and looked at me through brown bangs before she left. A moment later she turned around and waved, her hand held high in the air above her. I waved back as if we were friends, even though we weren't. Not yet.

I waited for her to leave. I waited until I heard the squeal and clang of the wrought-iron front gates. Then I knelt down beside Jamie's grave and wiped her name out of the dirt. In place of it, I wrote my own, etching into the dirt deeply. But I wrote my name different. My letters were tall and slanted. My letters were straight and fierce.

I came home and found I'd missed dinner. My mom was asleep, back in her and my dad's bedroom again, Andy was in the back field smoking a joint, and my dad was in the living room watching the Weather Channel. He could watch the weather report for hours, listening to the Muzak play, watching the words that told us what tomorrow would bring scroll across the screen forever. He'd watch it every night for a couple of hours before Andy and I started groaning. He'd eventually change the channel, but would never acknowledge our groaning was the reason.

After I sat down with a plate of meat loaf, he changed the channel without me asking, and a news brief about the search for Jamie's murderers came on. I wondered why the anchorman called them "Jamie Marks's murderers," the same way you might say Jamie's dogs, or Jamie's Boy Scout honors, as if he'd owned or earned them, so I asked my dad what he thought.

He didn't answer my question though. Instead he started muttering about what he'd do with the killers if it had been his boy. His face was red and splotchy, his plaid shirt unbuttoned, falling away to reveal a patch of hairy chest.

I set the fork down on my plate.

"What would you do?" I asked. "What would you do if it had been me?"

My dad looked at me and said, "I'd tie a rope around those bastards' armpits and lower them inch by inch into a vat of piranhas. Slowly! That's important. To let the little suckers have at their flesh."

He looked back at the TV.

I thought this was a good start.

"But what if the police got them first?" I said, hoping for something more realistic. "What would you do then?"

My dad looked at me again and said, "I'd smuggle a gun into the courtroom, and when they had those bastards on the stand, I'd jump out of my seat and shoot their god-damned heads off." He jumped out of his recliner and made his hands into a gun, pointing it at an invisible person in the room. He pulled the trigger once, twice, a third time. *Bam! Bam! Bam!* They were all dead, all the evildoers. Just like that.

I nodded. I felt loved, like I was my dad's favorite. I kept on making up different situations, asking, "What if?" over and over. What if the judge said they were innocent and you saw them eating at a restaurant afterward? What would you do then? What if they holed up in an abandoned ware-house with lots of firearms and hostages? What then? It didn't matter what I threw at him; each time he killed them dead. I wanted to buy him a hat with the words Best Dad in the World! printed on it. I couldn't remember the last time we'd talked. We were really close right then, for the first time in a long time, and I went to sleep that night still thinking of scenarios in which he could exact his revenge.

According to my dad, Gracie Highsmith's house was a split-level beauty. Whenever we drove past, he'd reminisce about the work his crew had done in the place. The house was white like ours, only with black shutters on the win-dows, and white wooden pillars holding up the porch roof. They had a circular drive too, black-topped with a maple tree in the center. "Very well to do, the Highsmiths," my mother always said when she was in a good mood. If she was feeling black, though, she'd just say they were rich snobs.

Their house was nestled in a bend of the railroad tracks where Gracie had found Jamie. She'd been out walking the tracks looking for odd pieces of coal or nickel when she found him. She hadn't seen his finger poking out of the gravel like everyone said. She thought she saw a glimmer, something shiny, so she'd bent down to sort through the rocks and when she lifted one away his blue eye was looking back at her. All of this she told me in her bedroom on the second floor of her house the next day. The room was painted bright yellow and lined with shelves of rocks, like a room in a museum. Only the bed and the white dresser next to it made the bedroom feel like a bedroom.

Gracie held out a fist-sized rock that was brown with black specks embedded in it. The brown parts felt like sandpaper, but the black specks were smooth as glass. "I found it in the streambed at the bottom of Marrow's Ravine last summer," she said. "It's one of my best discoveries."

"It's something special all right," I said, and she beamed like someone's mother.

"That's nothing," she said. "Wait till you see the rest."

She showed me a chunk of clear quartz and a piece of hardened blue clay; a broken-open geode filled with pyramids of pink crystal; a seashell that she found mysteriously in the woods behind her house, nowhere near water; a flat rock with a skeletal fish fossil imprinted on it; and a piece of rose quartz in the shape of a heart, which she said was her favorite. I hadn't realized how beautiful rocks could be. She made me want to collect them too. But they were Gracie's territory. I'd have to find something of my own, I figured.

We sat on her bed and listened to music by some group from Cleveland that I'd never heard of, but who Gracie obviously loved because she set the CD player to replay the same song over and over. It sounded real punk. They sang about growing up angry and how they would take over the world and make people pay for being stupid idiots, how they didn't need anyone or anything but themselves. Gracie nodded and gritted her teeth as she listened. Her head bobbed a few inches away from mine, her brown hair splayed out on the pillow.

I liked being alone in the house with her, listening to music and looking at rocks. I felt eccentric and mature. I told Gracie this and she nodded. "They think we're children," she said. "They don't know a goddamn thing, do they?"

Then we talked about growing old, imagining ourselves in college, in midlife careers, as parents then grandparents, then we were so old we couldn't walk without walkers. Pretty soon we were so old we both clutched our chests like we were having heart attacks and choked on our own laughter. We stared at each other, not saying anything, then looked away, as if we'd turn to stone if we looked any longer.

"What sort of funeral will you have?" Gracie asked a moment later.

"I don't know," I said. I'd never thought about funerals much. "Aren't they all the same?"

"Funerals are all different," said Gracie. "Mexican cemeteries have all these bright, colorful decorations for their dead; they're not all serious like ours are. On the Day of the Dead, families go to the cemeteries and picnic on the graves of loved ones."

"Where did you learn that?"

"Social Studies. Last year."

"I bet Mexicans never would have had a private funeral," I said. Too bad Jamie wasn't Mexican, I thought.

"I see graves all the time now," Gracie told me. She lay

on her back and stared at the ceiling. I watched as her chest rose and fell with her breath. "They're everywhere," she said, "ever since..."

She stopped to release a long sigh, as if she'd just made a huge confession. I worried she'd expect something in return, a confession of my own, so I murmured a little supportive noise and hoped that would be enough.

"They're everywhere," she repeated. "The town cemetery, the Wilkinson family plot, that old place out by the ravine where Fuck You Frances is buried. And now the railroad tracks. I mean, where does it end?"

I said, "Beds are like graves too," and she turned to me with this puzzled look. I suddenly wanted to kiss her. Instead I said, "No, really," and told her about the time my grandma came to live with us after my grandfather died. How one morning my mother sent me to wake her for breakfast—I remember because I smelled bacon frying when I got up—so I went into my grandma's room to wake her up. She didn't, though, so I repeated myself. But she still didn't wake up. Finally I shook her shoulders a little, and her head lolled on her neck. I grabbed one of her hands, hoping, but it was cold to the touch.

"Oh," said Gracie. "I see what you mean." She stared at me, her eyes glistening. The look on her face was scary, but I liked it. She saw that I liked it and in one swift motion she rolled on top of me, pinning her knees on both sides of my hips. I almost laughed, but her hair fell over my eyes, dimming the light.

She kissed me on my lips and she kissed me on my neck. Then she started rocking against my penis and I rocked back. I put my hands on her hips for some reason. The coils in her bed creaked. "You're so cold, Adam," she whispered.

"You're so cold, you're so cold." She smelled like clay and dust. As she rocked, she looked at the ceiling and bared the hollow of her throat. I wasn't sure if she was acting or if she was really getting somewhere with this, but after a while she let out several little gasps and collapsed on my chest. I kept rubbing, trying to keep the moment, but stopped when I realized it wasn't going to go any further.

She slid off me and went over to kneel in front of her window and look out.

"Are you angry?" I asked.

"Why would I be angry, Adam?"

"I don't know," I said. I wanted to ask what all that had been about, but she didn't turn around. "What are you doing?" I asked instead. It wasn't as good a question as, "What are you thinking?" I should have asked that one.

"He's down there again," she whispered. I heard the tears in her voice and went to her. I didn't look out. I wrapped my arms around her, my hands meeting under her breasts, and hugged her to my chest. "Why won't he go away?" she said. "I found him, yeah. So fucking what? He doesn't need to fucking follow me around forever."

"Tell him to leave," I told her.

She didn't respond.

"Tell him you don't want to see him anymore," I said.

She moved my hands off her stomach and turned her face to mine. She leaned in and kissed me, her tongue searching out mine, her hand cradling the back of my head like she was in charge of everything. When she pulled back, she said, "I can't. I hate him but I love him too. He seems to, I don't know, understand me. We're on the same wavelength, you know? As much as he annoys me, I love him.

He should have been loved, you know. He never got that. Not how everyone deserves."

"Just give him up," I said.

Gracie furrowed her brow, then stood and paced to the doorway. "I think you should go now," she said. "My parents will be home soon."

I craned my neck to glance out the window, but her voice cracked like a whip.

"Leave, Adam," she said.

I shrugged into my coat and elbowed past her.

"You don't deserve him," I said on my way out.

I ran home through wind and soon rain started up. It landed on my face cold and trickled down my cheeks into my collar. Jamie hadn't been outside when I left Gracie's house and I was beginning to suspect she'd been making him up, just like the rest of them. *Bitch.* I thought she was different.

At home I walked in through the kitchen door and my mother was waiting in her wheelchair by the doorway. She said, "Where have you been? Two nights in a row. You're acting all secretive. Where have you been, Adam?"

Lucy sat at the dinner table, smoking a cigarette. When I looked at her, she looked away. Smoke curled up into the lamp above her.

"What is this?" I said. "An inquisition?"

"We're just worried," said my mother.

"Don't worry," I told her.

"I can't help it," she said.

"Your mother loves you very much," said Lucy.

"Stay out of this, paralyzer," I warned her.

Both of them gasped.

"Adam!" my mother said. "You know Lucy didn't mean that to happen. Apologize this instant."

I mumbled an apology, rolling my eyes the whole time.

My mother started wheeling around the kitchen then. She reached up to cupboards and pulled out cans of tomatoes and kidney beans. She opened the freezer and tried to pull out ground beef. She couldn't reach high enough, so Lucy jumped up and hurried over to hand it down to her.

"Chili," my mother said, just that. "It's chilly outside so you need some chili for your stomach. Chili will warm you up."

Then she started in again. "My miracle child," she said. "My baby boy, my gift. Did you know, Lucy, that Adam was born premature with underdeveloped lungs and a murmur in his heart?"

"No, dear," said Lucy. "How terrible!"

"He was a fighter, though," said my mother. "He always fought. He wanted to live so much. Oh, Adam," she said, running the can of beans through the opener. "Why don't you tell me where you've been? Your running coach called. He said you've been missing practice."

"I haven't been anywhere," I said. "Give it a rest."

"It's everything happening all at once, isn't it?" Lucy asked. "Poor kid. You should send him to see Dr. Phelps, Linda. Stuff like what happened to the Marks boy is hard on kids."

"That's an idea," said my mother.

"Would you stop talking about me in front of me?" I said. "God, you two are ridiculous. You don't have a god-damn clue about anything."

My father came in the kitchen then, looking around like a policeman. "What's all the racket?" he said. His voice boomed, filling up all the space, so I put my hands over my ears and they all looked at me like it was *me* who had the problem.

"Why don't you just go kill someone!" I said. His mouth fell open like it does right before he starts in on us, so I made a break for it, opened the door behind me, and ran outside again.

I didn't know where I was going at first, but by the time I reached the edge of the woods, I'd figured it out. The rain still fell steadily, and the wind crooned through the trees like a song I'd heard my grandma once sing. Some song from the old country about a black bird that plucked a baby from its mother's arms and carried it away to the land of the dead. Leaves fell around me, red and gold stars falling through the mist. I pushed my way through the brambles until I could see a wall of twilight ahead where the woods broke and I could almost see the old railroad tracks.

His breath was on my neck before I could reach the spot though. I knew it was him before he even said a thing. I felt his breath on my neck, cold and damp, and then his arms were around my stomach like mine with Gracie and before I knew it he had climbed up on my back. "Keep going," he whispered, holding tight, and I carried him like that all the way to the place where Gracie found him.

That section of the railroad had been marked out in yellow police tape, so I knew it was the right place. But something was wrong. Something didn't match. The railroad ties hadn't been pulled up like I'd thought. And the hole where

Jamie had been buried—it was there all right, but next to the railroad tracks. He'd never been under those rails, I realized. He'd never looked up between the slats as trains ran over him.

Stories change. They change too easily and too often.

"What are you waiting for?" Jamie said, sliding off my back. I stood at the edge of the hole and he said, "Go ahead. Try it on."

I turned around and there he was, naked, no Boy Scout uniform at all, with mud smudged on his pale white skin. His hair was all messed up, one lens of his glasses shattered. There was a gash in his head near his left temple, black and sticky with blood. He smiled. His teeth were filled with grit.

I stepped backward into the hole. It wasn't very deep, not like Lola Peterson's grave in the cemetery. Just a few feet down and I reached bottom. I stood at eye level with Jamie's crotch. He slipped his hand down there and touched himself.

"Take off your clothes," he told me.

I took them off.

"Lay down," he told me.

I lay down.

He climbed in on top of me and he was so cold, so cold. I hugged him tighter, trying to warm his body up. He said there was room for two of us in there and that I should call him Moony.

I said, "I never liked that name."

He said, "Me either."

I said, "Then I won't call you that."

"Thank you," he said, and tightened those cold, wet arms around my back. He said she never let him hug her. I told him I knew. I told him she was being selfish, that's all.

"Don't worry," I said. "I've found you now. You don't have to worry. I found you."

"I found *you*," he said, pulling away to look at me.

"Let's not argue," I said.

He rested his cheek against my chest and the rain washed over us. I imagined as I held him that he was coming back to life, that somehow I could sustain him. I didn't look at him, but I could feel him clinging. Clinging to my body for life.

After a while I heard voices, faraway and tinny, like music on a radio turned down low. As the voices grew louder, I stood and saw flashlight beams coming toward us. My dad and Andy and Lucy. I imagined my mother wheeling in worried circles back in the kitchen. I imagined her holding her head between her hands, tearing her hair out, saying, "Get up! Get up and get him, goddamn it!" But she couldn't. She couldn't or wouldn't get out of that chair.

"Adam!" my father shouted, his voice cutting through the rain.

I didn't move. Not even when they came right up to me, their faces white and pale as Jamie's dead body. Andy said, "I told you the little freak would be here."

Lucy said, "My Lord, your poor mother," and her hand flew to her mouth.

My father said, "Adam, come out of there. Come out of that place right now." He held his hand out. "Well, come on, boy," he said, flexing his fingers a little.

I grabbed hold of his hand and he hauled me onto the gravel around the hole and I lay there, naked, a newborn. They stood around me, staring. My father took off his coat and put it over my body, covering me up. When I didn't move, he told me to come on, to just come on back to the house, so I finally got up and started walking down the tracks.

As we left, I looked up through the rain at the swirling dark. And although it was night and the sky was full of clouds, I saw something. A plane, or a part of the sky itself, falling through the air. I blinked and blinked, trying to make it go away. But after a few blinks, I knew it was useless. It was real, and it was coming down hard and fast. I saw it. God's finger was pointing at us.

And right then I knew I had better start to run.

THE BOY WHO HEARD SHADOWS

WHEN MY FATHER PULLED ME OUT OF THE GRAVE, Jamie didn't come with me. He stayed in the hole as we walked down the tracks. Pebbles rolled under my heels and toes; railroad ties scraped my bare feet. My father's coat was warm, but rough against my shoulders. It was a camouflage jacket he usually wore while hunting. It smelled of sweat, of bark and leaf and mildew, of dark mornings trekking through the woods to climb into his tree stand. I wanted it off as soon as possible, but it was cold and the rain pelted my bare legs, so I kept it on.

Lucy had kneeled down to grab my clothes out of Jamie's grave before we left and now she pushed them at me, saying, "Put your pants on. For Christ's sake, at least put your pants on." But I slapped her hands away.

I looked over my shoulder just once, to see if I could see him. He was still there, his head and shoulders rising out of the grave. He lifted one pale hand to wave as we walked away, then sank back down like a drowned person.

When I got in the van, I took the jacket off and laid it on my lap. My dad didn't say anything, just started the engine, wiped his brow, put the van into drive and pulled onto Highway 88.

I sat beside my brother in the back, staring ahead at the point where the headlights weakened and the gray road in front of us disappeared in the dark. I was trying not to feel, to numb myself to the point where nothing mattered, when suddenly—*pop!*—I found myself outside, flying over tree-tops and telephone wires. Below me, a sliver of light moved down the road like the blip on my mother's heart monitor. They were all inside that light, protected. And when I concentrated the roof of the van disappeared and I could see them in there: the father, the brother, the paralyzer and the body I used to live in.

The brother sat as far away from the body as possible, leaning against the sliding door. He breathed heavy on the window, fogging fingerprints into existence. The paralyzer rode next to the father, her head bobbing whenever the father drove the van over a pothole or took a turn too quick. She kept nagging the body, saying things like, "Just what were you thinking? Don't you care about anyone but yourself?"

The body didn't answer. It sat quiet and still while up above I imagined the paralyzer's car careening into my mother's: the smash, the crack of my mother's back, her blood spattering the windshield. The body didn't mention these things though. The body was better than that. I thought the paralyzer should consider herself lucky because right then the body could have opened its mouth and burned her alive with its words.

They were so far below, and me, I was in the clouds, drifting. Before the van reached its destination, though, I felt the tug. I had to come down, I had to drift back down through telephone lines and treetops, back into the van and back into the body. Then I no longer looked down, but watched as my father spun the wheel to turn into our driveway.

Light spilled from all the windows of our house, pooling on the front lawn and treetops. Normally my mother followed behind everyone, turning lights off, complaining about electric bills, but now she had switched on any possible source of light. She sat in the living room, holding the curtains of the picture window open with one hand, watching as we got out of the van.

We came into the kitchen through the garage entrance and a moment later, my mother wheeled in to meet us. She looked me up and down, shaking her head as if she didn't recognize me. "My God," she said. "What's happened? Why are you naked like that?"

I moved past her, not answering, went back to my room, locked the door, threw the hunting jacket on the floor and climbed into bed, still covered with grit from the grave. But even with the door closed, I couldn't shut them out all the way. Their voices moved like lines on a heart monitor, murmurs of worry and spikes of anger. My mother said, "Where did I go wrong?" which was the question she usually asked whenever Andy fucked up. I knew I'd arrived at a new level of trouble.

"He's got a lot of growing up to do," my father said. "You've babied them too much, Linda."

"It's not babying," said my mother. "It's called loving them, John. L-O-V-I-N-G. *Loving*."

"John has a point, though, Linda," said Lucy. "You can't coddle them forever."

I wanted to cut her face open. I wanted to watch blood drip down her cheek and ask how it felt.

"It's about time you people woke up," said Andy, his

voice full of vindication. "That brat gets away with every-thing."

"Hush," said my mother.

"See?" Andy snorted. "Even now you take his side."

"There are no sides in this family!" said my mother. My father grunted, but I couldn't tell if it meant he agreed.

Andy huffed and puffed, whining, so I figured it must have been a grunt of agreement. A moment later he came thumping down the hall and as he passed my room said, "You are such a fucking idiot, Adam." Then he slammed his door behind him.

"No more door slamming in this house!" my mother hollered.

"Bitch!" Andy shouted back. He started playing a heavy metal CD before she could yell again, and then I couldn't hear anything except guitars screaming. When my mom was a walker, she would have been down that hallway in an instant, ready to beat the living crap out of him, but she couldn't get to doors before they slammed now, so it would have been a wasted effort. There's an economy to move-ment when you're in a wheelchair. You have to pick and choose your battles.

By midnight Lucy was getting ready to go home to her husband, a man who ran an auto shop on the outskirts of town. His name was Doug but everyone called him Buck for some reason. As she opened the door to leave she said, "I'm sorry, but I have to get home to the child. Buck doesn't give a damn when I'm there, but he does when I'm not." When she shut the door, I let out a breath I'd been holding. I could breathe now that she'd gone back to the story she belonged to.

I tossed and turned after that, but no matter how I tried

I couldn't fall asleep. I stared at the ceiling, I stared into my pillow, I stared at the dark space in my head where I usually saw dreams. But nothing helped. The clock on my night-stand ticked through the hours.

My muscles twitched as if I'd run a long race; but it was my insides changing. Not my muscles. I could feel my blood rearranging, the DNA being rewritten, like Peter Parker turning into Spider-Man. I kept thinking I'd be some-one or something completely different by morning, but I couldn't imagine who or what. I whispered into my pillow, "You are no longer the person they think you are. You are no longer the person you think you are. You are someone else."

When everyone had finally gone to sleep and snores came from their respective corners, I got out of bed and went to the kitchen. I hadn't eaten, so I scoured the refriger-ator until I found some chili my mom had left. I warmed it in the microwave, making sure to turn the timer off before it dinged. I ate two bowls, one right after the other, then got ice cream out of the freezer.

I was scooping the ice cream into a bowl when I heard him cough—once, twice—and turned to find him on the other side of the counter where my mother used to stand and do things like chop vegetables and cut the fat off chicken. On my side of the counter was the kitchen; on the other side was the dining room, the mahogany table and the hutch my grandma left us.

Jamie stood beside the table. He was still naked, but his skin didn't glow like it had outdoors. In here he looked gray and dirty. A bruise covered his left cheek, fingerprints lin-gered on his neck. Somehow I hadn't seen them earlier. And there too was that gash near his temple, black and sticky with blood. I shuddered, but I said, "You made it," and smiled to make everything seem all right.

"Of course I made it," he said. And when he came around the corner I saw his mud-streaked legs and knees, scraped and bloody as if he'd been dragged around on them. He opened his arms as he came toward me and I almost ran out the door again.

I didn't though. I let him swing his arms around me. I rested my chin on his shoulder and told my body not to shiver. *It's nothing,* I told myself. *It's nothing.* And finally I was still again.

"I thought I lost you," I said into his neck.

"You can't lose me," he said. "You couldn't lose me if you wanted."

I pulled back and he adjusted the smashed glasses that sat on the bridge of his nose. Suddenly he looked older. A lock of hair flopped over the gash and I thought he didn't look like a Moony one bit. *Maybe,* I thought, *it's because he's finally out of that Boy Scout uniform.*

"What's the matter?" he asked.

I looked down and said, "I'm just a little worried."

"About what?"

"It's nothing to do with you," I said, "so don't sweat it." I waited before saying anything else. I wanted him to tell me something to make me feel better, but he just stared, face blank as a sheet of paper. I pretended to be interested in the view out the kitchen window. There was a pine tree out back and a grassy field with fence posts strung with barbed wire to keep our neighbor's cows in their pasture. When I didn't talk for a while he grabbed my chin and turned my face back, looking at me like I was something to be examined. "You up for playing video games?" I said.

His face lit up then, like he'd remembered something wonderful. But in the next moment his smile faded and he said, "I don't know how. We don't have a computer at my house. My mom and dad can't afford one. So I only know the programs we learned at school."

"Don't worry," I told him. "I have no clue how to do those computer programs you helped me out with, but I can show you how to play *Nevermorrow*."

So we went back to my room where I introduced him to the pleasures of staking vampires through their hearts for a good six hours. He was right though. He *was* a terrible player. He kept pressing the button to jump when he wanted to dodge, and he pressed the button to engage creatures that were too powerful for him to battle when what he should have done was turn his character around and run. Even with all of his mess ups, he somehow managed to complete the first level. And with my help, the next. And by the time we'd traveled down to the third layer of hell, morning light was slowly edging around the curtains of my window.

By then my eyes were dry and itchy, and I was making a lot of stupid mistakes myself: maneuvering my knight into death pits, going into rooms where demons ganged up on me. Making mistakes like that, you're never going to have a chance to get out of hell and win. So I admitted defeat and said, "I've got to get some sleep."

"Already?" said Jamie.

I said we'd been up all night, then turned off the computer and climbed into bed. He came over and slipped in beside me. I didn't say anything when he turned on his side to make himself comfortable. I just lay there, feeling his back touch my back, feeling the chill of his skin spark against mine. I used to wonder what it would be like if he'd have ever stayed over like I heard other kids talk about doing, but this wasn't how I'd imagined it happening.

I started talking about the game then, even though we weren't playing. Talking about the game felt very important just then. I didn't want to think about his body next to mine, bruised and broken. I explained the game about ten times, and he kept saying, "Okay, uh huh," and every once in a while his leg would brush against mine and I'd start to shudder again.

"I'm so happy," he said once, interrupting my lecture on how to fight goblin hordes. "It was lonely there for a while."

I waited to see if he'd elaborate, but when he didn't I came out and asked what I'd been wanting to know.

"Who did it?" I asked.

He turned over, then so did I. I was sure he was going to confess. He shook his head, though, looking very upset. "Don't ask me that, Adam," he said. "If you like me at all, don't ask that again."

"Why?" I asked.

He turned his back to me and sighed. "It hurts too much," he said. "It hurts too much to remember."

When she came knocking at my door the next morning I told my mom I was sick, and she said through the door that she'd send a note excusing me to the principal with Andy. She only let me sleep into the early afternoon, though, before she came around knocking once again. *Knock, knock, knock.* "Adam?" she said, her voice worried. *Knock, knock.* "Honey? Why is your door locked? Are you all right?"

"He's not coming out, Linda," Lucy said from the living room. "Not now anyway. Come watch soaps with me while he sulks."

Before my mother wheeled away, she said, "I'm setting your lunch down out here, honey. Please eat something for me." The TV came on then, tragic music announcing the beginning of the soap opera, and my mother and Lucy began to comment about who was sleeping with who, about who was possessed by the devil, their chatter turning into a mantra the longer I listened.

"He's a dog."

"She should really get a clue her man is cheating."

"Who would have thought she was a princess?"

And soon I fell back to sleep.

It was night when I woke again. The Weather Channel's Muzak was playing in the living room. I groaned when I heard it, then rolled over to find an empty space in my bed. Jamie was gone, but I could still see his muddy imprint on my sheets.

When I got out of bed, I found my room had been ransacked. All of my pants and shirts were strewn across the floor, their hangers with them, but my closet door was closed. I didn't understand why Jamie would have done this, but it had to have been him.

I was still covered with dirt from the night before, so I unlocked my door and slipped into the bathroom. I got in the shower and watched mud circle the drain until nothing ran off but clear water. Afterward I dried off and wrapped the towel around my waist. Shaking the last of the water from my hair like a dog, I opened the door to find my mother in the hall. She looked up and said, "Don't. You. Dare. Lock. Me. Out. Of. Your. Room. Again." Then she turned her chair around and wheeled into the kitchen where I could hear my dad's and Andy's forks clinking against their plates.

I went back to my room, locked my door again and sat down on my bed to open my Social Studies book. I was trying to find the entry on Mexican funerals Gracie mentioned, but there was no follow-up from the ninth grade edition, so instead of Mexican funerals I ended up reading about a tribe of people in Africa who spoke with clicks. I thought clicking noises were probably better than words anyway. Words never really work except for the person saying them. Everyone else hears whatever they want. I thought maybe I'd start clicking to people instead of talking too. That would be as good as saying, "How are you? I'm fine. My mom is paralyzed and my dad never talks. My brother hates me and there's this strange woman in my house who paralyzed my mom. Everyone thinks this is normal." You can tell people stupid shit like that all day and they'll just smile and nod.

After that I stayed up playing *Nevermorrow*, waiting for Jamie to come back. I got through the first five layers of hell by one in the morning, and was maneuvering my knight through a maze of dim castle halls when I heard something come from behind my closet door. I listened harder. It sounded like someone crying maybe. I wasn't sure. So I got up and went over and slid the door open, and found him on the floor in there with his legs curled up to his chest, his arms around them, crying without tears. "Jamie?" I said.

He looked up, frowning. "I tried," he said, "but I can't wear any of them. They're all yours."

"They're too big?" I asked.

He shook his head. "They're being used," he said. "I can't wear them like that."

I wasn't sure what he meant, but I told him he could wear my Cleveland Indians jersey that I never wore anymore, and found a pair of jeans and old running shoes I'd worn out last year. He couldn't believe I'd give them to him. "Are you sure?" he said, his hands out, fingers curling.

"Sure I'm sure," I said.

He put everything on in a hurry, as if I might change my mind, and I sat at the computer to continue playing *Nevermorrow*. He stood in the center of the room looking at the clothes he wore, touching them over and over, going on about how we wore the *same* size. "Who would have thought we'd wear the same size?" he said. "Isn't that great?" It was like he was happy we actually had something in common. He rested his hands on my shoulders and lowered his head next to mine, to get the same perspective on the computer I had. His bruised cheek brushed against mine, but I didn't shudder one bit.

I commanded my knight to open a door and three skeletal warriors who had been waiting for an ambush came at me with swords raised. I clicked the attack command and my knight took his Flame of Truth sword and slaughtered them, one right after the other.

"This looks cool," said Jamie. "What's it called?"

"*Nevermorrow*," I said. I didn't mention it was the same game he'd played the night before. Instead I paused the game and said, "Where did you go?"

"What's the matter?"

I spun my chair around to point at the clothes on the floor. "When I woke up, my room was a mess and you were gone. I just want to know what happened."

"Chill," he said. Just that. *Chill.* I was about to clock him for being an idiot when he said, "I was looking for a way out."

"A way out? So you tore my room apart?"

"I didn't mean to." A stupid grin slid up one side of his face.

"Have you ever heard of a door?"

"I can't go through that one," he said.

"Yeah," I said. "Right."

"I'm serious, Adam. I can go through it, but not to get where I was going."

"So you went through the closet instead?" I got up from the computer and sat down on the bed.

He came over and sat next to me, placing his hand on my leg, trying to catch my eyes. "Hey," he said. "I needed to find a dead space. That's the truth."

"Dead space?" I said. I didn't move my head, but I shifted my eyes to get a look at his face.

Jamie nodded at the door that opened on the hallway. "That door goes somewhere," he said. Then he nodded at the closet and said, "That one doesn't. Dead space. A door that doesn't go anywhere. Unless you know how to make a way out of no way."

"It goes to my closet," I said, "where my clothes used to hang."

"You know what I mean," he said.

"No," I said. "Actually I don't."

He rolled his bloodshot eyes and said, "If you don't believe me, I'll show you." He grabbed my hand and pulled me toward the closet. "Don't let go," he said. "And whatever you do, don't look back."

I nodded and he pulled me into the closet and slid the door shut.

"Don't talk," he whispered. "They might hear you, and you're not ready to be here yet. It could make them mad, so don't say anything."

"Who are *they*?" I whispered.

"The men with no skin," said Jamie.

As we took a few steps toward the back of the closet, I reached my hand out to brace myself, tracing my fingertips along the wall as we walked. But five steps later the wall dropped away and suddenly I was touching damp air and empty space and I wasn't inside my closet at all.

Voices murmured around me, soft and raspy, but I couldn't see anything. Something wet brushed against my arm and I jerked away, but Jamie held me tight. Something crackled underneath my feet, something like twigs snapping, something like dead leaves. Water gurgled nearby and I wondered if we were in a forest. In the distance wolves were howling.

After a few minutes Jamie stopped walking and I bumped into his back. A click, then hinges squealing. A square of light appeared, blinding me, and when my vision returned we were in another closet, looking out at a yellow room lined with shelves of rocks. "This is Gracie's room," I said.

Jamie nodded.

"How did we get here?"

"Dead space isn't what it looks like," he said. "You just have to know how to use it."

I let go of his hand and stepped over the threshold. I stared at Gracie's bed, the white quilt and fluffy pillows. I thought of her on top of me, rocking and rocking. I thought of her going over to the window and looking out at the maple tree in front of her house. That was where everyone said Jamie turned in circles, round and round the tree, looking up at Gracie's face in the window, waiting for her to let him inside.

I went over to the window and looked out. No ghost was down there though. He was with me instead. I wandered over to her shelves of rocks and picked out the heart-shaped pink quartz she'd shown me earlier and slipped it into my pocket. I wanted something of hers, something to remind me it had been real, even though she'd kicked me out.

"We shouldn't stay here," said Jamie.

"Where is everyone?"

"Downstairs," he said, looking around the room, from door to window to closet. "Come on," he said, adjusting his smashed glasses. "If she catches us here, she'll kill us."

He grabbed hold of my hand and we went back in the closet. Jamie pulled the door shut and darkness surrounded us again. We walked through that same place where I couldn't see anything but shadows passing, couldn't hear anything but soft murmurs and crackling, the sounds of water moving and wolves howling. We walked through that space where I couldn't feel anything but a bitter wind blowing against my face. Then Jamie slid my closet door open and we were back in my room with my clothes all over the floor. A pair of my running shoes lay at the end of the bed. I needed to start running before it was too late, but I didn't know where I should run to.

So I decided to look for a sign. Grandma would do that.

Wait until all your ducks line up, she always said, before you do anything. I had the running shoes and the body to take me wherever I went. I just needed to know where to run. I'd get a compass, I decided. I'd take clothes and food. Maybe a knife. Knives are useful. I got a pad from my backpack and started writing a list. Jamie lay on the bed and watched as I paced the room, making plans. A map. Also a flashlight would help. And I had something else to take with me, I realized. Inside my front pocket, I had Gracie Highsmith's pink little heart.

The next day I missed school again and, since my mom and dad didn't seem to mind, I decided to keep missing. I stayed in my room playing *Nevermorrow* with Jamie. We left my clothes on the floor. Usually he'd leave while I slept. I wondered where he went to, how many places a dead person could even go. After his reaction when I asked about his murder, though, I thought it was best to leave some things alone.

I didn't want to bother my mom now that she was in her wheelchair and things were hard for her, but several days after Jamie took me through dead space, I woke up to hear her making breakfast in the kitchen. I was hungry for the first time in days, and since she was making it anyway, I went out to ask what it was.

"Scrambled eggs," she said, not looking up from the pan. "Would you like some?"

I nodded and, even though she wasn't looking at me, she wheeled over to the refrigerator and pulled out a carton of eggs. "Only two left," she said. "That enough?"

"Plenty," I said. "Thank you." Her face lifted a little to hear me say something nice.

Andy came out and forked his eggs down in under a minute. "Gotta fly. See you in the loony bin, Adam," he said, then opened the side door and went out laughing.

My mother wheeled over with a plate of eggs. "Toast?" she asked.

I nodded. She wheeled over to the counter, untied a bag of bread, started reaching up to slide the bread into the toaster. She struggled trying to reach it, so I said, "Wait. Let me get that." I put my eggs on the table, took the bread from her and slid it into the toaster myself.

She looked down at her hands and sighed. "Thanks, sweetie," she whispered.

I leaned against the counter, waiting for the toast to pop while my mother stared at me. Her hair was tangled from sleep. Finally she opened her mouth and said something I should have known was coming, but as usual I was the last person to realize what was happening.

"You have an appointment with Dr. Phelps," she said. A moment later she added, "Today." Then she wheeled away, opening the refrigerator to pretend like something in there was very interesting.

"I'm not going," I said.

The toast popped out of the toaster.

"Yes. You. Are."

"No. I'm. Not."

She turned her chair around and said, "I'm your mother, and when I say you're going to see Dr. Phelps, there's no arguing."

"You can't make me," I said. I imagined her chasing me

around the house in her chair, her arms pumping the wheels. I could have outrun her when her legs were working. What made her think she could catch me now that she couldn't even stand up?

"No," she said. "I can't, can I?"

I sat down at the table to eat, feeling like a bastard. "Your father will be driving us to the doctor's office," she said a minute later. "Be ready at noon. You know your father doesn't wait around for anyone."

She didn't have to say anything else. She'd slapped down her last card and knew she'd trumped me.

I left the table, my food uneaten. I wanted to tell Jamie what had happened, but when I got to my room the bed was empty and the door to my closet was closed. He was gone again. I was alone again. On my way, as my brother said, to the loony bin.

When it came down to it, the visit with Dr. Phelps wasn't so bad, really. He had pale white skin with brown age spots that reminded me of some of Gracie's rocks. His head was bald except for a ring of grayish-white hair around the crown, so it looked like a bird's nest holding one large, age-spotted egg. He spoke with a rumble in his throat, as if everything he said might turn into a cough. But what was best about Dr. Phelps was his total ignorance. I could tell him anything and he'd just go along.

"So tell me, Adam," he said, very friendly. "What made you get undressed and get into the place where they found the Marks boy?"

"I was curious," I said. "My brother keeps taking people

back there. They have orgies there, him and his friends and their girlfriends. I thought I could hide there and maybe see some action."

"And your clothes?"

"Oh, those," I said. I waved my hand in the air as if to bat away such a silly question. "You know," I said, "I'm used to masturbating naked. I just wanted to be ready."

"I see," said Dr. Phelps. He was still nodding as usual, but I could tell he was maybe starting to catch on. So I decided to throw in some stuff I figured he'd like. "Also, well, I thought maybe about killing myself and I didn't want anyone to have to undress me. When my grandma died, my mother had to undress her and redress her in good clothes before the mortician came. I thought maybe I'd make it easier on her. Just be naked and then all they'd have to do is dress me."

His eyes lit up at that. Like some old lady at Bingo, all the muscles in his face came alive. "And what did you feel when your grandmother died?" he asked, excited. "Did that disturb you also?"

"Oh yeah," I said. "It really fucked me up. She was like my best friend in the whole world."

He smiled. Blinked his eyes and nodded. I could tell this was what he wanted, how it would be from now on. Me and Dr. Phelps, for however long my parents wanted to drag this out, wasting their money while I entertained him with the worst case scenarios I could imagine.

My parents came in after we were done, and my mother wanted to know if I should leave. "Not at all," said Dr. Phelps. "Nothing we talk about in here should be kept from Adam. No secrets, that's my policy." I thought maybe the fool wasn't so bad after all.

He told my parents I needed some time to myself.

"Adam's had a big shock. Some kids deal with death more directly than others," was his explanation. "Some time at home with his family is what he needs. Also three sessions a week, right here in my office."

My father didn't think we could afford the sessions but that two weeks off from school would be fine. My mother said, "Two sessions a week," and the deal was struck.

On the way out of his office, Dr. Phelps put his hand on my shoulder and said, "Death is difficult, Adam. But we all face it. Don't worry. Everything will be all right."

You stupid fuck, I was thinking, *do you think you're talking to an idiot?* Of course we all face it. I probably faced it more than *he* ever had. I got *in* there. Right in where they'd buried him, for Christ's sake. How close to facing it can you get?

But he meant well, I knew. They all did. All of the so-called grown-ups, the adults, the mature audience. They mean well, even if they make you feel like you don't know anything about anything, just because you're a kid.

So I did as suggested and spent more time with my family, trying to make everything seem normal. I sat with them in the living room and watched stupid reality television shows, which aren't really about reality at all really. Like that show where all the people get dumped off on a deserted island and have to eat worms and catch fish with their bare hands. My dad loved that show about as much as he loved the Weather Channel. He liked this one cast member who was a Navy SEAL, who painted his face with camouflage to go hunting in this one episode. He even made a spear. He found a wild boar somehow, even though in the previous episodes it didn't seem like anything lived on the island at all. You hear this snorting sound, and the camera pans to this wild boar, which is really a little pig probably flown in from America, and the Navy SEAL spears this baby pig and swaggers around like he's somebody. My dad thought that was the greatest thing in the world. I could tell he was imagining himself on that island, what he'd do to survive, who he'd ally with, who he'd try to get thrown off the island. He'd be a pig killer too. I could see him doing it over and over. Behind his eyes, the pig killing was happening.

All of a sudden, though, he snapped. "What the hell are you looking at?" he said. "Do you have a problem or something?"

I realized I'd been staring at him instead of the television like we're supposed to. He looked at me for a few seconds, but the longer he looked the more his eyes turned away from one another: the opposite of crossing. One went to the left and one went to the right. And my dad sat there, saying nothing, while his eyes turned their backs on each other. He finally shook his head, and his eyes went back into place. Then he slammed the footrest of his recliner down and left, mumbling under his breath.

I thought about telling Dr. Phelps about this, but in the end I didn't need his answers. I just remembered something my grandma always said. She said if a person can't look you in the eye, they're either lying to you, or else they're not able to see the person you are. "Don't be friends with these sorts," she told me. "They'll either hurt you, not understand you or both."

Andy was coming home every day with reports of what everyone at school was saying about me, but mostly I pretended not to listen. One night, though, a few days before I had to go back, he started in and wouldn't let up.

I was in the kitchen with my mom and Lucy, playing the normal boy, avoiding my father so he wouldn't have to avoid me, when Andy said, "Boy, you think what they said about Gracie Highsmith was something else, Adam? Ha! Ha! Ha!" He shook his head with this stupid grin on his face.

My mother shushed him from her wheelchair. Lucy scowled and said, "Andrew, don't talk to your brother like that. It's not nice."

"Ha! Ha! Ha!" Andy continued, and left the dining room before the paralyzer could scold him further.

"What a little dickhead," Lucy said as he left. I waited for my mother to say something, but she didn't.

So I said, "Hey, you can't talk about my brother like that. Andy's a dickhead, sure, but it's not your place to say so."

"Adam!" my mother scolded. "What on earth are you talking about?"

"You heard her!" I said. "Why do you just let her say anything she wants?"

"She was defending you!"

"She called him a little dickhead! That's line crossing! *You* can call Andy a little dickhead. *Dad* can call Andy a little dickhead. *I* can call Andy a little dickhead. But no way should Lucy have that right."

"Did you call me a little dickhead?" Andy said, coming back into the dining room. "Whoa. That is so uncool, Lucy. I thought you were on the up and up."

"I certainly did not call you a little dickhead," said Lucy. Her hand fluttered near her heart, bracelets clinking. She turned to me and said, "Adam, I have no idea what this is all about. I understand you don't like me for reasons which

your mother has forgiven me, but please respect our friendship and do not make up things about me like that. I'd
never! Never in a million years would I say such a thing!"

I was about to call her a liar when I realized Lucy was
telling the truth. Out of nowhere I heard it. I heard Lucy's
voice say, "Bastard. Little bastard." But her mouth never
moved, not even a twitch. Her red lips rested firmly against
each other. Her nostrils flared instead.

That was when I saw it for the first time. On the wall behind her—her shadow thrown against it. "Why won't you
let me live here in peace, you little bastard?" said Lucy's
shadow. I saw the mouth move on it instead. It raised one
hand to flip its hair over its shoulder, but Lucy herself never
moved an inch.

"I'm sorry," I said. "I thought . . . I must have misheard
you."

"Well, now," she said. "Thank you. I'm so upset you'd
think I'd say such a thing. You're family. I love you all." She
grabbed hold of her purse and pulled out her cigarettes. Her
hands shook and it took several tries before she could con-
jure a flame from her lighter. "Must need fluid," she muttered, not looking up.

I started to leave the room when her shadow spoke
again. "That's right," it said. "Move it on, brat. Get your ass
going before I get it gone for you."

I looked back as I turned the corner and found Lucy ex-
haling a cloud of smoke.

Jamie was playing Solitaire on the computer in my
room. My bed was unmade again and my clothes were still
strewn across the floor, and even though I thought I was

okay with that, I really wasn't. Only when nothing was going on with my family could I stand his mess. "What are you doing?" I said. "Why don't you ever clean up?"

Jamie didn't look at me. He kept clicking the mouse, flipping cards over, depositing them on other stacks. "I have top score now!" he said. A grin slid up one of his cheeks. He never smiled completely, only to one side. A lopsided sort of happiness.

"Hey!" I yelled. "I said, 'Why don't you ever clean up your mess?'"

He looked up. "What's the matter?"

"Lucy's shadow is threatening me, my parents are sending me to fucking Dr. Phelps and all you care about is fucking top score on Solitaire." I started picking up clothes, putting them in the closet. "Just don't throw shit around and leave it for me to clean up. And if you're going to sleep in my bed, make it after you're finished."

"I don't sleep," said Jamie. His smile faded as he took his hand off the mouse.

"Then what do you do? Why would you even lie down if you can't sleep? You don't make any sense!"

He looked away and I felt about *this* big: Put your thumb and index finger almost together, with just a sliver of space between them. That's how big I felt right then.

It was obvious, even though I didn't want to admit these things about him, but now it all came out:

Jamie didn't sleep. He didn't eat either. He didn't have to use the bathroom. He didn't have to breathe. He said, "I can't smell anything either, and sometimes I get so cold I have to burn memories to get warm again."

"Burn memories?" I said, and he nodded, looking down into his lap. "What does that mean?"

He lay down on my bed and started tossing and turning, his arms crossed over his chest, his face pinched as if he were in pain. "Yes," he said and, "I love you," and, "Why? Why? Why?" and, "Anything, anything, just let go."

I smelled something like hair burning. I couldn't see any smoke, but the room filled with the scent. His face contorted, the muscles bunched beneath his skin, his hands clenched his shoulders, and then—*bam!*—it was over. The smell of burned hair fled the room, gone in an instant, and the gash near his temple began to change. His face smoothed over, his skin flushed pink with heat. It was like he was alive suddenly, which made me think maybe he didn't have to be dead, that maybe we could find a way to make him live again.

"What memory did you burn?" I asked.

He shook his head. "I don't know. It's gone now. I couldn't remember if I wanted."

He cried then, quietly, no tears at all, and started to shake. "I have nothing left," he said. "It's all going away. It's all ruined."

I went to him and put my arms around him, holding him until he stopped shaking, like I'd made myself do that first night. I didn't shudder when I touched him now. I thought if I held him long enough, maybe he wouldn't hurt. But just like Gracie did at his grave, he kept sobbing.

He was right. He had nothing. Nothing at all. Hardly anyone could see him either, and after a while, when no one can see you, it can make you feel pretty bad about yourself. So far it had been only me and Gracie who had seen him, who had talked to him, and now Gracie was being such a freak.

In life, everyone at school had treated him like a loser.

He was good at computers and didn't dress normal. Everyone knew the Marks family didn't have money, but I wished they would've at least tried to get him clothes that might have helped him fit better. Instead he wore tennis shoes with the tongues hanging out, shirts a size too small. And the Boy Scout uniform didn't really help. And that's when it hit me, making me feel stupid in one second flat. That Boy Scout uniform—it wasn't what he wanted. It was just another outfit, and everyone had made fun of him for wearing it.

"I'm sorry," I said. Right then, right there, in my messy room that he'd made a mess, I remembered what Gracie had said that day in her room: "He should have been loved, you know. He never got that." She was right.

"It's okay, Adam," he said. He hugged me, his chin resting on my shoulder, his whole weight falling into my arms. I could feel his breath—his useless breath—cold on my neck, the heat from the burned memory already leaving his body. I patted his back and said I was sorry again and he said, "Forget about it."

I tried. I tried to burn that memory of my regret. But I wasn't dead yet, I was just on my way to dying, and it's harder to burn memories when you've still got life left. When you're alive, you have to learn how to live with things like regret.

The Facts of Death

GRACIE HIGHSMITH KEPT CALLING. ONCE, TWICE, a third time. Each time I told my mom to say I was sleeping. My mother didn't like that. "I think you should talk to her," she said. "She sounds like a nice girl."

"Look," I said. "Remember when Lucy used to call here?"

My mother nodded and went back to the phone. "I'm sorry, dear," she said. "He's sleeping. I'll tell him you called."

I thought I'd escaped her pestering, but then I was on-line a few nights before I had to go back to school and suddenly this box pops up with a message from someone calling themselves IgneousGirlinOhio and I open it to find this message:

"why wont u return my calls?"

So I write: "y do u care?"

And she writes: "come on! you know y!"

"no. i *dont* no y. i think u should be a bit clearer about your intentions."

She sends an angry face symbol.

I send a tongue-out face back.

"fine, b that way," she writes. Then IgneousGirlinOhio disappears, gone, just like that.

Good riddance. I was still mad at her for throwing me out of her house.

But then the thing I hadn't expected happened. The night before I had to go back to school came around and suddenly I wanted to talk to her. I wanted a friend. I thought about calling and saying, "Hey, what's up? How are your rocks?" pretending like nothing had happened. Like she hadn't missed school for weeks because she'd found a dead body, and I hadn't missed school for weeks because I'd found the same ghost she had, or that we'd kind of had sex but not really, or that I'd stolen her pink heart even if she hadn't noticed.

I couldn't, though. I'd stare at the phone, pick it up with an air of determination, dial each number like a major decision, and then—before the first ring sounded—I'd hang up. I told myself it didn't matter, that it was too late to call anyway. And besides, I thought, who knew what she was *really* thinking? Those phone calls she'd made—they might have been to yell at me instead of make up.

I'd seen that happen with my parents. They hadn't fought much after Lucy paralyzed my mother, but every once in a while the old spark flared up and my dad would say something utterly stupid. Earlier in the week it had been after they got home from an appointment with my mom's doctor. The doctor tried to get her to keep doing physical therapy, but my mom said she was fine, that nothing was wrong, the world was a wonderful place to live in, didn't he agree? She'd been going to therapy off and on, mostly at the insistence of my father, but now she wanted to stop being hopeful. "The damage is done," she told the doctor again, and once more my father grimaced guiltily.

When they got home, my dad was upset with her for

not trying more and said, "Why don't you just fucking die already, Linda?"

"Oh yeah?" said my mom. "That's what you want, isn't it? *Isn't it??* You just wait, John McCormick. Maybe I *will* go to therapy! Maybe one day I'll walk again, and when I do, I'll kick your stinking ass!"

They went their own ways for a few hours. Then my mom came to the garage, where we were working on the van. Andy was handing my dad wrenches and rags like a surgical assistant, while I sat in the driver's seat with my hand on the ignition, ready to turn the key whenever my father motioned for me to start it up. The door to the kitchen flung open and my mother sat there in her wheelchair, beer bottle in hand, her face looking sad and forgiving. "Hey," she said. "Hey, John?" My dad looked up from the engine. He was probably thinking she was going to apologize, but what he got was:

"You son of a bitch!" She hurled the beer bottle at him like a tomahawk. It nearly hit my father's head, but he raised his arm and it glanced off his elbow. Beer foamed out of the bottle onto the garage floor. "How *dare* you talk to me like that?" my mother shouted.

They screamed at each other until my mother's voice gave out, which meant my father was the winner. Then my mom wheeled backward, popped a wheelie and sobbed all the way back to their bedroom. A moment later my father stumbled toward the door with the bottle she'd thrown clenched in his hand.

Before he followed, he paused in the door and looked at us. He focused his attention on Andy and said, "You boys remember this. Remember what your father's telling you at this very moment. Don't get married," he said. "Don't ever marry."

Andy and I had heard this life lesson before. We just nodded. Then my dad headed back to their bedroom to either fight some more or maybe make up.

I figured what use would talking be if all Gracie wanted was to act like my parents, yelling and telling each other they weren't worth anything?

So I put myself to bed instead of calling. But again I couldn't sleep. I flipped my pillow from the warm side to the cool one, I tried making my mind a blank slate, I even tried counting stupid sheep. But whatever I tried didn't help.

It wasn't until four in the morning that my eyes started to flutter, and then I was off, off, off, running in the direction of darkness. And then suddenly I saw a point of light in the distance. A voice that seemed familiar called for me to come. So I went toward it, toward that light.

As I grew closer, the darkness broke around me and I found myself outside the house, running down our back road toward Highway 88. Someone ran beside me. I looked over and saw it was my grandma, her knees lifting under her floral nightgown. "What are you doing here?" I asked.

She looked over and smiled, her arms flaring like pistons. "Sugar," she said. "I'm here to tell you one thing, and that's to keep going and don't look back."

"I don't know where I'm going, though."

"You'll have to make a plan," she said.

"I've been trying, but I can't think of anything. I have a list, though. I'm bringing a knife."

She huffed and puffed before saying, "First thing: run in

the right direction or else you'll get lost. Second thing: ditch the ghost."

"He needs me," I said immediately.

"Nope," she grunted, shaking her head. "Only thing he needs is to get his butt on to where he needs to go."

"You don't understand," I said. "It isn't fair what happened to him."

"No, it's not. But it's a fact of life."

"What is?"

"Death," she said, and as soon as the word left her mouth she started to fall behind. I didn't think to slow down for her either. I kept going, one foot in front of the other. Before she was too far behind, she shouted, "You go that way, boy, and you'll learn those facts the hard way. You'll be on your way to dying before you can blink twice."

"Love you, Grandma!" I shouted. I blew her a kiss over my shoulder, then turned back to the dark road ahead.

The road stretched on without end before me, a gray strip of pavement thrown down in darkness. Treading the center line like a tightrope, I ran all night, watching my feet eat up the miles, one after the other. I ran until my legs began to ache and my side cramped. And even then I kept running. By the time I woke up, I was more tired than before I'd fallen asleep. And confused. *Run*, Grandma had said, *and don't look back. Go in the right direction*. But whatever the right direction was, I wouldn't figure it out before morning, when I'd have to go back to school again.

"Up, Adam! Get ready. Your brother's outside warming up the car."

I blinked my eyes to find my mother sitting in my doorway. After seeing my eyelids flicker, she backed the chair up and turned it around. One of her wheels squeaked against the floor, then she wheeled herself down the hall into the kitchen. I thought I smelled sausage, something greasy definitely, but that was all I could make out.

I pulled myself out of bed and my feet hit the hardwood floor with a thump. The floors looked all right, especially when morning light edged in and turned the wood a buttery color, but I missed the carpet we had before the accident. How soft it was and how in the morning you could set your feet down without the floor creaking.

Clothes. Nothing special. I put them on: jeans, a T-shirt, a flannel shirt unbuttoned, socks and shoes. Navigating these choices took up most of my thoughts. For some reason my zipper seemed unfamiliar, my shoelaces as problematic as an algebraic equation.

When I finally got everything zipped, buttoned and laced, I joined my mother in the kitchen. She was on the phone with my aunt Beth in California, where it was way early. My mother was nodding, saying, "Mmm-hmm. I know, Beth, I know! I don't know what's got into him." I rolled my eyes. While they talked, she rolled over with the cordless phone propped between her ear and shoulder, handing me a plate of pancakes and bacon. Not sausage, but I'd guessed pretty close.

When she hung up the phone she said, "Aunt Beth said she loves you and that she'll see you at Christmas. And that you better talk to her like you used to or she'll give you a beating to remember."

"Just broadcast everything, why don't you?" I said.

"Your aunt loves you. She's just worried. You know she doesn't have any kids of her own. You and your brother are like her own children."

"Whatever."

My mother scowled. "Why do you have to be so negative?"

"Why do *you* have to be so negative?"

"*I'm* not negative," she said. "*You're* negative."

"Then why won't you go to physical therapy?" I asked.

"Don't start acting like your father!" she said. Reaching up to remove the frying pan from the stove, she grabbed its handle and dropped it into the sink, where it sank below the soapy water.

"Where's Lucy?" I asked. Lucy was a safe point of conversation. If she wasn't at our place, it seemed somehow not normal.

"Still at home. Seeing how you're set on fighting with her, we thought it best you got off to school before she came over."

"Figures."

"What do you mean by that?"

"Nothing," I mumbled. I swallowed a triangle of pancakes.

"If you don't mean something when you're talking," my mom said, "don't say anything at all."

I set my fork down and gulped the rest of my milk in one swallow. "I'm out of here," I said, and grabbed my backpack.

"You haven't finished your breakfast."

"I've had enough."

I'd had enough and I hadn't even gotten to school yet. Outside, Andy waited in his car, an old Malibu Classic from the early eighties that he'd restored with my dad. They did things like that together. The car was his baby, midnight blue with a lighter stripe of blue dividing it. Very cool in a retro sort of way. The inside smelled of smoke and marijuana. Andy had tacked a Confederate flag to the inside roof, even though we weren't from the South. My brother only allowed one type of music to come out of his speakers: heavy metal. Still, it was better than riding the bus with all the junior high kids who did nothing but chatter about nonsense.

I could see it all happening in slow motion. The hush falling over everyone, the bus driver staring at me as I climbed those steps. Then conversation returning, filling the bus, buzzing. Whispers would begin to make their way up to where I'm sitting behind the driver, who's eyeing me in the rearview mirror. *Crazy,* they'd call me. *Fuckup. Freak.* All the words I suppose I deserved fluttering around me, lighting and landing on me like a horde of flies.

Riding with my brother was definitely the better option.

Andy peeled out of our driveway, throwing gravel as he pressed down on the gas. He slid a CD into the stereo and rolled his window down a crack. From his front pocket he pulled out a pack of Camels and a silver lighter my grandma had given him. The lighter had been my grandfather's during World War Two, or so we'd been told. Andy lit a cigarette and blew smoke out the window real harsh. He didn't look at me, just turned the music up loud enough to vibrate the car.

My brother didn't hold on to my grandfather's lighter out of any sentimental attachment. He'd asked for it because there was a skull and crossbones engraved on one side and on the other side were the initials F.U. My grandfather's name had been Francis Ulster. Andy thought it was funny our granddad's initials were shorthand for "Fuck you." Sometimes he and his friends would smoke a joint after school and when they'd ask Andy for his lighter, which they called Fuck You Francis, he'd say, "Here you go. Fuck you." Or he'd say, "Do you mean fuck you and your mother too?" All of Andy's friends were jealous of the lighter, which gave him an endless supply of fuck you jokes. No one got that lucky.

I never thought it was funny, though. I couldn't help but think of the real Fuck You Frances, the girl who was buried in the old Wilkinson family cemetery on the outskirts of town. Andy had never been good at making connections though. He never saw signs, ghosts or shadows. He was, in effect, a blind and deaf boy. Unfortunately he could speak and lived in the same house with me.

As we drove to school, I looked out at the passing fields, at the brown earth graying, at the broken yellow stalks of corn stubbling the ground. Crows scavenged through the remains of a late October harvest, picking up their heads to watch as we rushed past. I started counting them like my grandma and I used to do when I was little. Years ago she'd taught me a rhyme that went something like:

> *One for sorrow,*
> *Two for joy,*
> *Three for girls,*
> *Four for boys,*
> *Five for silver,*
> *Six for gold,*
> *Seven for a secret*
> *To never be told.*

I counted four crows and wondered what would come of the answer. Boys could mean anything, and my grandma would have predicted something from it. But they could mean nothing too. It was just an old rhyme.

When we arrived at school, the buses were already lined up in the parking lot. Kids swarmed out and into school, chatting, holding books against their chests, slung across their backs in backpacks or casually rested on one of their hips. You could tell which ones had found some kind of group to be in and which ones hadn't. The ones who hadn't yet mostly hurried around with anxious expressions, the ones who walked the hallways leisurely had probably already found a clique. Or at least they were good at making it seem so.

Consider Marty Chapman, president of my sophomore class, captain of the baseball team, discus thrower, straight A student, leisurely hallway walker. He was the guy everyone wanted to be. He walked through the halls with his head held high, a smile ready for everyone.

You could always count on Marty Chapman for a hello and how's it going, so when I got out of Andy's car, I headed in his direction. I needed a hello and how's it going right then, even if it *was* from Marty, who said hello to basically anyone. If Marty acknowledged me, the rest of the day would go fine. I'd take tests and walk through hallways unnoticed. A ghost.

So I walked right up to him and said, "Hey, Marty. How's it going?"

And this was his reply:

Marty's mouth dropped open, but he only blinked his eyes a lot while his lips squirmed. I could see that H forming, the "heh" of hello about to roll out of the back of his throat. Then quickly he turned his head in the opposite direction and walked away in a hurry.

After this, I began to panic a little.

As soon as Marty walked away, my stomach twisted. I could feel it coming on me then: that slow burn in the center of my chest from when I was a little kid and had trouble breathing. Underdeveloped lungs, my mother called it. Her miracle child. What a joke. I was no miracle. I was a freak who'd climbed into a hole where a murdered boy had been hidden. One look from Marty Chapman was all I needed to know how everything would go.

I breathed deep, though, like the doctor had taught me. I thought about air and snow and cold and how easy it is to breathe in winter, when breath steams and you can see it isn't just an idea, that your life is right there in front of you, flickering in and out like a snake's tongue. Jamie still needed me. I couldn't let Marty Chapman or anyone get to me. And I still needed to talk to Gracie, to touch her again if she'd let me. If she wasn't afraid of me, I would touch her, or let her touch me (which is what happened really). And pretty soon, my breath started coming on its own again.

I walked into school even though I knew Marty's reaction was only the beginning, and I was right: everyone stared. Heads turned from conversations in progress, lifted from the depths of lockers. I made my way down the hallway, and as I walked, everyone parted.

Before I even reached my locker, I heard the names. All the words I'd imagined being whispered on the bus followed me through the hall. Here they were. But they couldn't touch me. I was ice and rock with no entry. I looked at the words and stopped them in midair, plucking them from their trajectories before they could get inside me.

I sat through Chemistry and History and English, not looking up from my book unless I had to, not even when Mrs. Motes asked me what sort of story Edgar Allan Poe invented. I knew the answer and she knew I knew it, and even when I finally muttered, "The detective story," she wouldn't let up. She kept calling on me for questions until I finally started saying, "I don't know. I don't know. I don't know."

"Sure you know, Adam," she said. "Come on. What's the significance of the house coming apart at the end of *The Fall of the House of Usher*?"

I said, "Its foundation was unsound."

"You're thinking literally," she said. "Now really. Why does it fall apart at the end? What is Poe saying?"

I said, "Poe's saying everything comes to an end, and that's about all that's logical in the world."

"Close," said Mrs. Motes. "What does this stand for?" There was some clicking on the chalkboard, then the chalk being set back in its tray. "Adam?"

I looked up. She'd written the words *ad infinitum* on the board. "I don't know Latin," I told her.

"It's a shame they don't offer it anymore, it's an important language," said Mrs. Motes.

Right then Elizabeth Moore, who sat two seats over and had her commentary ready as usual, said, "Umm, I think Latin's a dead language, Mrs. Motes."

"I know that, Elizabeth."

And Elizabeth, smirking, said, "Well, then. What's the use of knowing it?"

The room went quiet. Outside there was sunlight and trees to look at. A crow lingered in an old maple, hopping from branch to branch. *One,* I counted in my head. One for sorrow.

"Ahem," said Mrs. Motes.

I turned back to her.

Mrs. Motes moved a stray piece of salt and pepper hair out of her eyes and said, "Just because a language is dead doesn't mean it's not important. A lot of the English language—*your* language—has roots in Latin. Poe often used it in his writing to good effect. The language may be dead, or more correctly, dying, but its ghost still haunts your grammar and vocabulary."

Elizabeth Moore didn't say anything. I turned around to look at the crow again and just then it took off in a whir of feathers. Mrs. Motes, making another plea for my attention, said, "*Ad infinitum* means to go on forever, Adam." A moment later she sighed, frustrated or sad, or feeling both of those things, and when I turned back to her, I found she'd been looking out the window with me.

At gym time, I headed straight to the locker room. If you played sports for the school you had a locker in the gym so you didn't have to keep bringing clothes back and forth from home as often. All of my warm-up pants and shirts were in there, along with an extra pair of running shoes. I hadn't put them on in weeks. They sat at the bottom of the locker, their toes touching. I imagined an invisible kid wearing them instead of me.

I hadn't been coming to cross-country practice for weeks. After a while the coach had stopped calling to ask if I was still on the team. But even though I wasn't running for him anymore, I still thought of myself as a runner. I just wasn't running around that cinder track in back of the school. I was running on my own time now, on a track no one but I could see.

The second bell rang and in swarmed the rest of my gym class, pulling off school clothes, hiking sweatpants on in place of jeans. I was almost ready, sitting on a bench, lacing my shoes up, waiting for the coach to come out and tell us to hurry, when I heard Matt Hardin, our school's best basketball player, say my name. He didn't call my name like he wanted to ask a question; he said it loud enough so I'd hear him talking about me on the other side of the lockers. I couldn't make out what he said, but I didn't care. I told myself, *Ice, rock, air, breathe.* I reminded myself to ignore everything.

So I was sitting there, ignoring Matt Hardin, lacing up my shoes, when he came around the corner still in his underwear, running his fingers through his frosted blond hair. Steve Carroll and Jesse Logan followed, his lackeys, and when they arranged themselves around me, Matt said, "So, McCormick, what the fuck's your problem?"

I didn't say anything, just threw my clothes inside my locker and closed the door. *Ice, rock, air, breathe.* I looked toward the door to the gym. A kid opened the door to leave and the sound of basketballs bouncing and shoes squeaking came in. Then the door closed and it was only our own voices in the locker room again. I started heading for the door.

Before I could go anywhere, Matt Hardin's hand landed

on my shoulder. "Hey," he said. "Don't fucking walk away from me when I'm talking to you, faggot. What the fuck's your problem? You got a thing for jerking off to dead people or something?" He laughed, but his hand stayed on me.

I craned my neck so I could see him over my shoulder. I could feel my face twisting. I tried to stop myself from saying anything, but fire unfurled in my blood, ran down my spine, the opposite of chilling, and I went and said, "Fuck you, Hard-On," through gritted teeth, a name I knew he hated, and ripped my shoulder away.

He pushed me and said, "Don't talk back to your fucking elders," even though he was only a year older.

I looked down at his shadow, which lay between the feet of Steve and Jesse, and concentrated on it, searching for its voice, trying to coax it into talking. But it wouldn't talk. I'd only heard Lucy's shadow, but I was in a pinch so I squinted and tried looking inside Matt's instead of just listening. It was dark in there, and furry, but there was no barrier, so I went in, searching, picking up and discarding things until I finally looked back up with what I needed.

"What do you care what I jerk off to, Matt?" Cocking my head to the side, arching my eyebrows, I said, "What? You want to watch me?"

Hardin's face was confident before I said what I'd found in his shadow, but afterward his eyes widened and his face went red. Then his fist came up under my jaw and my head went back and my teeth rattled. Above me, the fluorescent squares of lights in the ceiling suddenly blinded me.

He was on top of me in a second, but I shoved him off and into the lockers, then scrambled over before he could collect his thoughts and grabbed a fistful of his frosted blond hair. Once, twice, a third time. *Bam! Bam! Bam!* I smashed his precious head into the lockers while Jesse Logan called for the coach and Steve Carroll said, "Get the fuck off him, asshole!"

Someone grabbed hold of me and pulled me off, but I kept my eyes on Hardin, glaring, my breath coming hard. He didn't move from where I'd left him crumpled on the floor.

"McCormick!" Coach shouted. I shrugged out of his hold. "What the hell are you doing?!"

"He hit me!" I said, and wiped blood away from my lips to show him the proof.

"That's no reason to bash his head against the lockers," Coach shouted. "Now settle the hell down and consider yourself lucky *I* caught you two jerkoffs. Otherwise, you'd both be out of school for the next two weeks!"

Hardin pulled himself up and moved past me, his eyes never leaving mine until he turned the corner, back to his side of the lockers. I went for the door to the gym again. But before I could go anywhere, a hand clamped down on my shoulder.

"McCormick," Coach said. "My office. Now."

I followed him back to his office and he sat me in the chair across from his desk. I slouched down like the burnout kids do whenever they get in trouble and stared at a calendar of track meets that hung on the wall behind his head. I'd missed four weeks, a month full of red X's, and didn't care.

"Why aren't you running?" Coach asked.

"I still run," I said.

"Well, why aren't you running for *me* any longer?"

"I don't run for anyone," I told him. "Not anymore."

"That's a shame, McCormick. I need you. The team isn't

doing so well. I know you've been having some problems lately, but—"

"Don't," I said before he could finish. "Just don't. I appreciate it, but really. You have no clue."

"Why don't you tell me about it?"

I looked away from the calendar and met his eyes. They were brown and crinkled at the corners. The hair at his temples was graying. I searched his face, but nothing in it told me he'd have answers.

"You wouldn't understand this," I said, and got up.

"We're playing touch football," Coach called behind me. "But I think you'd better run laps instead, McCormick. You've done enough touching for today."

It was then, a few minutes later, as my legs propelled me across the cinder track, as my arms pumped and my fists clenched and unclenched, as I breathed in and out, *Ice, rock, air, ice, rock, air,* with the grayish-black cinder track before me, my feet eating up the distance, my muscles using what had been called up in me, that I finally realized how Hardin, and everyone else, had found out I'd gone into the place where Jamie had been buried.

Who else would know why I'd been absent from school except my brother?

At lunch, I sat alone at a table in the far corner of the cafeteria, sipping a cola and eating potato chips, trying not to think about how much my brother hated me. But there weren't enough things to distract my attention. So I took a notebook from my backpack and chewed on my pen for a while. Then my head started to fill with the first clear thoughts I'd had in weeks and this is what I wrote:

Things I Know about the Dead and Other Observations

1. My father is a man who can't talk to me like I'm a real person.
2. Contrary to popular belief, mothers can easily miss early warning signs of problems concerning their children.
3. When you're dead, you don't have to care about anything, unless you want to.
4. People aren't what they seem, whether they're dead or living.
5. The dead want the world of sight and sound and smell and taste and touch more than anything else.
6. The dead aren't as polite as the living. They'll make messes of your room.
7. When you're dead, you can do a lot to the living and not care, because what can the living do to the dead anyway?
8. My mother's friend Lucy is *exactly* what she seems, and I've known that from the start.
9. The dead aren't mannerly. They drop in unannounced without apologizing.
10. The dead will take whatever you give them.
11. The dead will take whatever they want, even if you *don't* give them permission.
12. When you run a lot, you don't get into trouble because you're always in motion. And if you're fast enough, when you *do* fuck up, no one can catch you.

After the last bell rang, I walked to my locker, pulled out my jacket and left. Outside Andy was already in his car, music pounding. I got in but we didn't look at each other, as usual. I concentrated on breathing instead. *Ice, rock, air, breathe,* I told myself. *Ice, rock, air, breathe.*

The next thing I knew we were pulling into our driveway and after he turned the car off I opened my door, threw my backpack on the ground and ran toward him as he climbed out his side. I flung myself at him like a wrestler and then it was the two of us in a tangle of limbs, bloody lips blooming, voices rising higher and higher: "You motherfucker, you motherfucker! You told everyone! How could you? I'm your brother! I hate you! I hate you!"

Then my mother shouting from the front door, "Stop it! You boys stop fighting this instant!"

Behind my mother, Lucy appeared. "Boys! Boys!" she shouted. "I'm calling the police! I'm calling the police on the both of you this very instant!" She actually shook her index finger at us and her plastic bracelets rattled against each other.

Andy was on top of me, pounding my face in, spitting, "I'm going to kill you, you fucking faggot. I'm going to fucking kill you!"

My mother wheeled down her ramp, her face full of fury. I kneed Andy in the crotch and his eyes twisted inward. "Fuck you, Frances!" I shouted. "How you like that?"

My mother shrieked, "Do not dishonor your grandfather's name, you little sons of bitches!"

Then my dad pulled into the driveway behind us, home from a long shift at the construction site. Andy and I got a few more punches in, and then my father was in the mix with both of us. He pulled Andy off and said, "That's the end! That's it! Finito!"

"Adam started it!" Andy yelled. "He came at me out of nowhere!"

I lay on the ground, burning. Inside me a dead language roiled like molten lava. If I opened my mouth, the dead language would wipe this house, these people, their shadows, right out of existence.

My father said, "Is that true, Adam? Did you start this?" He kept his eyes on Andy. I waited to see if he'd look at me, but he didn't.

"Answer your father right this minute," said my mother.

A group of crows landed in the field across the road, their heads cocked, cawing curses, staring greedily, like I was their next meal.

I pulled myself up, my face dripping with blood, speckled with bits of gravel. *They have two days,* I was thinking. *Maybe three. In a week,* I thought, *Thanksgiving will be here. But not me.*

"That's right, little one," said Lucy's shadow. "Go ahead and say what you're thinking. You know you want to."

But I didn't. I decided words were no longer necessary with these people. I turned away, ran past my mother and into the house, where I locked myself in my bedroom.

Jamie was on my bed. He sat up and said, "Are you ready?"

I nodded. "But we have to wait until they're not paying attention."

"They never pay me attention," said Jamie.

"They'll wish they had now," I said.

"Why are you angry, Adam?"

"Don't go sounding like fucking Dr. Phelps," I shouted.

A tear collected in the corner of his eye, trembled, then evaporated before it could even leave a watery trail behind.

I looked down and said I was sorry. "It's not you. It's

them. Me and you are okay. Okay?" I went over to sit beside him. "Hey," I said. "Everything is going to be all right. I just have to get out of here somehow for that to happen."

He turned to face me. I held my hands in front of me, between my knees, and stared at him.

"You're right," he said. "You have to get out. And I know a place you can go."

"Where?"

"The Wilkinson farm. Frances will let us stay there for a while."

"Frances?" I said.

"Yeah. You know. Frances."

"You mean Fuck You Frances?"

"Yeah," said Jamie. "She'll put us up, no problem. It'll be perfect."

"Perfect," I repeated, spitting the word into my cupped hands, where it rolled around like a marble. Going nowhere fast. Going nowhere at all.

DEAD IS DEAD IS DEAD

FOR THE NEXT FEW DAYS, WHILE I WAITED FOR JAMIE to return from the Wilkinson farm, I went to school like everything was normal. Now I rode on the bus, though, instead of with my brother. My father had declared us off limits to each other, which was fine by me, although I'm sure it annoyed Andy that he couldn't torture me one-on-one any longer. Not that he needed me to be around in order to torture me. He'd managed to do a good job of that in my absence.

The one difference between that first day back and the next ones, though, was that things weren't as difficult. Word spread fast that I'd slammed Matt Hardin's head into a locker until the coach pulled me off him, and also the school bus had passed our house while Andy and I were beating the hell out of each other in our driveway. Now when I looked at people who'd been saying things about me the day before, I could see their bones turn to jelly inside them.

Gracie still hadn't come back to school and because everyone was afraid of me I couldn't ask anyone what happened to her. I finally asked the principal's secretary if she was sick, and the secretary told me she no longer attended. She'd been pulled out by her parents.

When the bus dropped me off at home later, I went straight to my room and dialed her number. Only this time I didn't hang up. I had questions to ask. Gracie was an expert on all things local, so once we got past the initial: "Hey, it's me. Adam."

And her: "Hey. What's up?" Very noncommittal.

Once we got past all that awkward starting-to-talk-again phase, I asked her the question that had been nagging me since Jamie said we'd be staying with Fuck You Frances.

"Do you know anything about her?"

"You mean Frances Wilkinson?"

"Yeah. What do you know?"

"The same thing everyone knows. Is this why you called, Adam? To find out about a ghost?"

"No. I was just curious."

"I know the story, sure. You've *really* never heard it?"

"Never," I said. That was a lie, but I wanted to get as much information as possible, and also I wanted to hear Gracie talk. I liked listening to the crazy stuff she'd say without thinking. I wished I could talk like that, but I wasn't good at it. "I guess I'm out of the loop," I said as an excuse.

"You're always out of the loop," said Gracie. "You're in outer space most of the time. But that's okay. I like that. Anyway. Here's what I know. So listen up.

"There was this girl named Frances Wilkinson, and like most kids she lived with her parents. This was sometime around the 1930s or '40s, I think, and Frances was thirteen or fourteen when all of this happened.

"The Wilkinsons lived in that gray clapboard house on the hill that slopes down into Marrow's Ravine. I don't think anyone's lived there for at least twenty or thirty years now, but people say they've sometimes seen a little girl go past the front window as they drive by."

"Spooky," I said, and Gracie said:

"Wait. It gets better. Next to the house, the Wilkinsons had a family cemetery. It's still there even now. There are five headstones: one for the mother, two for her stillborn babies, one for Frances's father, and then the one for Frances herself. There used to be a wrought-iron fence around the place, but it's mostly falling down now.

"From what I've heard, Frances Wilkinson was crazy. They say you could see that in her even as a child. She frowned a lot and wouldn't try to be friends with anyone at school, and was constantly trying to run away. And when they'd find her and bring her back home again, she'd look even worse than when she'd left.

"I found some pictures of her once. You know, all those old newspapers they keep in the library. She didn't look much like her parents, that's for sure. Mr. Wilkinson was tall with a beard and mustache. Mrs. Wilkinson wore these floral print dresses, and in the two pictures I saw, she's wearing an apron, hands folded at her waist. In the same pictures Frances is frowning, her face turned down but her eyes turned up to stare at the camera. She looks kind of devil-child freaky, really. She has the same dress on in both pictures too, a copy of her mother's, but tied at the waist with a sash instead of an apron. They weren't well-off, you can tell, but apparently they were hard workers and attended church every Sunday. They look like any family from back then, really, just even more country. So when Frances suddenly murdered her parents, everyone around here was super freaked out.

"Supposedly she used her mother's butcher knife. First she did in her father while he slept, then her mother while she was taking a bath. Then she stabbed herself in the stomach on the front porch.

"This was on a Sunday before church started, and later that day their pastor drove out to find out why they hadn't been to services that morning. A massacre, he reported. And the whole town couldn't believe it. Just like nowadays. Something bad happens and there's a collective gasp. I don't know why people here are like that, always trying to pretend like they don't know bad shit happens in the world.

"I heard about Frances one Halloween from a friend of my dad's, but he didn't have details so I went to the library and looked her up on my own. Then I started to get it, how some people are just crazy, you know. Why even now people know her story and why my mom always shakes her head when we pass by that rotten shack with the family cemetery next to it. I started to get why people still go out there.

"What's supposed to happen when you go there is, you gather around Frances's grave and all in time together call out, *Fuck you, Frances! Fuck you, Frances! Fuck you, Frances!* to call her up. Afterward nothing will seem too different, but when you try to leave you'll feel a strange force keeping you. When you turn back around she'll be there, wearing her raggedy dress and tattered shoes. Her face is dirty from the grave and her red hair blows around like Medusa snakes. And her eyes. Her eyes will be pinched, half-shut, like she's judging you. She forces you to lower your head then, while she spits on you for defiling her grave. And it's only after she's finished that she finally lets you leave the place."

Gracie took a deep breath after she finished. "That's about it," she said. "I've touched it up a little."

"Of course," I said, very civilized, even though her way of telling it was a trademark flourish, like the curly letters she used to spell her name on Jamie's grave. I asked her my other question after a moment of silence where it felt like we were both thinking about everything Gracie had said. "Hey," I said. "Are you still angry at me?"

Gracie snorted. "I'm not mad at you, Adam. God, you are so spastic! Get a grip. Better yet, come over. I don't like talking on the phone."

"Why?"

"I think my parents bugged the line."

"Why would they bug the line?"

"Because they don't trust me. They're homeschooling me now, you know. I won't ever be in school again. They blame my finding Jamie's body on the dangers of public school systems."

"What does public school have to do with it?"

"Nothing," she said. "I didn't say they made sense."

"That sucks."

"Yeah," said Gracie. Then, "So what are you doing right now?"

I was on my bed looking at the ceiling, turning Gracie's rose quartz heart over and over in my hand, imagining Gracie doing the same thing, turning a rock end over end with her fingers. I didn't tell her I had her heart-shaped rock. I said I was at my computer playing Solitaire.

"Oh." She sounded disappointed. A lull crashed into our conversation for a while and the phone grew hot against my ear. Finally Gracie sighed and said, "Are you coming over or what?"

"Sure," I said, and left straightaway, slipping out while my mother and Lucy watched TV, pedaling the six miles on my ten-speed as fast as I could go.

When I got to the Highsmith house, I leaned my bike against the maple tree out front and before I even knocked Gracie opened the front door, took my hand and led me up to her bedroom. Her parents weren't home again, and before we said anything she was on the white quilted bed, motioning for me to follow.

Then we were kissing, my bruised lips meeting her chapped ones, her hands slipping under my shirt. I shivered when her fingers touched my stomach and she flicked her tongue in my mouth like a snake. She rolled me over on my back, got on top of me and started to unzip her pants. She was already rocking, but I said, "Wait." She made a puzzled face, eyes scrunched up like she was going to say she didn't wait for anyone. She stopped, though, and I said, "Let me do that."

She smiled when I took the tab of her zipper and pulled down on it like we were in a movie. I rolled her off me and onto her back, grabbed her jeans at the cuffs and pulled while she pushed them down at the waist. I was thinking, *Oh God, Oh God, Oh God.* But in a good way. I hoped I was doing everything right.

Once her pants were off, she started to pull my shirt over my head. I got lost in the neck but she tugged and it slipped over my head like a magic trick. Then we were like a centaur and a mermaid: half of our bodies bare, the other half covered.

"Do you have a condom?" she asked.

"A condom?" I said. "Why would I have a condom?"

She made a face like I was stupid. "So I don't get pregnant, stupid."

"Pregnant!" I said. "Come on! I don't have a condom!"

"Well, then," she said. "We'll just have to keep this strictly no penetration."

I thought about this for a moment. I wasn't sure if I knew what she meant, but I said, "Sure. That'll be great."

She smelled like sunflowers. I didn't actually know what sunflowers smelled like, but she smelled like that word.

If Gracie was nervous, I couldn't tell. I mean, I'd never been touched like this by anyone, but she seemed to know what she was doing. She worked briskly, and I thought maybe she was doing everything without hesitation because she was used to seeing scenes like this in movies and books, used to hearing about it from other kids at school maybe. Whatever the reason, she knew how to touch me like she knew how to talk to me: without making things weird.

She unbuttoned my pants and unzipped them like I'd unzipped hers. Then it was my turn to shimmy out of my jeans while she pulled them the rest of the way off. She lifted her shirt over her head and she wasn't wearing a bra, so her breasts were right there suddenly. I sat in my boxers with my penis pressed tight against the front. Gracie pulled those off too. "Pretty," she said, lowering her head toward it. "You have a pretty penis, Adam," she said.

I didn't really know how to answer, so I said thanks and that her breasts looked really creamy.

"*Creamy?*" she said, giggling.

"Yeah. Creamy. Like white chocolate."

"That's sweet," she said. Then her mouth covered my

penis, hot and wet. My breath shuddered in my throat as
her lips went down, down, down the length of it and suddenly I couldn't feel the rest of my body. I was dick. Just
dick. Everything else disappeared.

"Oh my God," I said, but it came out a whisper. I said it
a few more times over the next few minutes. My eyes rolled
back and I watched the blades of the ceiling fan standing
still above us and then there was this blinding, bright light
for a second, then my body returned, quivering like a
plucked harp string.

Gracie pulled a tissue from a box on her nightstand and
spit into it. After throwing the tissue in the wastebasket, she
said, "God has nothing to do with it."

She stretched out next to me, curling into my side. I
could tell it was my turn to do something, so I reached
down and slipped my finger inside her. She moaned a little,
closing her eyes while I searched around. She was wet and
warm, her hair soft and brown. After a while she opened her
eyes and said, "Will you kiss me?"

I said, "Sure, I'll kiss you!" and leaned in to kiss her
while I touched her down there.

After we finished kissing she said, "That's sweet, Adam,
but will you kiss me down there?"

I was stunned. Even though she'd done that for me, it
hadn't occurred to me to do it back. But it didn't seem like
it'd be a big deal so I said, "Yeah! Sure, I'll kiss you down
there!"

So I moved down the length of her body until I reached
the place. Closing my eyes, I slipped my tongue inside a little and her back arched. She moaned a bit too and that
made me hard all over again. Just a sound from her and I
was ready.

I pressed my face closer, searching with the tip of my tongue, the flat of it, flicking and pressing like I'd heard you were supposed to do. And after a while of this, she shuddered like I had, quivering until it was all done and over. When she settled, she released a long breath and said, "Come up here and hug me."

We stayed in bed for a while, listening to our breathing, not sure of what we'd done or if we should have done it, but also it wasn't like we had done everything possible so I didn't feel all that worried. I was thinking about the word sunflower and how it had to smell like sunflowers, like Gracie, because that word kept coming into my head. Not the sound of the word but the image, the word itself: sunflower. I saw the rocks lining the shelves of Gracie's room and remembered the pink quartz heart I'd stolen. I decided I should give it back, but not right away. I'd wait and see how things developed. There were plenty of other things I could collect without stealing. Words even. Those would be good. No one else wanted them, so I'd collect them. My first word would be *ad infinitum*, I decided. And my second would be sunflower.

"Aren't you all smiles?" said Gracie, and she was right. I was smiling like crazy.

She asked me how things at home were going, and I said, "Not so good. I think I'm leaving."

"What do you mean? Where will you go?"

"Jamie is talking to Fuck You Frances," I said. "He says we can crash with her."

Gracie narrowed her eyes. "So *that's* why you were asking all those questions. What the fuck, Adam! Why are you still messing around with Jamie Marks? He's dead! Don't you get it?"

"I'm not *messing around* with Jamie," I said. "God, you

sound like my grandma. He's had it rough. You of all people should understand that."

"Don't guilt-trip me," said Gracie. She got out of bed and started putting her clothes back on. First her underwear, then the pants and T-shirt. Snip snap, just like that, my nakedness was the only remaining evidence that anything extraordinary had happened here. "I don't need anyone to tell me who to feel sorry for."

"Don't feel sorry then," I said.

"I won't," said Gracie. But she hesitated, folding her arms across her chest, peering toward the window where the light was failing from late afternoon to evening. The tree out front was bare, its branches black after a cold November drizzle. "But why the Wilkinson farm?" she finally asked.

"I have to get out," I said. "I have to get out or else I'll go crazy."

"Why don't we go somewhere worthwhile, then?" she said, casually inserting herself into my plans. "Why shack up at that run-down farm? It's stupid."

"Well, where would *you* go, Miss Know It All?"

"Somewhere I've never been before. Someplace wonderful," said Gracie. "Where haven't you been before, Adam?" Her face lit up as she asked and suddenly it was like a game of Three Wishes. What would I wish for? Where would I go?

"California," I said without having to think too hard or too long. "My aunt Beth lives there, but she always comes here to visit. She says it's like another country. There are all sorts of people there. From China and Mexico and Russia. From all over. Going there would be like going to Disney World, I think, only realer."

"Let's go then!" said Gracie. And the next thing I knew

she was on her dad's computer, looking up train schedules. "My dad works for Amtrak," she said. "We can buy tickets through his account."

"Just like that?"

"Just like that," said Gracie. I leaned over her shoulder while she typed in our names, addresses and telephone numbers. I wasn't sure if she knew what she was talking about, if we could actually just order tickets like that, but I figured at least it was another possibility. "We can leave this coming Sunday," she said.

"Are you serious? You're a genius," I said, and bent down to kiss her.

"Why, thank you, sir," she said, putting on a Southern accent.

I said, "My pleasure, missus."

Then we got naked again and everything was sunflower sunflower sunflower for a good half hour.

Before Gracie's parents came home from counseling, I was on my bike and pedaling back to my house like a madman. I whirred past farms and fields and falling down barns, calling things out as I passed.

"Crows!" I shouted as I sped past three of those black scavengers wandering in a pasture. "Maples!" I yelled as I passed a line of maple trees, buckets strapped to their trunks, collecting sap to be steamed into syrup. "Cows!" I hollered as I spun past the Morgan's dairy. "Telephone pole! Clouds! Pond! Broken down Ford Escort that has sat in that same damned ditch for over a year now!" I was delirious with naming, my head so filled with words that when I got home I trudged in through the door sort of singing them.

My mother was in the kitchen making lasagna. When she heard me come in singing she turned her chair away from the stove and laughed. "What's got you happy all of a sudden?"

I said, "Nothing in particular," as if I hadn't just had a little sex with Gracie, as if I hadn't just felt the word sunflower open up inside me and face the light. I passed through the dining room, where my father sat at the table reading the sports section, rattling and harrumphing, not looking up or saying hello, and continued back to my room.

Andy was asleep in his bedroom. He took three-hour naps because school was such a huge drain on him, or so he told my parents. Really he was just coming off the high from the joints he smoked after school. I never said anything because I liked him like that, down for the count, drooling. This way I didn't have to hear his comments about how I was a troublemaker and how everyone at school thought I was a freak, and how did I think our parents liked having a psycho for a child? I suppose he had his own best interests at heart when he poisoned them toward me. Then they didn't notice all of his own fuckups. Like D's and F's on report cards and after school detentions. It didn't matter. Even if they knew, my father would just say, "Boys will be boys," and my mother would look skeptical, but she'd never disagree.

I, on the other hand, had "problems socializing." I had "difficulties with healthy interactions." I "appeared in a constant state of melancholy." I "rarely engaged teachers in discussions." The guidance counselor was spying on me for Dr. Phelps now, who preferred to have observations of my behavior outside of our sessions. Although I wasn't told I was being spied on, I figured it out pretty quick. On those first few days back at school, after the fight in the locker room—which the coach never reported but everyone knew about—the guidance counselor always seemed to be in the periphery of my vision, notebook in one hand, pen in the other, staring. With all the focus on me, Andy's bad grades and general disinterest in attending classes were forgotten.

When I looked in his room, I found him asleep on his back, arms draped over the sides of his bed, head tilted back on the pillow, snoring. His jean jacket hung on the doorknob. This is when I got the idea to pay him back for busting my lip and making things worse for me with my parents in general.

I slipped my hand into the front pockets. First one, then the other. But I found only gum wrappers, cold coins and grit. I took the jacket off the knob and searched the inside pockets until I felt the cold metal of my grandfather's lighter. Jackpot. I took it in the hot palm of my hand and set the jacket down before going on to my room.

Jamie was waiting at my computer, his head cupped in one hand, staring at the screen-saver fish floating back and forth. I closed the door and locked it before sitting down on my bed and asking, "How was Frances?"

"Frances was Frances," said Jamie. He moved the mouse and the screen saver disappeared. "She said we can stay as long as we want, but she's not happy about it."

"Why?"

"Because," he said. "You're not dead, Adam. She's a little skeptical."

"Not dead?" I said. "What's that supposed to mean?"

"It means she thinks you're probably not very clued in,

that's all. Ignorant, is how she put it. 'The living are so ignorant, Jamie,' she said. 'How can you stand them?' "

"And what did you say?"

"I said she was generally right, but that you're different.
Don't worry. Just be yourself and she'll find out she's
wrong."

"Well, she's wrong in more than one way," I said, remembering what my grandma had told me. "I'm on my
way to dying, and that has to count for something."

"That's true," said Jamie, apparently not impressed. I
suppose to a dead person, dead is dead is dead. "In any case,
she said we can stay there. Are you ready to go yet?"

"I'm ready," I said. Even though I'd made plans with
Gracie, I wanted out now. "But we should wait until everyone goes to sleep. Then we'll have a head start."

Jamie nodded. Then we didn't say anything for a while,
just stared at each other, him at the computer, me on the
end of the bed, one foot tapping. He tilted his head to one
side and his eyes shifted down then up. He seemed to be
searching me for something. His nostrils flared as if he
could smell a change. He adjusted his glasses and stared at
me like I was an obscure painting in a museum until I finally said, "What the hell are you looking at?"

"Nothing," he said calmly. "You just seem different. Are
you okay?"

"Sure I'm okay," I said. "I'm completely okay. Why
wouldn't I be okay?"

"I don't know. But if you're okay, I'm okay."

"Okay!" I said.

He rolled his eyes, got up and came over to lie on the
bed beside me. He took his glasses off and frowned. "I suppose I don't need these anymore," he said, his voice like ice

melting. He looked so desperate, staring at those glasses, the one lens busted out by whoever murdered him. He folded them and placed them on my nightstand. "I see the same without them anyway," he said. "Everything is equal now. Nothing is getting worse or better. This is how things are going to be forever, aren't they?"

"Don't think like that," I said. "Things are going to be good again. We'll make them good again. You and me, okay?"

"How can we make them good again? It's over," he said. "It's all ruined." He turned to face the wall, breathing heavy like he was trying not to cry, so I put my arms around him and curled my legs to fit behind his and held him until he stopped hyperventilating. When it was over, he turned to me and said, "What would I do without you, Adam?"

I just shrugged. "You don't have to worry about that. You'll always have me."

"We'll have each other," he said, and we hung on to each other like that until night came, and it was safe for us to go out into the dark.

FUCK YOU FRANCES

WHEN IT WAS TIME TO LEAVE, WHEN THE HOUSE WAS quiet and everyone asleep, I grabbed my backpack with the two changes of clothes and the supply of food I'd foraged from the kitchen, and left through the side door farthest from everyone's rooms. As I inched the door shut, as I crept down the gravel driveway, as I stopped at the mailbox and turned around to take one last look, I whispered goodbye to everything as I passed by. The mercury light attached to the garage was on, casting everything in its purple-white light. My shadow stretched out on the gravel drive before me, tall and narrow, a bigger me than I was used to. "Are you me from the future?" I asked, but it only shook its head.

"What do you think this is?" it said. "There's no door number three. No growing up now. That's the path you've chosen."

"Whatever," I told it. "Fuck you too." Then I hopped on my bike and rode toward Highway 88.

As I rode from Highway 88 to Fisher Corinth Road, I looked at all the farms and houses, their windows dark, the creeks in the pastures shining in moonlight, and imagined I was the last man on earth and all of town was just the leftovers of the world I once lived in. At the end of a dust-stone back road off Fisher Corinth, it was waiting for me, the Wilkinson farm, gray-blue under moonlight, shambling, rotting, ready to fall over or else in on itself.

Moss grew over the base of the house and the porch sagged in the middle. The barn off to the side had fallen in so that it looked like one gigantic funeral pyre waiting to be lit. The family cemetery lay off to the side, headstones chipped, worn down by years and weather. They tilted toward each other, off center a little. The wrought-iron fence surrounding them was rusting, its gate on the ground in front, and a weeping willow grew in a far corner, the branches draping everything in shadow. A cold wind came and stirred the leaves, making me shiver. Then voices, soft voices, drifted out from beneath the willow tree. I walked closer and saw them, two silhouettes beneath the branches: Jamie and Fuck You Frances.

I cleared my throat and the talking stopped. Jamie looked over and waved. "Hey!" he called. "You made it! Come inside the gate."

I was a little nervous. I wondered what she'd be like. Mean and crazy? Sweet and disturbed? Personable or more of a bitch? Most kids had done this before turning fifteen or had avoided it altogether. I'd been an avoider, mostly because I'd thought visiting Frances's grave was stupid. It didn't seem much use to come here and call her up just so she could spit on you.

Jamie met me halfway through the cemetery. Frances hung back at the edge of the tree, her dress blowing around her legs, her hair lifting in the night air. She held her hands clasped near the sash at her waist, the way Gracie described her mother standing in the photo. I couldn't see her face in the tree shadows. I imagined a death's head, a skull covered with a thin layer of skin, an emaciated concentration camp victim. I tried to make her out over Jamie's shoulder, only half listening to what he said, but at the words, "We'll stay in the barn," he caught my attention.

"The barn?" I said, turning back to him.

"Yeah. The barn. It looks fallen down, but there's plenty of room in there and it'll be shelter from the wind. Wouldn't want you catching cold. Also no one will see you from the road if someone drives by."

"Okay," I said, then turned my attention back to the girl in the shadows. She was silent and still. "Are you going to introduce us?"

"Sure," said Jamie, looking over his shoulder. "Sorry. She's shy, so give her a break."

"I'm shy too," I said, and Jamie raised the eyebrow near his damaged temple.

"Come on," he said. And we walked back to where Frances waited.

No death's head stood beneath the tree like I'd imagined. As I came closer, I saw a small girl, face round, lips full, her hair tangled from not having combed it in years. Her dress was in rags, just like the story Gracie had told me. But other than that, she looked normal. Just poor and dirty. I guess I was a little disappointed. *This* was the crazy girl who had murdered her parents? She didn't look scary. She just looked sad.

"Frances," said Jamie. "This is my good friend Adam. Adam, this is Frances."

"Nice to meet you," I said, but her sad face suddenly turned into a scowl.

"Enchanted," she said. "I'm sure." Jamie told her not to

start anything and I decided right then she was mean and crazy, not strange and disturbed, and I would sleep with one eye open unless I wanted her to gut me like she did her parents.

She didn't say she was sorry, just sat down on the ground in front of her headstone and picked at the hem of her skirt. You could tell it had been pretty once, with a light floral print and a lace collar. Now, though, it was yellow-gray like the paper in my grandma's old Bible. The little flowers on it had faded so you couldn't tell what color they once held.

Jamie sat down beside Frances, crossing his legs Indian style. The grass was damp. When I sat down the wet seeped through my jeans. I didn't want to appear ungrateful, so I didn't say anything. Frances looked at me, measuring, before finally saying, "So. I hear you're on your way?"

I could tell she was ready to pounce on any evidence of my stupidity so I said, "Yeah, I'm not sure how far along, but I'm not smelling things so well, and my mother's friend's shadow keeps harassing me."

Frances shrugged. "Not that far," she said. "You've got some time left to enjoy living. After that it's all downhill and then you'll be stuck like me and Jamie."

"I'm not stuck," said Jamie. "I mean, Adam and I aren't stuck, are we?"

"No way are we stuck," I said, and he smiled.

Frances sneered.

"The two of you have a lot of unjustified optimism," she said. "Oh well, it's your funeral."

"Famous last words," I said, realizing even as I said it that it was somehow wrong. Frances blinked and looked puzzled.

"Sure," she said. Just that. "Sure."

"It's cold out," I said, changing the subject. I opened my backpack and pulled out the blanket I'd stuffed in there. Even though it was thick, the wind whipped right through, making me wish I'd stayed at home in bed.

"Isn't that nice?" said Frances, getting up, circling me like a drill sergeant. "I wish *I* could feel the cold. Go ahead. Complain. Poor baby. So cold out, isn't it? You have no idea how good that even feels, do you? You don't know what you've got there, the cold. Ignorant. The living are so stupid. Really, Jamie, I don't know why you insist on playing with him like this."

Jamie stood up and said, "That's enough, Frances." He dusted off the back of my pants—I mean his pants, since I'd given them to him—which were wet like mine, and said, "Come on, Adam. I'll build you a fire."

He ducked his head under the former entrance to the barn and I followed him into the dark, where my eyes were useless and all I could sense was the sound of small animals shuffling. It reminded me of dead space. I shivered. The ground was lumpy and uneven. I tripped on something, a rock probably, and told myself to remind Gracie she might find rocks for her collection out here.

Jamie said, "I'm just gathering some of the drier wood and hay." His voice boomed and echoed, as if we were in a cavern. "Come on," he said. He grabbed hold of my hand and I let him lead me out.

We went behind the barn where he went about instructing me on how to set up a plank of wood with a groove in it. He had me tie a shoelace to both ends of a bowed stick. Then I put hay in the middle of the plank and stuck a stick in the groove of the wood and spun it using the

stick with the shoelace tied to both ends. After a few minutes, a small plume of smoke rose from the hay and an orange glow grew in the center. Jamie said, "There you go.
Finally. A fire."

I was impressed. I'd forgotten he'd been a scout and
knew about survival tactics. Maybe the Boy Scouts weren't
so lame after all.

I gathered hay and made the fire bigger, then put planks
from the barn down so we could sit without getting wet. I
also made a litter from the boards to lie down on. We were
pretty efficient, he and I. Survivors. We could have gone on
that television show on an island in the middle of nowhere
and lived happily ever after. Or as happily ever after as you
can be when you're dead.

After we'd spent an hour or so trying to make the place
comfortable, Frances wandered back to join us. Jamie sat on
one side of the fire, I stretched out with my blanket on the
litter, and Frances looked back and forth between us, smirking like a cat. "Playing house, are we?" she said, sitting
down beside Jamie.

"No, we're not *playing house*," I said. "We're just trying
to make things more comfortable. Excuse us for—"

"For what?" Frances snapped. She already knew what I
was going to say, though. She was just toying with me.
"Excuse you for what, Adam? Would that be excuse you for
living?"

"You are such a bitch!" I said.

Frances snorted. "I might be a bitch," she said, "but
you're a *sniveling* bitch. A sniveling bitch boy who doesn't
know how good he's got it! What do you think you're doing? Face it. You're just slumming."

"Shut up, Frances," said Jamie. Unlike me, he was calm

and collected. I was sick of Frances and hadn't even known her for two hours.

It was when she told Jamie, "No, *you* shut up. This is *my* property, and it's *me* doing *you* a favor, remember that!" that I went off on her.

I sat up and said, "You think you're so much goddamn better than everyone, don't you? But just because you're crazy doesn't give you the right to treat people bad. You can't talk to people like they're nothing!"

"You don't know anything about it," said Frances. "I suggest you lie back down and speak when you're spoken to, bitch boy."

"Fuck you, Frances!" I shouted, and she came at me with fists ready.

I stood to defend myself, but before Frances reached me, Jamie grabbed her around her waist from behind. She struggled, kicking and screaming, her dress flapping, but Jamie held her tight.

"You can go!" she shouted. "The both of you can just go to hell! I don't need this!"

Right then we heard a loud bang, then someone muttered a curse and we stopped fighting, all of us, to look where the cursing came from.

It was coming from the house. Someone was in there. Things clattered, crashed, scraped across the wooden floor. A man's voice, deep and sandpapery, shouting something I couldn't understand. I flinched when he hollered. So did Jamie. The only one who didn't was Frances. She narrowed her eyes like a hawk that's spotted its prey. "It's *him*," she said. Her voice sounded like winter coming.

"Who?" I asked.

"Her father," said Jamie.

"Excuse me," Frances said, and headed toward the house. As she left, I noticed she held a large butcher knife in her hand. I had no idea where she'd gotten it. It was just there all of a sudden, like the knife was a part of her, a part that she knew how to make invisible if she wanted.

She walked through the backyard and around the side of the house to the front. I asked Jamie, "What's she doing?"

"What she does every morning," Jamie said.

"What does she do every morning?"

Jamie looked down at the shoes I'd given him and shifted from foot to foot. I could tell he knew what this was about but didn't want to say. I started to wonder what else he knew that he wouldn't tell me. Who else did he know like he knew Frances?

"She kills her parents," he finally said.

Screams and curses filled the house now. Jamie and I moved closer and, as we came to the front, I heard water splashing. I figured this was the part where Frances finished off her mother. "Why does she do this?"

"It's her thing, Adam," Jamie said. "Leave it be."

A moment later Frances stumbled through the screen door onto the porch, her dress covered in blood, her hands covered in blood, her face streaked with it. She breathed heavy, her mouth hanging open like a dog's on a hot summer day. Her eyes were half closed, as if she were drugged, and she squinted at us as if she wasn't sure if she really saw us. Then she took the bloody knife and plunged it into her own stomach. Heaving, she crumpled onto the fly-coated porch. And the longer I looked at her, the more she seemed to get smaller, curling in on herself, curling around the knife in her stomach like a piece of paper burning inward from its edges.

"Jesus!" I shouted. "Why the hell did she do that?"

Jamie put his hand on my shoulder. "Calm down," he said. "It's her own business."

"How can you say that?" I said. "That's so fucked up!"

"Give her time," said Jamie. His hand moved to my back and he started to rub it. "I'm sure she'll answer your questions."

An hour later Frances struggled up from the porch, pulled the knife out of her stomach, wincing as the metal slipped from the wound, and proceeded to the cemetery where she sat at her grave, silent until Jamie and I joined her.

"Did you enjoy the show?" she asked.

"What the hell's wrong with you?" I said immediately.

"That's not the question you really want to ask," she said.

"What do you mean?"

"What you really want to ask," said Frances, looking away from her grave, turning her gaze on me, "is an entirely different question. Go ahead," she said. "Ask it."

"Why do you keep doing that?"

She'd been smirking, but now she looked sad and desperate. "Well," she said. "The answer is complicated. See, my daddy, he wasn't what you'd call the most upstanding gentleman. In fact, he didn't have one ounce of gentleman in him. Everyone around here was afraid of him. Even if my mother showed up at church with bruises, no one would do or say a thing. I didn't have bruises, really. He didn't hit me like he hit my mother. He'd touch me in other ways instead."

Frances looked down at her lap where her hands rested. Her knife had disappeared and I hadn't even seen her move it.

She returned to telling her story and the more she told, the worse the story got. I had a hard time hearing it. I won't go into details because we know this story. We know this story better than we ought to. But I couldn't have stopped her from telling it if I wanted. The words rolled off her tongue one after another and I could tell she'd been telling it for years, had turned it into something round and smooth, like one of Gracie's streambed pebbles. As she talked her face remained smooth. No tears. No crack in her voice. Nothing. It was weird to watch her tell those things so calmly. So much that, when she finally finished, I said, "I don't understand. Why aren't you crying?"

She looked up from her empty hands. Now it was her turn to ask, "What do you mean?"

I said, "Why aren't you crying?" again, and this time my voice started to quiver.

Frances didn't say anything. She sat there and smiled that cat smile again. After a while I said again, "Why aren't you crying? If I told that story, I'd cry. I mean I'd really, really cry, damn it. Cry already, why don't you?"

"You know I can't," she said through gritted teeth. "Why don't *you* cry for me? Why don't you cry like a baby for me? What's the matter? You only do that for Jamie? Is that it?"

"Shut up," I said. "You don't know anything about it."

"Oh really?" she said, grinning. When she realized how much she could bother me, she looked at me pitifully and said, "What's the matter, boy? Can't stand the heat? Maybe you need to get out of the fucking kitchen."

"I'll show you heat," I said, and stood up.

"Adam, what are you doing?" Jamie said.

I didn't answer. I'd be like her, I thought. I'd play her game and see how she liked it. Miss Guided Tours of Hell, I thought. Let's see what she thought of some real heat.

My blood felt thick and poisonous, moving slow and slick like a fire was building inside me. And the more Frances smiled, the more I thought about what she'd said. And the more I thought about what she'd said, the more I burned.

It was morning. The sun was on the horizon, the tree-tops flaring. Birdsong had started, doves and blue jays, a coo and a cackle. When I reached the front porch, I took my grandfather's lighter out and rolled the sparker with my thumb. A flame came up, yellow-red, bending in the wind. I held it to a piece of wood dangling from the porch roof and kept it there until the wood started burning. I helped the flame move farther up the plank until it had a life of its own and, finally, there was a fire.

Then Frances was running at me. "Stop!" she screamed. "Stop, you motherfucker! Leave my house alone!"

She was too late, though. First the porch was on fire, then the front entry. Then the entire house sparked and fumed and went up like fireworks had been set off inside. The house was so dry-rotted, hardly a minute passed before the windows filled with smoke.

"You son of a bitch!" screamed Frances. She pounded on

me with her fists, her eyes scrunched up even though no tears would come. "That was mine!" she screamed. "That was the one thing that was mine!"

Jamie pulled her away from me. When I met his eyes, they were dark and disappointed. He said, "You'd better go, Adam," real soft. Then he put his arm around Frances, who shook and sobbed, to walk her back to the graveyard. Back to her grave.

Playing House

I GRABBED MY BACKPACK AND LEFT THE WILKINSON farm as soon as Jamie told me to go. *Bastard,* I thought as I hopped on my bike and rode to the end of the road. How could he side with her? I was fuming as I rode away, but soon after I turned down Fisher Corinth I heard sirens blaring in the distance and put my feet down on the road to stop. Someone had seen the billows of smoke rising over the trees behind me, a black stain on the morning, and called the fire department.

Fuck. I hadn't thought about that. I bolted into the woods, afraid of being seen on the road. All I needed was to get caught and subjected to further sessions with Dr. Phelps, not to mention the varieties of possible juvenile delinquency violations I was collecting. I could just imagine myself being shut up in one of those detention centers where all the bad kids went. No fucking way was *that* part of my future.

An hour later I was waiting just inside the woods across the street from Gracie's house. Her parents were still home, so I waited until they left for work to dash out of the trees and knock on her front door. When Gracie answered, still sleepy-eyed, I said, "Can you hide me?"

"For Christ's sake, Adam," she said, her eyes widening. "Get in here. Quick. Before someone sees you."

I was being a burden, I knew, but I had something to give her in exchange for putting me up, a gift she'd cherish forever, like one of her precious stones. The true story of Fuck You Frances. So I didn't feel too guilty as I slipped through the door to safety.

"You're all covered with mud and blood," Gracie said as she walked me up the stairs to the bathroom. She wrinkled her nose, which made me feel bad, being someone people would wrinkle their noses at. I hoped Gracie just thought I smelled bad and wasn't thinking I was a bad person. "God, Adam," she said, turning on the shower. "What the hell have you been doing?"

I was too tired to answer. My blood still lagged, heavy from burning down the Wilkinson house, so I just shrugged and let her take over. She stripped my sweat-soaked shirt over my head and unbuttoned my jeans, then said, "Take everything off and get in the shower." Gracie left the room and I got out of my jeans, pulled off my underwear and stepped into the spray, leaning against the cold tiles for support.

Closing my eyes, I listened to the water spatter, and after a while I started to feel calm. Too calm, I guess, because pretty soon it happened again. Suddenly I felt that—*pop!*— happen, and slipped right out of my body.

Bumping up against the ceiling, I looked down at the body leaning against the wall of the shower. Mud and blood sluiced off the flesh as if it were a cow carcass hanging from its hook in a slaughterhouse. Some of the blood was maybe from fighting with Frances and some was from crashing through a thicket of thorns in the woods on the way to

Gracie's, but all of the blood came off together, turning the water pink as it circled the drain.

The body looked ready to fall into a heap, but it stayed standing as I crawled along the ceiling, looking for a way out. Finally I gave a little push and drifted through the ceiling into the attic, which was full of boxes and dust spiraling in shafts of sunlight, and then—*pop!*—I slipped through the roof into the autumn morning air.

I couldn't feel the chill. I couldn't feel the wind that stripped the last remaining leaves from the trees just days before Thanksgiving when people would give thanks for the food they must eat and the water they must drink and the love they must make in order to make the families they needed to protect themselves from death and being alone in the world. I couldn't feel any of that as I floated above the Highsmith house, above the body I'd lived in for fifteen years.

Up here, I was spreading, my arms stretching to both sides of the horizon, my head growing wider and flatter while my legs flipped around like a whale's tail behind me. Looking down, I saw into the Highsmith house as if it were a dollhouse, the wall cut away to reveal the interior: the living room and bedrooms, the stairs leading from floor to floor, the different dolls in their different rooms, living their plastic lives out with their plastic dogs and their plastic cats and their plastic milk bottles and their plastic frying pans frying plastic eggs in the kitchen.

In the basement of the Highsmith dollhouse, the girl was stuffing the body's clothes into a washing machine. She threw in a capful of detergent and slammed the lid shut. Then she ran upstairs to the kitchen. Then she ran upstairs from the living room to the second floor hallway, where she ran to the bathroom, her tiny lips moving. She was saying the body's name, she was saying, "Come on, Adam. Get out of there. You need to go to bed and sleep."

As soon as she said the body's name, gravity took hold and I plummeted like a rock dropped from heaven. Down I fell, back through the dusty attic, back through the ceiling and into the bathroom, back into the body like an elevator jerking to a halt. I blinked and heard her calling. "Come on, Adam. Get out of there. You need to go to bed and sleep."

I turned the water off. Sliding the frosted door open, I found Gracie waiting with a towel. I stepped into it, drying my hair and face, then wrapping it around my waist. Gracie took my hand and led me to her room, put me in her bed, and left me there, clicking the lights off behind her.

I slept more deeply than I had in weeks. But even in sleep I couldn't shake what had happened. Over and over, I dreamed of burning down the Wilkinson house. I kept lighting that piece of wood dangling from the porch ceiling, Frances kept calling me a motherfucker, and Jamie kept saying I should leave. Each time he said that, my stomach clenched and I buckled, waiting for him to take it back. He never did. He'd just turn and walk Frances back to her grave again.

I was grateful to wake in the late afternoon to Gracie's face above me, wisps of her brown hair brushing against my face. "Wake up, Adam," she whispered. "My parents will be home soon. Wake up."

I sat up, rubbing the sleep out of my eyes, and asked what time it was. "After four already," said Gracie. "I need you to be invisible when my parents get home."

"Where should I hide?"

She pointed to her walk-in closet. "In there," she said. "In case one of them comes into my room for something. It probably won't happen, but better safe than sorry."

I didn't want to hide in the closet. I didn't want to sit in the dark and think about wet flesh or wolves howling, but Gracie was right. We needed to be careful or else we'd never escape. So when her mother pulled in the drive ten minutes later, I stepped into the closet. Before Gracie closed the door, she flipped a switch and a light came on overhead, so at least I wasn't in the dark.

I was in there for what seemed like forever, and to tell the truth it was the biggest bore of my life. No books, no music, no games. Since I had a lot of things on my mind and some time to burn, I started thinking about my problems, lining my ducks up in a row, as my grandma would say. *Bing, bang, boom.* I lined them up and shot them down, one right after the other.

The first thing I thought about was how I was slowly but surely becoming a criminal. Not in any bad way, like a murderer or a rapist. But in ways that people don't really understand or talk about a lot. I had committed the crime of not keeping things normal. I had committed the crime of not doing. Most crimes are when people do what they're told *not* to do, but my crime was against *not doing* things we're *supposed* to. I didn't listen to my parents. I didn't go to my appointments with Dr. Phelps. I didn't stay at home like a good fifteen-year-old. I ran away from it instead of running with the track team. I was a not-doer, as opposed to evil-doers, but somehow they got lumped together. And now, on top of all the not-doing, I'd burned down a house. Even though the house had been abandoned for something like seventy years, that was no excuse. By the standards of the living, burning down houses, even abandoned ones, is not good behavior.

The second thing I thought about was how Gracie was so loyal. For a girl I'd barely spoken to for most of my fifteen years, for a girl who seemed to distrust people in general, who suspected the worst in every situation, she was quick to share secrets, quick to rub her body against mine, quick to understand from the right angle that my fuckups weren't really fuckups. You don't find people like that too often. Not so easily at least.

It made me feel bad really. You know, hindsight being twenty-twenty. After I showed up on her doorstep, reeking of smoke and scratched up from crashing through the woods, I felt like the fool she'd been calling me since we'd met at Jamie's grave. So far I'd stolen a heart-shaped rock from her, stolen Jamie maybe (I wasn't sure about this, since he didn't seem like he was going to stay with her anyway) and worse, I'd ignored her phone calls after we'd almost had sex. And all the while, she'd been opening herself up to me, making plans for a mutual escape, taking me in when I needed a place to hide. That's friendship and love rolled into one really. Gracie was on my side, unlike *some* people. I'm not just talking about my family either. I had one more fact to add to the list of my education in death so I grabbed my notebook from my backpack and jotted it down while I hid in the closet:

13. The dead are just as untrustworthy as the living. They will close ranks when it comes to choosing sides.

After I'd spent a few hours doing all that thinking, Gracie came back with a ham sandwich, which was the most wonderful thing in the world. I hadn't eaten in over twenty-four hours and even though I wasn't feeling too starved, I devoured it. Afterward we curled up on the closet floor, kissing, stroking each other before falling asleep with some of Gracie's clothes bunched under our heads as pillows. Gracie set her alarm for five in the morning, so she'd be able to slip into her bed before her parents came in to wake her. She was always thinking of things like that. I was glad we were in this together; for the first time in my life, I felt like I could depend on someone.

In the morning her alarm shot off beeping like there was no tomorrow, and Gracie staggered to her bed as planned. An hour later, also as predicted, her parents were moving around. The shower turned on and downstairs a kettle whistled. Then there were footsteps on the stairs and suddenly someone knocked on Gracie's door and before Gracie could say anything, Mrs. Highsmith came in.

"Grace," she said. "Get up, Grace. It's time to start the day. You need to finish your algebra lesson, and don't forget about that essay on *The Diary of Anne Frank*. I want that before we go to your aunt and uncle's. Come on now. Get moving, Grace."

Ugh. What a nagger. I mean, my mother woke me up too, but she just made sure I was up in time to catch a ride with Andy. She didn't lay out the next three days like she was my secretary or something.

After Mrs. Highsmith left for the library, Gracie opened the closet and before we started the day we got into bed and the word sunflower opened up again. By now the letters glowed gold and brown in my mind, and they had gotten bigger since last time I saw them. Sunflower was now the size of the letters on the covers of my schoolbooks. I imagined they'd just keep growing until one day they'd be the size of a billboard. There'd be a huge advertisement. Nothing else would be on that board except the word sunflower. People would drive past and suddenly have an urge to pull off the road at a place five minutes down the highway where you could park in a shaded semi-private area and take some time with whoever was with you to figure out what that word meant.

Afterward we went downstairs and sat on the couch in the living room and talked. "They're not that bad," said Gracie, referring to her parents. "They just don't get me." Her mom worked as a librarian in the little one room library in our town square, next to the Rexall pharmacy, and her father worked at the Cleveland Amtrak an hour and a half away, where he was in charge of the mechanics. "My dad used to be a mechanic too," she said, "but now he's in charge of the others."

From the looks of their house they made a good living. They had leather furniture and this white carpet that left whiter footmarks behind when you walked on it. And all these plants and ferns in the corners, by the staircase and between chairs. They had paintings of landscapes hanging too. And the dining room was just one room, not split with the kitchen by a prep island. And their kitchen—everything in there was steel. Everything in there gleamed.

My mom would have loved a kitchen like the Highsmiths'. Our kitchen was all fake blond wood cabinets with huge knobs on them from the eighties, which was the last time my parents could afford changing things, and the island dividing the kitchen and dining room was scarred up with knife marks. I hadn't noticed these things the first couple of times I'd been over, but I'd really only seen the front entrance for all of two seconds before Gracie had rushed me up to her bedroom to look at rocks and learn each other's bodies. Now, though, I had a chance to see the house while filling Gracie in on what had happened the previous morning. She said, "Details, Adam," so I gave them, including the truth about Frances. The one thing I didn't mention was how Jamie had sided with Frances. Whenever I thought about that, my throat swelled and my eyes felt like they were going to pop out of their sockets, so I left that part out.

After I told her about Frances, Gracie just stared down at the carpet. "Wow," she said. "How fucked up is Fuck You Frances."

Gracie was thinking about what Frances's father had done, I knew, how no one had helped her or her mother, how our story didn't even come close to the why of what she did. We called her crazy and never wondered what had made her that way. I could see the story changing in her. Her eyes shifted, her bottom lip trembled. Then Gracie said, "That poor girl."

"Don't get too compassionate," I said. "She was a bitch too."

"Well, that's just because she's been totally fucked over! I'd be pretty bitchy if all that shit happened to me and then on top of it I had to kill them every morning for all of eternity."

"No," I said. "You didn't hear me right. She doesn't *have* to kill them. She does it because she *loves* it. It's all she has, she said. She could stop if she wanted."

Gracie stared at me, then back down at the floor. A few

minutes later, she looked up as if the conversation had never taken place and asked if I'd like some breakfast.

She made toast, sausage and eggs, and we sat in the dining room to eat like we were her parents: me at one end of the long shining black table, her at the other end staring back. We were very quiet, the only sound our forks clinking against the plates and our glasses of orange juice being set down after taking a drink. There were place mats under our plates that matched the burgundy walls, and these little wooden rings that held cloth napkins until we slipped them out and unfolded them onto our laps. I did everything right, placing the napkin on my lap, eating small mouthfuls, taking sips instead of gulps, being considerate as I passed the salt. I just imitated how I thought people like the Highsmiths ate. And I was right. I matched Gracie manner for manner and she never blinked.

After breakfast, Gracie took my plate into the kitchen. I followed and found her already washing things up. "Wow, you clean up fast."

"I don't want to leave them. If my parents came home and saw two plates, they might wonder why I'm dirtying so many dishes."

"Would they really notice something like that?"

"Mmm-hmm," she said. "They're big noticers. But they only notice little things. Don't worry. I'm good at covering what they'd notice. They'd never notice a person living in their daughter's closet."

We laughed at that. Then Gracie turned off the water and wiped her hands dry with a towel.

"How did she do it?" she asked. She focused on wringing the towel through her fingers. "How did Frances work herself up to killing them?"

"I guess she'd just had enough," I said. "Everyone has limits."

"I know. But still. She was so young. It must have been horrible. She must have felt so alone."

"Stop," I said, and Gracie looked up.

"What's the matter? Did I say something wrong?"

"No. It's just... Be careful. That's the kind of talk that got us into this in the first place."

"I was just wondering."

"I know. It's not that. It's the caring."

She nodded. "I know," she said, turning away, looping the dishtowel back through the cupboard handle. "I know."

In the end it took only an hour for the Wilkinson house to burn to cinders. I read it in the newspaper after breakfast. The house burning was on page three. On page one, on the top half of the paper, was a picture of Jamie. "Possible Suspect in Child Murder Apprehended" the headline read, and my heart did a backflip. There was no real information other than what the headline said: that they'd found a man in his thirties who might have been Jamie's killer and further investigations were ongoing.

On the bottom half of the front page was a picture of me. That headline read, "Local Boy Goes Missing." They mentioned Jamie too, about how my parents were afraid something could happen to me like him. There was also a lot of garbage about how I was messed up and seeing a psychologist and about how to contact the police if anyone found me. There was no reward. I didn't expect one. My parents didn't have enough money to reward someone for finding me even if they wanted.

"Looks like you're getting famous," Gracie said, reading over my shoulder.

"Yeah," I said. "Famous for being a weirdo."

"You're not weird," she said, looking up from the paper. "It's them. They're the weird ones. There are just more of them than you. More of them doesn't make them normal."

It was strange to have an entire day with no parents around to bother us. We watched TV, me at one end of the couch, Gracie stretched out so her head rested in my lap. She let me have the remote, which felt awkward. For the first time in my life I had control of the channels and it wasn't even in my own house.

We watched game shows and when the local news came on at noon we started making out. Then this anchorwoman began talking about the suspect in Jamie's murder being apprehended and we broke away to listen. We wanted information that would change the way we understood his story. But the lady didn't have much to say except it was a man in his mid-thirties who had been arrested, possibly a drifter, and that they'd let us know more as soon as possible. Same old, same old.

Afterward they interviewed Jamie's mother. She hadn't been talking for the past two months, since all of this started, but now it seemed like she'd gotten mad and finally had something to say.

They interviewed her at the Marks house, which I'd never actually been in—it was nice to put an inside to the outside I'd always watched while running past. At first the camera showed the gray unpainted house with all of those dog coops around it. Yellow straw spilled from the coops and the dogs ran back and forth in the muddy yard. They took a shot of the tire ruts from Mr. Marks's eighteen-wheeler too, and it was all a sad sight, but even sadder once they went inside.

She sat in the living room, which was about the size of my bedroom. In there was an old TV with an antenna on top, a ratty couch with a print of faded flowers, a chair that didn't match and a bookshelf with nativity figures on it instead of books: Mary and Joseph and the baby Jesus in the manger. Everything seemed pushed together, like there wasn't enough space in there but they were going to make everything that belonged in a normal living room fit.

Mrs. Marks wore a gray sweater with holes in it, and as she talked you could hear the dogs outside, barking and howling. She said things that made me think she was questionable. She said things that made me wonder if she *really* knew her son.

"So tell me, Mrs. Marks," said the anchorwoman, "how would you describe Jamie?"

"He was a sweet boy," said Mrs. Marks. "He was always trying to help with one thing or another. I never had to worry about him doing things he wasn't supposed to be doing like some kids do these days. He was a Boy Scout and always on a project, getting those badges. I confess I never understood why he liked the scouts so much. But I figured I was doing something right if all my son wanted was to be a Boy Scout."

"And how do you feel now that a suspect has been taken into custody?"

"I'll tell you this much," said Mrs. Marks. She sat up and adjusted the folds of her hole-filled sweater. "I hope they've found the man who murdered my boy, because then God's vengeance can be carried out. Jamie won't have died in vain any longer. He would have appreciated that."

Mrs. Marks smiled real smug after that little speech. I rolled my eyes. "What a load of crap."

"What do you mean?" Gracie asked.

"That woman is totally using Jamie's death to give testament to her success as a mother. He was so sweet, she says, and of course we have to say, *You poor woman.* He was a Boy Scout, she says, and of course we have to say, *What a shame.* She might as well have asked everyone to take pity on her. Sure Jamie's sweet, but what does that have to do with her? People are either sweet or they aren't. And the way she talked about how his death could mean something if the killer was brought to justice. I mean, what a bunch of crap! Even if that man turns out to be the killer, it won't make things meaningful. Jamie won't have suddenly died for any good reason. He'll still be dead. Big fucking deal. It won't change his story."

"Okay," said Gracie. "Calm down."

We spent the rest of the day eating potato chips and drinking cola, watching soap operas like we were my mom and Lucy. Playing house. I didn't understand what was going on in the soap operas, but by the end of each episode, I had figured out everyone's fucked up relationships. There were so many divorces and secret romances and children who were raised by one father but were really someone else's. And people in comas who had been in comas like five other times, as if this were the normal course of events. Also every show had an evil man or woman who lived to ruin the lives of others, which made a kind of sense, I thought. This one evil woman named Gina reminded me of Lucy. She kept trying to bust up this all-American family at every turn, but they held strong against her plots to unravel their love for one another. She always looked like a fool in the end, which made me mad because I was like, *Fuck.* Soap opera people can keep their shit together but not my stupid-ass family.

Around five o'clock, Gracie said her mom would be getting home soon and that I'd better get back in the closet. This time I took a book from the bookshelf in the living room so I didn't have to think about things so much.

I got comfortable in the closet and started reading the book I'd chosen, which was about this kid who goes to a prep school and is always getting into trouble and hating on the world, but he can afford to spend all kinds of money taking a trip into New York City, running away from his problems. It was interesting but I kept thinking, Why the hell is he complaining? It's not like it was *hard* for him to get where he was going. He didn't have to lie, steal or cheat someone out of money. He just left and no one missed him because it was a boarding school he attended and it's Christmas break, and his parents don't miss him because they're used to other people taking care of their kids. So this kid has his own money and can break cash out whenever, for trains and cabs or to get drunk or to rent a room and get prostitutes to mess around with. Of course he's sorry after doing these things, but then he just goes and does something stupid again and really doesn't have to worry because he has enough money he can make a new life and forget about the one he's just fucked over. At the end, he's in therapy. Whatever.

It was after I'd finished reading that I heard people downstairs yelling. I tried putting my ear to the floor but the sounds were muffled, so when the yelling didn't stop, I got up and crept over to the door and opened it a crack. I could hear the voices better, but still not enough, so I pulled it open a little more and listened harder.

It was Mr. Highsmith yelling at Gracie, and she was yelling back. It became clear in no time that they were yelling at each other about me. Mr. Highsmith's voice boomed and echoed up the stairwell, clattering to a halt outside of Gracie's door, and I had to just stare at it and keep quiet because if I made my presence known everything would be over. There'd be no escape into the unknown, where maybe things were better.

These were some of the things he said:

"If you know where he is, you had damned well better tell us, young lady!"

And:

"Just take one look at that goddamned McCormick family and you know there's trouble. That Linda is a nutcase, always going around with Lucy Hall, who *paralyzed* her for God's sake! And the father certainly isn't worth a day's work."

And:

"I don't want to hear it. No girl of mine is going to associate with a piece of trash like Adam McCormick!"

Things like that are enough to make a person feel pretty bad, and I started to feel that way pretty quickly. I hung on the doorknob and twisted it as Mr. Highsmith went on about me and my family, his voice stumbling around like a drunk in the hall. Some of the stuff he said was true, which made me feel a little sick. I thought of myself as a good observer of my flaws and hadn't even noticed a lot of things he had, which made me think there were maybe even more things about me and my family that I didn't know were wrong. The only thing that saved me from breaking out into a mad dash from the Highsmith house right then and there was all the stuff Gracie yelled back.

"I have no clue where Adam is and even if I did I wouldn't tell you!"

And:

"You're just so ignorant you don't even know it! You're just a silly old train mechanic who thinks he's better than other people!"

And:

"Adam McCormick is a good person. He has integrity, unlike *some* people. You don't know anything about him. If you did, you'd shut your mouth and see everything those newspapers and these stupid gossips are saying is a load of shit. But it's so much easier to judge others, isn't it, Daddy? You're so stupid! Sometimes I wish you weren't my father!"

Mrs. Highsmith broke up the argument. "Enough!" she shouted. "There's no reason to fight. Gracie, your father simply asked you a question because he's worried. That boy is on the loose. We're concerned. There's no reason to get angry."

"Adam is not on the *loose,* Mother," Gracie corrected. I could hear her teeth gritting as she spoke. "He's just another kid who people are pushing around because they can, like you guys are doing to me right now."

"You think you have it so rough?" Mr. Highsmith grunted. "You better learn respect for your elders, young lady, or I'll give you something to cry about!"

Gracie came thumping up the stairs suddenly, so I ran

back to the closet. I clicked the door shut just as she was coming into her room. I pretended like I was sleeping, so when Gracie opened the door, tears staining her cheeks, I was able to wake up and say, "What's the matter?"

"Nothing." She sat down beside me with her knees pulled under her chin. "Just my stupid parents. They know you and I started hanging out a few weeks ago and they were worried about that stupid article in the newspaper."

"It's no big deal," I said. "They're just being parents." I didn't let her know I was upset because I'd never heard what other people thought of my family. I mean, I suspected things. It's just hard to hear it come from someone's mouth unfiltered because they don't know you're around.

Gracie sniffed, so I patted her knee and kissed her. After I pulled away, she looked at me, her eyes shiny with tears, and said, "Adam, I love you."

I gave her a blank stare, I'm sure, because she finally looked down into her lap and said, "I just want you to know that."

"Thank you," I said. I couldn't say it back, but I took it, the word love, and placed it beside sunflower and *ad infinitum*. As soon as I did that, a slight pulse began to beat a rhythm against my leg. I looked down and saw the outlines of Gracie's heart-shaped rose quartz in my pocket, thudding and thudding, growing soft and warm. Each thud was the word love, over and over, and it beat against my leg from then on.

Gracie didn't spend the night in the closet. She was afraid her parents would come in and want to apologize or expect an apology. That's how things worked in her family.

In mine we didn't apologize, not even when we knew we were wrong or had been mean to each other, so I really didn't believe Gracie until about half an hour after she ran upstairs someone came knocking. She scrambled up from the closet floor and grabbed a pair of pajamas hanging from the back of the door so that when her mother came in a second later, it looked like she'd been in there getting ready for bed.

"Grace," said Mrs. Highsmith. "Are you okay, honey?"

"What do you want?"

"Your father's very sorry, sweetie. Please come down and watch television with him and let things smooth over."

"I'm tired," said Gracie. In the mirror, I could see her standing beside her bed, clutching her pajamas to her chest.

"Well, come down and say goodnight at least," Mrs. Highsmith pleaded. "You know your father won't sleep until he knows the two of you are on good terms."

Gracie sighed. "Fine," she said. "I'll be down in a minute."

When her mother left, she came back in the closet. "I'll have to stay in my bed tonight," she said. "But listen. In the morning, my parents and I will leave to eat breakfast with my aunt and uncle in Youngstown. Then we'll probably go shopping or see a movie. That's what we do on Saturdays. But you and I have to be in Youngstown right after midnight to catch the one A.M. train. So I need you to do a few things while we're gone."

"Sure," I said. "Whatever you want."

"Okay," said Gracie, "so this is what you need to do."

In the morning the Highsmiths left like Gracie said and, after it felt safe, I came out of the closet and went into her parents' bedroom to open the middle dresser drawer like she'd told me. Inside were piles of Mr. Highsmith's folded white underwear, but as soon as I pulled up the top layer, I found the white envelope like Gracie said I would. It was slim so I didn't expect much money to be inside, but when I sat on their king-sized bed and shook the money out onto the bedspread, it was fifty and hundred dollar bills that drifted out. Fifteen hundred dollars. I'd never seen so much money in my life.

I tried to figure out how much to take. Gracie hadn't been specific. I needed to leave some so Mr. Highsmith wouldn't notice, but I had to take enough to make sure we'd be okay. Five hundred, I decided. That left a decent amount in the envelope, so if Mr. Highsmith opened it to look inside he'd see enough bills to think nothing had been tampered with. Five hundred dollars would be enough, I figured.

After stuffing the money next to Gracie's heart in my front pocket, I returned the rest, then put the envelope back neatly, tucking down the folded underwear as if I were Mrs. Highsmith herself. That had been simple enough.

For the rest of the day, I picked at leftovers in the refrigerator and watched television until it was time to hide again. When the Highsmiths came back that night, I was asleep on the closet floor. Gracie left me like that until it was near midnight, when she shook me awake and said, "Adam, it's time. Come on."

She had packed a purple backpack full of clothes and food and some money of her own. She slid it on her back and lifted her finger to her lips as she walked to the door. I followed, stepping lightly down the staircase, through the living room and kitchen, out the back door.

"What now?" I whispered, and Gracie grinned, her teeth glistening in the moonlight. She held up a set of keys and they shone as bright as her teeth.

She got into her mother's car and put it in neutral. Then we pushed it while holding on to the doors. Gracie steered the wheel with one hand and when we were on the road, she got in and I pushed the car a while longer just to be safe.

"Far enough," said Gracie finally, and when she turned the ignition, I jumped in too. Then she flicked the headlights on, shifted the car out of neutral, and suddenly the rose quartz in my pocket began to thud fast and hard. "Hold on," she said, pushing down on the pedal. And like that we drove out of town, into the dark of an unknown country.

A PLACE YOU'VE NEVER BEEN

WE DROVE OUT OF TOWN IN LESS THAN FIVE MIN-
utes, then dipped through Vienna, the next town over,
small like ours, with the same town square and the same
cannon from World War Two sitting on the green, the same
paint-flaked band shell no band played in anymore and the
same Super Duper grocery store on the corner where everyone stopped to get gas on Sunday evenings, the same back
roads running like capillaries from rural routes to main
streets and the same churches with the same people in them
on Sundays, praising or kneeling or crossing themselves,
the same fields of corn that, the farther out we drove, slowly
began to fade until they completely disappeared.

Past the local airport, this sorry excuse for a terminal in
the middle of a hayfield, the landscape began to change and
we entered Liberty, a town where nothing but fast food
restaurants and shopping plazas sprawled as far as I could
see. According to Gracie, this was where the Jewish people
in our part of Ohio lived. Well, here and Cleveland, she corrected herself a moment later. I tried to notice if anything
looked particularly Jewish, but I wasn't sure what Jewish
things looked like.

Then Gracie took a left on a road called Gypsy Lane and

a right on Fifth Avenue, and that's when I began to realize when roads are called lanes, avenues and boulevards, you know you're no longer in Kansas. Trees and lampposts lined the streets and just like that, we had entered Youngstown.

As we passed apartment complexes and houses that looked like Spanish villas and gothic mansions, I thought of Mrs. Motes teaching *The Fall of the House of Usher* and wondered how long it would take for those places to fall apart. A park appeared on our left, a square of trees and playgrounds and tennis courts like an oasis in the middle of all those huge Victorians, taking up an entire block. And just across the way was a huge building with stone pillars holding up the roof and wide steps that led down to the sidewalk. I said, "That building looks Greek, not Jewish," and Gracie said it was Stambaugh Auditorium, where she and her family sometimes went to see plays.

Then we drove down a hill and were suddenly surrounded by the college campus. It wasn't much. Not like I'd thought it would be. Four or five story buildings without decoration, not classy like the one that looked Greek. I'd seen advertisements on television for the university since I was a little kid, but it looked bigger on TV than in real life. I blinked and we had passed all the way through campus. On the other side, in the downtown, there wasn't much to see either. Mostly the buildings looked like they'd been built a hundred years ago and were ready to fall down. Like the Wilkinson farm, they were waiting for a fire to be lit.

We stopped at a red light on the corner of Commerce and Fifth, where a few people roamed the streets, drifting out of bars or walking aimlessly, bumming cigarettes or money. One guy sat against the wall of the city playhouse, under the Stage Door sign, and although I'd never seen a real homeless person before, as soon as I saw him, I knew that's what he was. He sat there, chin tucked against his chest, like he was asleep or drugged out of his senses, and then—blink—the homeless guy disappeared and there was this kid there instead.

This kid wore dirty clothes, ripped up jeans, and had the yellow hood of his sweatshirt pulled over his head like a boxer. I watched him for a moment until suddenly he pulled off his hood and looked up at me. When our eyes met, my gut twisted. I had no word for this feeling. It was like déjà vu, only in the opposite direction. Because what I saw when that kid pulled down his hood was me.

Then the light shifted, Gracie pushed on the gas and I looked at her for a moment to see if she'd seen that other me. Her eyes were fixed on the road in front of us, though. I wasn't sure whether I wished she'd have seen me too, or if it was better that I'd been the only one to notice.

We crossed a green iron bridge and entered an area that seemed to be nothing but empty parking lots, tunnels and bars with motorcycles parked out front and leather-vested men and women going in and out of them. Gracie drove through a tunnel, pulled into a parking lot soon after and said, "We've got to hurry. The train will be here in ten minutes."

Not spotting any tracks, I said, "Why don't you drive us to the station then?"

Gracie was already getting out of the car, though, starting to run. "It's down the street," she called over her shoulder. "I don't want to leave the car near the station. It'll give them a clue to where we've gone. Come on!"

I was amazed by the way her mind worked. I was really lucky, I thought, to have been given the word love by someone like Gracie. If she knew what she was doing when it came to making plans like this—to run away and make it possible—then she must have known what she was doing when she gave me that word.

It was strange in this place: a weird mix of concrete and nature. The sky spread out above us like carbon paper, but the streetlamps drowned out all the starlight. On one side of us the downtown skyline loomed on the horizon, its rooftops jutting up and down like a row of rotten teeth. On the other side an oil-black river flowed, its surface moonlight-rippled. Trees lined the riverside, their leafless branches reaching toward the sky like the arms of beggars.

Gracie had a few strides on me, but I caught up with no problem. She didn't know how to pace herself. She pushed too fast for too long, so her breath was unsteady. When we ran back into the tunnel we'd driven through, her Doc Martens echoed. *Clip-clop, clip-clop.* Like a horse and carriage. "Slow down," I shouted, my voice echoing with her boots. But when she looked back her eyes were narrowed.

"We don't have time!" she hissed over her shoulder.

Once we left the tunnel, we crossed the street and ran down a little drive with a sign at the entrance: Youngstown's B&O. And as we ran down the curve of the drive, the building became visible: two stories of whitish-brown brick set into the hillside where the rails rested on their ties.

I stopped at the front doors, which had frosted designs around their borders and log chains wrapped through the brass handles. The place looked pretty ritzy. When I cupped my hands together and pressed my face to the glass, all I could see was the shadow of a circular bar and some stools surrounding it. "The downstairs is a restaurant," said Gracie, breathing hard. "Upstairs is where we wait to get on."

I followed her up a set of attached steps that led to the rails on the hillside. "The doors upstairs will be open so we can wait inside," she said. "There'll be a security guard there and some bathrooms, but there aren't enough people using this stop to make it worth opening a station with actual Amtrak people working. My dad used to work here, but they shut it down and moved him to Cleveland."

We reached the top of the stairs and a moment later a whistle blew, piercing the night. We could see the round light in its grill a ways in the distance. We stood there with our backpacks casually slung over our shoulders, acting normal, and I thought for an instant, *We're going to do it, we're going to get out,* but soon a security guard came out of the building to ask if we were here for the train and I closed my eyes for a moment before turning around to face him, wondering why the hell people always had to be in a kid's business.

Gracie looked away from him, so the guard turned to me. I nodded and offered him a smile, hoping that might make us less suspicious. He was a little black guy with a security badge on his forearm, like a police badge, which made me anxious. His shadow twitched, shuffling around on the platform, reaching for the gun holster at its hip. He had a walkie-talkie. The walkie-talkie worried me too. Especially when it squawked and a voice asked questions I couldn't make out. I thought he might radio someone about two kids trying to catch a train without their parents, so I decided I'd better do something to make him my friend for the next five minutes.

"Does the train have a dining car?" I asked.

He nodded and said that it did. That was a mistake on my part, though, because now he felt like he could ask us even more questions. "You kids here alone?" he asked. But before I could answer, Gracie turned back to him again and took over.

"No," she said. "Our parents are down in the lot, waiting for the train to pick us up. Our mom's in a wheelchair." She said this like my mom was her mom, which made me feel like she was trying to steal my mom, but I got over it pretty fast. "It would be too hard for my dad to get her up here," she explained. "We're visiting our grandparents for Thanksgiving."

"That's nice," said the guard. He peered around the corner, searching for the wheelchair-bound mother waiting in a car with her dutiful husband that Gracie had brought into our story. But when the guard looked back he said, "You say they're down there?"

Gracie and I nodded.

"Well, I don't see a soul down in that lot," he told us. "I'm sorry, but I'm going to have to have you kids come inside until we can figure all this out."

That was it, I thought. It was over. In another minute the train would pull in and we wouldn't be on it when it pulled out. I was already imagining my parents coming to get me, my mother's hurt-filled face, the angry dip in my dad's forehead, Lucy trailing behind, shaking her head in disappointment while her shadow gloated. I suddenly felt like I was going to throw up and put a hand on my churning stomach. But while I was getting ready to give up, Gracie opened her mouth and said, "That's not necessary, sir. They're down there. Really. We'll get them for you if that's what's needed."

The guard gave Gracie a suspicious look, one eyebrow arched, torn between distrust and not wanting to get in trouble if he was wrong. I saw the round light of our train as it drew nearer, felt the tremor in the tracks. I hoped he'd side with not wanting to get in trouble like most people. After a moment, though, he spoke into his walkie-talkie. "Yeah, this is Gordon over at the B&O. I got a couple of kids here saying they're supposed to be going to visit their grandparents for Thanksgiving and their parents are down in the lot, but I don't see anyone down there. Can you send an officer over?"

The radio fizzed and crackled, then a voice came out. "Sure thing, Gordon. Hold tight and someone will be there in a minute."

"Thanks," Gordon radioed back.

"No problem," said the radio.

"Sorry, kids," he told us, "but if your story checks out, we'll still have you with your grandfolks on time."

"Thanks," I said lamely, tipping back and forth on my heels. Gracie winced at me like I was stupid. And when Gordon went to put his walkie-talkie on his belt, she nodded toward the steps we'd come up and then in the next moment she was sprinting down them. I looked at Gordon, who'd gone wide-eyed, and said, "Don't worry, I'll get her!" and was off and running too, leaving him at the top shouting at us to come back.

Before I reached the bottom, the staircase was rumbling and by the time I reached the lot, the ground trembled beneath me. When I looked up, our train came thundering out of the east, sliding down the tracks behind Gordon like a silver curtain. When it came to a halt and stopped squealing, I heard Gracie calling ahead of me.

"This way, Adam!" she shouted. She was already at the other end of the lot, running back to where we had ditched her mother's car. I ran after her, watched her enter the flickering tunnel before me. *Clip-clop, clip-clop,* her boots echoed again, and when I caught up to her in the empty parking lot she was already in the car turning the ignition. In the distance I heard the whine of police sirens and got in fast. Gracie put the car in gear as soon as I was in, and we took off with my door still swinging. First down a side street, then another and another, left and right and left again, until we were far from the station, lost in the labyrinth of look-alike streets in the suburbs of Youngstown.

When we finally made our way to a street Gracie recognized, she pulled the car over for a moment, leaned her head against the wheel and said, "Fuck, fuck, fuck, fuck. I can't believe this. Fuck!"

"Calm down," I said. "It's not the end of the world yet."

"But what are we going to do, Adam?" she said, her voice rising with each syllable. "We're fucked. That's it. That's all. That train was our one chance out of here and we blew it."

"We didn't blow it," I said. "Besides, we got out. That's something."

"Who died and made you an optimist?" she said.

"That's not what people usually call me," I said. Coming from Gracie, it sort of made me want to smile. "By the way," I said instead, "where are we?"

Gracie nodded toward an old Victorian house across the street from where we were parked and said, "That's where my aunt and uncle live."

She'd been so angry with herself but suddenly at the mention of her aunt and uncle's house, she dropped into some hazy field of memory and began telling me stories. It was as if she'd been saving them for some other time but wasn't sure if she'd have that chance now, so they all tumbled out of her mouth at top speed. If it had been my brother, I'd have thought he was high, but Gracie had something high about her naturally. She told me about how her dad sings opera in the shower, but never anytime else. About how her mother threatens to leave when she thinks Mr. Highsmith isn't paying her enough attention. About how her aunt and uncle are drunk all the time and spend their weekends in alcoholic stupors and you can practically see the fumes exit their mouths when they talk. About how every Saturday she and her mom and dad go to visit them and her parents drink with them and give her money to take the bus into town to see a movie while the adults play cards and drink their heads off. I interrupted her at that point and said, "You mean like, before we left, when you and your parents went to Youngstown, you were at the movies by yourself?"

Gracie nodded.

"I thought you did all that stuff as a family," I said. "The way you put it, that's what it sounded like."

"Yeah, well," said Gracie. "Sorry if I gave you the wrong impression. That's Saturdays. Mom and Pop and Aunt June and Uncle Eddie sitting around the card table with their drinkies." She laughed, "Ha! Ha!" then shook her head, looking miserable. "I'm sorry, Adam," she said. "It wasn't supposed to be like this."

"I don't mind," I said. "I mean, I've never been to Youngstown. I'd say we were successful. We can save California for some other time."

She turned to me and I saw she was looking at me like

kids at school did when I used to ask about Jamie. "You've got to be kidding me," she said. "Right?"

I shook my head a little, then looked down at my hands in my lap and pretended like they were really interesting at just that moment.

"You mean," she said, "you live approximately one hour away from Youngstown and have never ever, not even once, been here?"

I shook my head again.

"What's wrong with your parents, Adam?"

"That'd take all night," I said, looking up again.

She nodded, seeming to understand this more than anything else, and put the car in drive again. Before pressing down on the gas to take us back into the empty streets, Gracie looked at me and said, "We've got all night. And I want to know. So. You know. Why don't you tell me?"

As she drove us out of Youngstown and back toward home, I started talking, slowly at first, trying to figure out how and where and what to even begin with, and after a while it all started to flow into one story, all these threads I'd thought belonged to different ones, and then I was telling her things I'd never really talked about before except a little bit with Jamie.

"My parents aren't any better, really," I told her. "They fight all the time and they're really stupid. It's like they don't have any words or something. They just scream and holler and call each other stupid fucks and shit like that, and then they're sorry about it later. That's how my mom got paralyzed."

Gracie looked over for a moment, interested. "What do you mean?"

So I told her. I said, "They'd been fighting that day, my mom and dad, all about how my mom didn't work and sat around the house all day doing nothing and how my dad didn't think that was fair since he slaved away at the construction company and for what? For a wife who kept getting fatter and two kids who were stupid and useless and how he wished we'd never been born and how he wished he'd never met her and gotten her pregnant like the cow she is. And then he went and said, *You are such a waste, Linda,* and my mom said, *Oh yeah? You think so? Well we'll just see about that.* Then she got into her car and peeled out of our driveway. She was going to Abel's, or so she said, to get a beer and find herself a real man."

"No way," said Gracie, her eyes wide.

"Halfway there, though, she got in a head-on collision with Lucy Hall, who was on her way home that night, drunk, it just so happened, from Abel's. She'd had a fight with her husband that day too, and had gone there and drank her way into a stupor, rubbing up against any tub of country lard that came across her. And then when she left to go back to her stupid husband she hit my mom and paralyzed her. I hate her."

"Adam," said Gracie. "Why didn't you tell me all this before?" She put her hand on my knee and kept the other on the wheel's twelve o'clock.

I shrugged. "I guess I thought everyone knew," I said, remembering all the stuff Mr. Highsmith had said about my family.

She shook her head. "No, Adam. Not everyone knows."

"Who cares about that stuff anyway," I said. "We have each other. That's what's important."

Gracie smiled. It was the closest I could come to saying what she wanted to hear, I knew. She nodded and said, "You're right. We have each other."

After a while of silence and me staring out my window as we passed the fields I'd thought I'd never see again a couple of hours earlier, I turned to Gracie and said, "What do you think he's doing right now? Do you think he's okay?"

"Who are you talking about?" said Gracie. She wouldn't look over at me. She kept her eyes on the road.

"You know," I said. "Him. You don't talk about him anymore. What happened?"

"I made a decision, Adam. I made a decision not to."

"Not to what?"

"Not to see him anymore. I told him to go away. I told him I didn't want him. I told him I chose something else."

"What did you choose?"

Gracie looked over briefly, the sunflowers behind her eyes flaring, the petals unfurling. "You," she said.

"But you could have had us both," I told her, and she turned back to looking ahead.

"I don't have what he needs, Adam," she said. "And neither do you."

"He just needs to be loved," I said. "Don't you remember?"

"He needs more than love," said Gracie. "You can't give him what he really wants. No one can."

We didn't talk for a while after that. I went back to staring out the window at the fields and town halls and maple trees and the brief flicker of Sugar Creek as we passed over one of the many bridges that crossed it, and when it was obvious that we were headed back home, I asked Gracie, "Now what?"

"There's only one thing to do now," she said. "Regroup."

"What does that mean?"

"It means you go back in my closet," she said, "while I pretend like tonight never happened."

"That's a plan?" I said.

Gracie nodded, spinning the wheel as she rounded a bend. "That's all we've got right now, Adam," she said. "We'll have to wait until we can figure out something else. Otherwise they'll know we left together and then we're both screwed."

"Okay," I said, "the closet." I was sort of getting used to it anyway.

We drove to town slowly, taking our time in case we passed a police car so we wouldn't seem suspicious, speaking only when one of us thought we'd made a wrong turn or knew a better way. By four in the morning we were back in town sighing as we passed by the high school and town square and reaped fields of corn, the stalks broken and trampled. Gracie knew where all the local cops hid in order to catch speeders, so at those places—the volunteer fire department, the oil well drive right around the curve on Highway 88, the church parking lot—she drove extra careful. When we finally turned onto her road, we thought we were home free, but as we drove over the railroad tracks next to her house, we saw a police car sitting in the circular drive ahead of us. "Fuck," Gracie said under her breath. "They're here already. This isn't happening. It can't be." She stopped the car and killed the lights.

"Don't worry," I said. "I'll say I made you do it. It'll be my fault. Just switch seats with me. I'm already in trouble for running away. This way is easier." I was going to list more reasons for her to let me take the blame because I sure had enough reasons, but before I could get the next one out, she held her hand up and shook her head.

"Stop," she said. "I've got a better idea." I looked at her, my mouth frozen mid good reason. She looked at me with the most serious face I'd ever seen before and said, "Get out of the car and run into the woods, Adam. Now. Quick. Before they come outside and notice us."

I stared at her for a second, then reached over the back seat and grabbed my backpack. When I opened the door, I turned back and said, "What will you do?"

"I'm going to try and convince them I went on a joy ride by myself. They don't necessarily know you were ever here."

"But then you'll be taking all the blame."

Gracie rolled her eyes. "That's right. But it's better than both of us. Now go! Find someplace to stay. Then contact me somehow in a couple of days. Okay?"

"How?"

"How should I know?" said Gracie. "Just do it. I'll be looking for you."

I went to leave again, but I didn't feel right about it. I turned back and said, "Thanks." Just that. What else could I say? Her plan would at least give me some time to figure out something else. So I leaned over and gave her a fast kiss. Her heart beat hard in my pocket as I pulled back and slung my backpack over my shoulders. It was a good thing I was ready to bolt because at that moment the porch light of the

Highsmith house suddenly came on, lighting up the front lawn, and a second later a cop came out, followed by Mr. and Mrs. Highsmith.

"Go!" Gracie whispered, all harsh. So I did. I went. I ran as fast as I could, looking back only once, briefly, to see Gracie pull the car into the drive as her parents and the cop hustled off the porch to meet her. Then I turned and ran down the tracks into the bitter November night.

It only took me a few minutes of running down those tracks before I realized I was running directly toward the place where Jamie's murderers had buried him, and thinking of that reminded me of the night I saw God's finger coming at my family, which made me feel even more desperate. Now when I looked up I could barely see any stars, let alone God's finger. I wondered where it had gone. It had probably reached earth by now and was seeking me out, just trying to get a good shot before it really let loose. It made me think of my dad the hunter and his survival tactics and strategies he always taught us while telling us what happened on his hunting expeditions and how when a deer realizes it's been spotted it'll run for the thickest cover possible to hide. I thought right then I better make like a deer before God had a clear shot at me, so I ran off the tracks and straight down into the blind dark of the woods below.

It was so dark in there, it felt like when Jamie took me through dead space. I kept holding my hands up in front of me, pushing branches away as they scraped my face, starting at the sound of twigs snapping, stumbling over dead branches that lay scattered over the hills and hollows of the woods. It all made me want to stop and bargain, to say, *Look God, you don't need to use your finger with me, say what you want, just put the finger down and let's talk peacefully*. But I knew that was useless. My grandfather had been a bargainer and my grandma always said that it got him nowhere with his cancer and he was in pain until the very end. She tried to tell him her various tricks for outrunning misfortune over and over, but it only made him mad because he didn't believe in washing the floors with salt water or burning something you loved in the oven so that something that was making you sick would go away. It only revived the same argument they'd been having since they married when she was sixteen and he told her she'd be Protestant now and she said no way, take the kids if he must, but she wasn't setting foot in that place. She was Catholic, but like in this really weird way apparently, which my mom says Catholics are in general because they tend to believe in a lot of magical stuff that she doesn't believe in, which to me isn't the smartest argument in the world because she has no proof there isn't magic in the world, she's relying on an invisible faith that magic *doesn't* exist, which is the same thing in my opinion as having faith that it does. In any case, it was an old battle in our family and I knew from my grandfather's failed prayers that it did no good to bargain. God will do as He pleases. With my grandfather, it turned out He wanted him to suffer for months and months before He finally let him go.

I was deep in the woods and had stopped running for a while because I had no clue where I was anymore and I was tripping way too much, falling on my face and picking wet leaves that smelled of mulch and insects off my cheeks so I thought I might as well slow down now. If the cops knew I was in here, they weren't going to find me right away anyway. I mean, hell, it took them two weeks to find Jamie's body. I wouldn't call that efficient.

But thinking that made everything just a little worse and I congratulated myself on making being in the woods late at night, unable to see, breaking branches and snapping twigs and rustling leaves around even more scary than it already had been. Now I couldn't stop thinking about Jamie's murderers, about Jamie's murder, and how it was in here, who knows—maybe on the very spot I was standing at that moment—that they did whatever it was they did to him. Smashed the one lens of his glasses, made that deep carve into his left temple, dragged him around on his knees until they bled, and the bruises on his neck, their hands pushing the air out of him. If it had been me, I'd wondered, would I have escaped? I looked around now, not able to see two inches in front of me, and knew for sure they would have done me just the same.

I kneeled down on my haunches, watching my breath steam a little. It was getting cold, but it didn't bother me much. I could feel it, but for some reason I didn't mind. Maybe I just had a lot of adrenaline pumping through me, and that was keeping me warm. *What are you going to do now, McCormick?* I couldn't even find my own shadow in this dark to ask for its advice. Not that it had ever been any use to me before.

After my mind began to quiet, though, I heard something. At first I thought it was light. I didn't know what that even meant, but I thought, *I hear light. Where is it?* And when I stopped breathing for a minute to listen harder, I realized what I heard was the sound of water running. A small trickle. I stood, trying to hear what direction it came from, because the only water that ran through town was Sugar Creek and if I could find Sugar Creek, I could find shelter. A place only I knew about. That was what I needed. Someplace no one knew existed but me.

Walking slowly, trying not to make any noise, I picked my way toward the sound of the stream. It grew louder and louder until eventually it seemed like I was surrounded by the sound of water and then the next step I took—*splash!*—I was in it on my hands and knees, saying *Fuck fuck fuck,* like Gracie had earlier, but happily. Once I pulled myself out of the creek and back onto the bank I waited there in the dark until the sun began to rise a while later, shooting rays of light down through the leaves that hadn't fallen yet. And then I got up and followed the sunlight dancing on Sugar Creek's dark surface until I came to the covered bridge where the old railroad tracks ran through and the creek went under, and there I crossed over to the other side and kept on going, farther and farther, until I reached the Amish loggers' camp.

The camp was just a cutout circle in the middle of the woods where a bunch of Amish men had been hired to cut down trees back when I was a little kid. After they were done, I'd come here and play in their camp a lot, imagining it was another world, that I was an astronaut on the surface of Mars trying to figure out a way to make the land habitable and make homes for people to live in. There was a lean-to shack the loggers had built to get in out of the rain and that had been my fort after they abandoned the place. It was still standing, leaning against an elm tree for support, and the three huge mounds of orange sawdust I used to climb and roll down were there too, only now they were browner and smaller and smelled more like rot.

I couldn't remember the last time I'd come, but I was glad to be here again, back at my old fortress in the woods where no one would ever think to find me. It wasn't a place I'd never been, like we'd planned for, it wasn't like California at all. But maybe it would be better, I thought, to come to a place where no one I knew had ever been instead.

Shadows in the Moonlight

THE SHACK WASN'T MUCH. MADE FROM PLANKS OF old, unpainted wood, now gray with age, it sagged to one side a bit more than it had the last time I'd seen it. That had to be five or six years ago, when I still came to the woods to get away from everything, before I started running. Other than the sagging, there was also no longer a door in the doorway, just a pair of rusty hinges where the old one used to be. The window cut out of one wall was still there, but its flap had been removed or more likely was probably torn off during a storm and blew away. The flat roof covered in tar paper was mostly fine too, except it was green with moss now. When I was little, I used to climb up there by sliding out the window and standing on the sill so I could pull my-self up and lie down to read comic books on the sun-warmed tar paper. I wanted to go up there now, but it was probably moist with all that moss, and I was pretty damp from falling in the creek already.

I sat inside on a three-legged stool instead and thought about the tree house my father had built for my brother and me when I was six or seven. Andy and I would sit in it during the summers and read comic books, trading them back and forth. We were each allowed two comics monthly. I got

Spider-Man and the *Uncanny X-Men,* Andy would always get *Cloak and Dagger* and the *Incredible Hulk.* It was the one thing we never fought about, the one time in our lives when we acted like real brothers. Even so, when I found the shack in the woods after the Amish loggers left, even though I thought maybe it could be another place for both of us to get away, I never told Andy. We knew how to share when it came to comics and the tree house my dad built, but I knew in the way that my grandma taught me how to know things that I'd need a space of my own to get away to someday.

Through the doorway I watched brown autumn light fill the clearing, orange and red leaves glowing like falling stars as they drifted down to the forest floor. The wind was bitter this late in November, but I only noticed when I thought about why I didn't feel it as much as I should have. Even though my jeans had rips and tears in them, even though my running shoes were still soggy inside from falling in Sugar Creek, even though I only had on a jean jacket and a hooded sweatshirt underneath for warmth, if I'd taken all that off I still wouldn't have shivered as long or as often as I probably should have.

There was an old steel cot in one corner of the shack that didn't have a mattress anymore, just a long rectangle of rusty springs basically, but I thought I might be able to make it into a bed with a little effort. So I went outside, got some wood planks and took them inside to put on top of the springs. Then I opened my backpack and took out my extra clothes and spread them over the planks for a little layer of softness. When I tried to sit down, though, the bed squealed like someone being murdered, so I braced myself and slowly let more of my weight rest on the bed until I was sure it wasn't going to fall apart beneath me. Then I pulled my legs up on the cot too.

Looking up at the ceiling, I saw a maze of webs in a shaft of sunlight, glittering from corner to corner, and in the center was this huge black spider that looked like it could have kicked the shit out of Charlotte, the spider that helped Wilbur the pig in that book *Charlotte's Web*, which I read when I was around ten years old maybe and had thought was pretty cool except I always felt bad because Charlotte was so nice and tried to bring Wilbur special attention by spinning webs above him to spell out things like Some Pig! and everyone would read the messages in her web and go crazy over Wilbur because of what they said. But I always thought the truly amazing thing was that a spider could read and write. No one seemed to get that, though. Then she had babies and died, yet another sacrifice it seemed we were supposed to feel okay about, but it was a huge disappointment to me and somehow reminded me of my mother except my mom had babies and didn't die. She had Andy and me and got paralyzed instead.

So I wasn't alone after all. I was living with Charlotte. No big deal. I could share a shack with a spider.

Rummaging through my bag, I found I still had the five hundred dollars I'd taken from Mr. Highsmith's underwear drawer along with a knife, a flashlight, a bag of cereal and an apple. I wasn't very hungry so I left the cereal in the bag and took the apple, crunching my way through half of it before it started to taste sour and I put it down. The other half sat heavy in my stomach and if I made the slightest move on my makeshift bed it sloshed around inside me like a huge load of gravel, making me double up on the cot, so sleeping that afternoon as I'd planned for didn't happen.

Since I couldn't sleep, I decided to think about other things I wanted. Hopes. Wishes. I didn't have many hopes or wishes for my life at that moment and those I did have were mostly things like how I hoped I could run fast and far enough away to get out of the range of God's finger as well as out of the range of my crappy family. Other than that I also hoped Gracie was at home writing her report on *The Diary of Anne Frank* right then, because if she was it meant she'd been able to convince her parents and the cops that she'd gone on a joy ride alone and they would still have no clue where to look for me. For all they knew, I was far away, not even near town anymore. Kids can get pretty far in a few days when they're on the run. Cops know that. If they were smart cops (which is rare I think, and so I added that to my list of hopes and wishes) they'd assume I wasn't anywhere nearby and Gracie could go back to studying at home alone and her parents would begin to trust her again and in a couple of days we'd be able to see each other, maybe.

It'd been about a week since I'd left home, give or take a day, but I'd already started to lose track of time. Now I found myself looking toward the quality of light to judge if it was morning, noon or evening. Night was easy. You can't mistake a moon and the stars spread out over the trees like a banner for anything other than night. So as the light faded from afternoon to evening and the dark came out and night birds began to rustle in the branches above, I put my list of hopes away and slept a little more easily. At least until I started to dream.

A place unfolded inside me that looked exactly like the place my body was hiding in the shack in the woods surrounded by trees as they lost their leaves and the air was full of their drifting colors. I woke up inside that shack, only this time the shack was inside me, and I walked out into the woods and down to Sugar Creek, where I kneeled and took a long drink of cold water, lapping at it like a dog.

There were other dogs too. Wolves were howling. I heard their voices all around in the woods and it was late and evening was coming on fast. Soon it would be night and the men with no skin that had been around the first time Jamie took me into dead space would come out and they'd find me where I wasn't ready to be, like Jamie had said. And then there they were, clambering through the brush, pushing aside branches until they were on both sides of Sugar Creek, stretching their arms out toward me. One said in a voice like someone who's just woken from a nightmare, "Say something. Say anything," and held his trembling hands out as if he was waiting for me to give him something to eat. I turned from him, but ran only a few steps before I knew I wasn't going to be able to get away. They were surrounding me, begging me to speak, their hands clenching and unclenching as they reached out.

"They're mine!" I shouted. "Mine!" And then they were on me and I couldn't breathe or shout because they were holding me down while the one who asked me to say something stitched my mouth shut with a needle and string.

"If you won't share," he said, "then you can't have them either."

I woke up for real then, shivering and cold for real too, though it wasn't from the cold air or the lack of a blanket or any real way to keep myself warm out in the woods. It was the men with no skin who had touched me and made me shiver. Like Jamie had made me shiver that first night he came to me.

I sat up and the cot screeched. It was deep in the night,

but as I looked around I thought I could see vague shadows moving under the moonlight that filtered through the trees. I didn't speak to them. I wasn't ready to be where they were, so it was better to pretend like I didn't exist and to say nothing at all. I kept all the things I wanted to say inside. Instead of saying them, I thought them in my head, where no one but I could ever hear them.

Is that you? I thought hard, looking out at the shadows. *Are you out there?*

The next morning I woke to sunlight falling through the window. The woods were full of chirping already and when I sat up and went to the doorway, I saw the white tail of a deer lifted high as she jumped into a thicket of thorny brush and trees and sped away. She must have heard the cot as I got out of bed. "Sorry," I said. I couldn't hear her rustling in the brush anymore, so she was either out of hearing range or playing it safe, hiding.

I felt a bit hungry so I got the bag of cereal out of my backpack and had a couple handfuls before it was completely gone. Luckily I was already starting to feel full again. Two handfuls of sugary cereal shouldn't have made me feel full but the other option was eating the other half of the apple I'd tried to eat the day before, which I found at the bottom of my bag and took out to throw into the thicket where the doe had jumped away. Maybe she'd eat it and I wouldn't feel so bad for scaring her. One thing I didn't have much patience for anymore was people scaring other people. Like how Frances loved weirding me out with her story about why she killed her parents every morning and to tell the truth, that is just not cool. That's crazy.

I was a little worried though because without the cereal and apple I had nothing to eat and I started to wonder if I'd have to eat crayfish from Sugar Creek or figure out what roots and plants were okay to chew on. Maybe I wouldn't do so good on that survival show after all. I only had a few things I knew how to do to survive in this world. The one I was best at was running, and that wasn't proving to get me very far. Maybe if Jamie was still with me, we could have put our heads together and come up with something. Or Gracie. She always seemed to know what to do. I was always the one without a clue. But they weren't with me, and I knew I'd better think of something fast because at some point I would eventually need to eat again.

I didn't want to stay in the shack anymore so I grabbed my backpack and started heading for Sugar Creek. The woods were peaceful that morning. Only a slight breeze blew, but you could tell that it was carrying winter on it, that somewhere down the line snow followed its trail. It was only a matter of how long it would take to reach here. A few weeks, I figured. And by then I'd hopefully have found somewhere to stay other than the old Amish logging camp. Even if I was still here when snow came, though, it was still better than home, where there was basically nothing but trouble waiting.

As I walked through the covered bridge, my shoes knocking against the wooden planks, then along Sugar Creek where the banks were soft beneath my footsteps, I thought about home. I didn't know how to feel about that word. I mean, I had the shack in the logging camp, which was sort of like home but not really because it was just a place to keep me out of the wind and rain for the most part. It didn't have anything comfortable about it and wasn't the safest place either. And that's when I realized the two most important things about home are comfort and safety. And knowing that those two things were a big part of the word home helped me understand that the home I'd left hadn't been my home either because it wasn't comfortable or safe and hadn't been for a while. If there'd been a chance before that moment that I'd have added the word home to my collection of words, it was gone now. There are too many things you can't trust about that word, so from there on out I'd settle for words that didn't hold false promises. *Shelter,* I thought. That was what I had now. That was the word I'd add to the others.

I was starting to understand what my grandma had been on to with her warnings before she went and died. She'd known this was coming, but not even I, who usually understood everything she said, even her strangest visions, could see what she saw in the time before she died. How could we? We weren't on the road she was on right then. But now I was, now I saw the path she'd been able to see when life was abandoning her.

But even if I'd been able to see what she saw, it didn't matter. No one but my grandma ever listened to me, and if I talked about visions and stuff like my grandma used to do, it would have been even worse. My dad always said if I listened to her my head would rot. Probably he was saying that right now even. *That boy's head is rotted from all of your mother's crazy talk!* He probably thought that's why I got into Jamie's hole too. But getting into that place wasn't because of my grandma. That had nothing to do with her. Nothing at all.

As I sat down on a stump beside Sugar Creek, I thought about sitting down beside him in computer lab, how we sat at the last two computers in the back corner of the room where no one could bother us, and even if we talked our teacher Mr. Gardner couldn't hear us. Or if he did hear, he didn't say anything. Probably he could see from my tests that I didn't understand computers as easily as Jamie, so maybe Mr. Gardner thought I was at least smart enough to get help. And if that's the case, then it's Mr. Gardner who gave us that period of being able to talk without everyone being in our business.

There was this one day I finished our assignment pretty fast and, since Mr. Gardner let us do what we liked after we finished our work, I logged on to a chat program I belonged to so I could play a puzzle game it had. I'd barely begun to play when suddenly a box popped up with a message from someone called Lonewolf who wrote, "move the green tile to the last row on the bottom right of screen."

I could feel my brows knitting together above my eyes and thought, *Who the hell is this? No one ever messages me.* But I moved the tile anyway and totally won practically before the game even started.

So I typed back, "how did u know I ws playing a game?"

And Lonewolf replied, "b/c I was watching you."

I looked slowly over to my right and Jamie turned his face in my direction, already smiling. "Jerk," I snorted and punched his arm when he chuckled at me, but he only shook his head and kept smiling.

"You don't think too quick, do you, McCormick?"

"I guess not. I mean, no. Not about everything."

"Good thing you have me around to watch your back."

He went back to doing whatever he'd been doing before and I thought about him watching me without me knowing it and somehow that made me feel safe, thinking maybe someone was looking out for me.

But he'd been the one who needed watching. Not me.

By the time late afternoon came around, I got up from my seat by Sugar Creek and started walking toward the tracks. The light was fading into the gloaming hour. That's what my grandpa always called the part of the day when there was no sun and no moon, but somehow light from both still filled the air, a gold purplish brownish light, a light like a bruise, he called it. I thought there was something true in that, how light can be like a bruise, painful like a bruise too, to look in the direction of light, to see it without squinting or shielding your eyes. My mother used to tell us not to look into the sun or we'd go blind, but sometimes I looked right at it, even though she said it was dangerous. Thinking of that made me feel like crap, though, because it just reminded me of all the other things I did that I wasn't supposed to do and made it seem like I had this criminal history or something. I always did the wrong thing if given the chance. I got into graves. I listened to shadows. I fought my own brother. I burned down houses. I ran away from home. I don't know why I reached for edges, but I'd reach every time. And the desperate thing was that I didn't plan most of these things. They just happened. Which was even more frustrating because it all seemed hopeless. Out of my hands.

I made myself stop thinking about it. I was on the railroad tracks, hands in my pockets, trudging toward Gracie's house. When I reached the road where the old tracks ran across and curved behind the Highsmith house, I kept close to the tree line, even though it was dark, in case there were cops still waiting for me.

But there weren't. In fact no one was waiting outside the woods for me. Mrs. Highsmith's car sat in the circular drive outside the house and the lights were on inside, making the windows look like squares of butter. I saw Mr. Highsmith wander across the front window on his way to the kitchen and thought about how everything in his kitchen gleamed, how everything was so new and fiercely clean. I imagined him making a sandwich, even though he'd already had a fine supper made by his fine wife, the town librarian, who also homeschooled their fine daughter and kept his fine house in such fine order. Who could ask for more than his blessed peaceful little family? He was so happy, spreading mayonnaise across the bread, smiling like a fool. How had he got so lucky?

I looked down at my feet and shook my head. What was Gracie thinking, getting caught up with someone like me? She was in way over her head, I thought, and I realized then that this was one thing I knew that she didn't.

I started walking toward town, still staying inside the trees, where I could hide and no one could see me.

A half hour later I was behind the fence in back of the high school looking at the track on the other side where I used to run. The school was dark and empty. Everyone had gone home and all the sports practices were over. I climbed over, wedging the toes of my shoes into the little diamond-shaped spaces one at a time until I was at the top, where I pulled myself over and landed on my feet in a crouch like

Spider-Man, looking around to see if anyone had spotted me. When it seemed safe, I took off running around the track until I was out of breath.

I walked the baseball diamond and soccer field, I walked the perimeter of the octagon-shaped gym, I hung out in the empty faculty parking lot in back and looked through the windows of the woodshop where all the machines you could cut yourself on sat in silence, their blades gleaming, hungry for the next kid to put his fingers too close as he slid a piece of wood through their teeth. Andy was good at woodshop, but I only took one semester because it was mandatory and after that I switched to typing. When I told the woodshop teacher I was transferring, he wanted to know why. I told him I was planning on going to college and needed to know how to type. He was nice about me leaving and said in that case typing would be a skill I'd need for sure. I didn't tell him I had no real intention of going, but he'd probably thought I was lying or deluded anyway. No one in my family had gone to college and I'm pretty sure that was obvious to everyone. I was even more sure after hearing how Mr. Highsmith talked about us when he didn't know I was living in his daughter's closet.

I was getting a little hungry so I went back to the garbage Dumpsters behind the cafeteria loading dock and flipped open a lid to look inside. There were pizza slices and burgers still in their wrappers and French fries in cups from today's lunch in there, so I climbed up on the closed side of the Dumpster and let my torso and arms and head drop down into that dark space to fish for food.

It smelled like any Dumpster, but not as bad as I remembered. I figured if I only took things still in wrappers like burgers, it wouldn't be so bad. So I grabbed three burgers and a salad in a plastic container with an Italian dressing pack and a plastic spork taped to the top and brought my haul back up to the night to sit on top of the Dumpster and eat.

I started with a burger, which was cold and goopy in my mouth but it filled my stomach faster than I thought it would. I packed the other two and the salad in my backpack and climbed down again to head back to the woods so I could reach the town square under the cover of tree shadows.

The good thing about living in a small town in Ohio where pretty much everyone works in factories or else on farms is that most everyone is in bed by ten at night. So by the time I made it to the town square where the cannon sat beside the stone wall that listed the names of war veterans from our town who had died in their various wars, by the time I reached the band shell sitting beside the duck pond just waiting for an occasion to have the school band play something festive inside it, pretty much everyone was either getting ready for bed or was already off and dreaming. So I was able to walk unnoticed across the square to the telephone rack at the front of the Super Duper grocery store and call the Highsmith house and hope as the phone rang that Gracie would be the one to pick up.

But the voice that answered when I called, saying "Hello?" all worried, then again, "Hello? Is anyone there?" after I didn't say anything, belonged to Gracie's mom. I could tell it was her by the grown-up voice. There's always something worried and overly concerned in adult voices. If you listen, you'll hear it. There's not much difference between kid voices and adult voices besides this tremor in the throat. In women it's what lets the nagging mother voice exist. In men it's what allows the grunting, outraged voice.

Probably that tribe in Africa that clicks in order to speak has nagging mother clicks and grunting, outraged father clicks too. Something happens to the voice when people become adults and—*bam!*—suddenly you're a worried voice person. I'm pretty sure this has to be universal.

So when I heard Gracie's mother's worried voice, I hung up and rolled my eyes, sighing. Jesus, lady, I thought. Why can't you go to bed like everyone else and let your daughter answer the fucking phone already? Don't you have work in the morning or something?

I waited a few minutes, watching the square for cars, cops in particular, then picked the phone up again, threw my change in and dialed once more. Two rings later and a voice came on, only it wasn't talking to me, it was in mid-sentence.

"It's my friend Melissa. You remember Melissa! She came to Stars on Ice with us two years ago? Yeah, it's *that* Melissa. Okay, I'll tell her not to hang up like that again. She's just shy. Sorry. Okay, I won't be on late. Okay, I love you too! Goodnight!"

"Hello?" I said when the voice stopped talking.

"Brilliant move, Melissa," Gracie answered. "I mean, don't just hang up on my mom like that. She won't bite, you know."

"Sorry," I said. "I just got scared."

"Well, you're lucky they like you, Melissa." Here Gracie's voice fell to a whisper. "Even if you are a bitch and I haven't been friends with you since I caught you spreading gossip about me and that guy from Lakeview's baseball team last summer. I mean, Jesus, I don't even like baseball! It's got to be the most boring sport in the world."

"Anyway," I said.

"Anyway," said Gracie. "Where are you?"

"I'm down at the phone rack in front of the Super Duper."

"Town square?" said Gracie, her voice rising a little before she caught herself and lowered it again. "What the hell are you doing there? Someone will see you."

"It's okay, there's no one around. The store is closed. It's a weekday. Not that Saturdays get jumping around here either."

"Hot time on the cold town," Gracie said.

"Yeah," I said. "So what's up? Did they believe you?"

"Of course they did, Melissa. Why wouldn't they? I mean, they're extremely disappointed and upset but somehow they did. They forgave me."

"Good," I said, though it took me a moment to realize Gracie was changing my words because a parent was patrolling nearby.

"What about you? How's school going?"

"I'm in the woods."

"The what? Why?"

"I'm staying in an old Amish logging camp about an hour's hike from your house. There's a shack back there. It's okay. It's better than the Wilkinson farm."

"Well, I guess that's true," said Gracie. Then: "What about food? Just because you're on a diet doesn't mean you should stop eating."

"School lunch was dinner tonight," I said, and she about flipped out on me.

"Melissa!" she said. "What the hell are you doing eating school lunch? I mean, how? Really? I mean that. How?"

"I got it out of the Dumpster. Don't worry. It was just a

burger and it was still in its wrapper. It's not the end of the world."

"Still, that's just gross. You don't know what they put in those burgers, Melissa. I mean, my mom and dad took me out of that school and the one thing I absolutely don't miss is the burgers."

"Got any better ideas?" I said. "Know of any upscale Dumpsters I should try?"

"In fact I do," said Gracie.

"I was hoping you'd say that. Where can we meet?"

"Hmm," said Gracie. "That's really hard to say right now, Melissa. My parents are really busy."

I imagined Mrs. Highsmith standing in the hall in her nightgown, trying to look like she was doing something, not prying, just wondering what to do with that hall light. Maybe she should change it even though it still works. Or that phone stand, maybe it needs dusting even though she'd just been getting ready to go to bed. "I understand," I said. "How about the edge of the woods near your house tomorrow? Around noon. My bike is there."

"Sounds great," said Gracie. "And I'm really glad you called, Melissa. It's been forever. Let's try to do something together soon, okay?"

"Okay," I said.

Then Gracie hung up and I was left in front of the Super Duper holding a phone with a dead connection wishing I could still talk to her, only for real, not through all that stupid Melissa code. I stood there holding that phone to my ear like an idiot for a full minute before I realized I was looking at my own reflection in the window of the grocery store and feeling sorry for the kid in the glass.

It was depressing to see him holding that dead phone, his hair totally messy like he'd just got out of bed, his eyes bruised and baggy like he'd been in a fight or hadn't slept in weeks. His sweatshirt and pants had holes in them, and there were weird stains on his jeans and jean jacket. Maybe he got them when he dove into the garbage Dumpster for dinner. Maybe he got them in the woods. It looked like his clothes belonged in Jamie's wardrobe. It looked like he was the kid they found murdered in a shallow hole by the railroad tracks.

I dropped the phone and let it swing on its metal cord. I wrapped my arms around his chest to hug him because no one else was there to do it, which made me want to cry a little, seeing this kid with shaggy, fucked-up hair and bruised eyes with my arms hugging him in the reflection of the Super Duper grocery store window, next to a sign that advertised a sale on window cleanser and tomatoes. I almost believed I wasn't alone for a moment, looking at that, but in the end I wasn't able to convince myself.

"No," I said, pulling my arms away. "No crying. No being stupid," I said to my reflection. I thought about how I looked better like this anyway, in clothes that were stained and filled with holes. I looked better like this than I ever did when they were fresh and crisp and new. With these clothes, I looked like how I felt on the inside: messed up, trashed, like I belonged in the Dumpster with the food I'd taken. Now, I thought, people can look at me and really see me.

The next day I reached my bike hiding inside the tree line near the Highsmith house a little earlier than I'd told

Gracie to meet me. I didn't sleep much the night before, but I felt fine when I woke. And I didn't feel hungry either, so I still had the Dumpster burgers and salad for later. What I really needed at the moment was to see Gracie, so when she came out her back door and looked around, searching the line of trees as she came toward it, when her eyes found mine and she smiled and came running, I felt immediately better. She came crashing over the branches lying on the ground until she reached me and I caught her as she threw her arms around me and we hugged like I wouldn't let myself hug myself the night before.

"Adam," she said, "I can't believe this. Why is this all so fucked up?"

"I don't know."

"I think maybe you should go home. It can't be that bad. Can it?"

I pulled away and didn't answer, just turned around and picked my bike up from the ground and started looking at it like it might need to be fixed, maybe oil on its chain, maybe a new tire was necessary.

"Adam, listen," she said. I looked up at her. "I'm sorry, okay? I'm just worried. I've got food in the house for you. Are you hungry?"

I shook my head.

"How can you not be hungry?"

I shrugged and looked away again. I could have explained in detail how I was not hungry and why, but it probably would have made her more worried than she already was.

"Okay," she said. "I'm going to pack it for you. Then we'll take it to your place in the woods. Okay?"

I looked at her again. "Okay," I said.

She came back ten minutes later wearing the purple backpack she'd had on the night we planned on running away to California. "All set," she said. "Let's get going." And I led her across the road, down the railroad tracks and into the woods, the same path I'd followed the other night when she'd told me to run and let her deal with the cops and her parents.

As we walked along Sugar Creek, Gracie pointed out several No Trespassing signs that the owner, Mr. Osborne, had posted on tree trunks. "Maybe this isn't the best part of the woods to stay in," she said, but I told her Mr. Osborne was so old that hardly anyone saw him come out of his house anymore.

So we kept on until we reached the logging camp and when Gracie saw the shack and the mounds of sawdust and the trees towering around the place, her mouth parted in surprise before she smiled and said, "It's not what I thought. It's great, actually."

I took her inside and we sat on my makeshift cot and the first thing she saw was Charlotte up in her web, which freaked her out a little. "That's Charlotte," I said. "She won't hurt you if you don't hurt her. She's *some* spider, you know."

Gracie wanted to know how I knew about this place, so I told her about how I found the camp when I was little, after the Amish left it. My dad had complained because Mr. Osborne had hired them to cut out some of the bigger trees and my dad thought he should have hired people from town to do that. This meant my dad thought Mr. Osborne should have hired him, because technically the Amish were part of our town, they just stuck with each other instead of mingling with us too much. Everyone knew my dad did odd jobs when he wasn't working, so he was upset about not being given the work. And after hearing him go on for weeks about the Amish in the woods, after hearing him go on about how they had finally left, I came back to see the place myself, following the logging ruts they left from the roadside into the woods.

I loved creeping around those first few times, feeling their presence still in the camp, seeing the empty potato chip bags and plastic cola bottles they'd left behind, finding the hammer they'd forgotten and the button from someone's suspenders on the floor beneath the cot. Even though the Amish that had been here were alive in the world, it somehow felt like I was visiting a haunted place, like at any moment one of their ghosts would show up and scare the hell out of me or else tell me a dark secret. It didn't occur to me until I was telling Gracie about all this and her face was growing more worried as I detailed how I spent so much time at the place that it had been me who'd been doing the haunting, that even then I'd been on my way to dying.

"Adam," Gracie said. Just that. Then she said nothing at all for a full minute. While I waited for her to say whatever was on her mind, she tilted her head to the side and stared at my face like I was a painting in a museum that needed to be looked at hard and for a long time before you could begin to really see it. Slowly she reached out and touched my cheek with her fingertips. Her hand was so warm. I pushed against it like an animal, nuzzling. "You're so strange," she said.

Still staring, she leaned over, making the cot shriek, and kissed me. Then we stretched out on the planks with my extra clothes as a mattress and kept kissing and touching and, even though it was the end of November and the wind was stripping the leaves from the trees, bringing snow in its wake, I saw nothing but sunflowers growing out of the leaf-littered floor of the woods, sprouting and opening up like film on fast-forward. As they grew the sunlight faded, but their petals still glowed as the dark draped itself over the woods.

We opened up and took our clothes off too. Light came from our bodies like light from the sunflowers outside, gold and dark like honey. "I'm so cold, Adam," Gracie said, so I pressed against her harder. I don't think I could warm her no matter how hard I pushed against her, though. My skin was cold now, no matter what the weather.

"Do you see them too?" I whispered.

"See what?" She looked nervous all of a sudden.

"The sunflowers," I said. "All around us."

She grinned but didn't say whether she did or didn't. She only said, "You're so strange," again. Then she pulled me down to kiss her over and over, wherever she liked, until it was so dark I couldn't see the sunflowers unfolding any longer, until I could only see the shadows moving around out in the moonlight as we moved around inside, making our own light to find our way by.

TRESPASSING

IT WAS LATE BY THE TIME GRACIE REALIZED SHE'D stayed too long, that her parents would be home and totally worried about where she'd gone, and as I led her out of the woods with my flashlight lighting the way, she was so angry all she did was say how she shouldn't have come, how her parents were going to kill her, how she didn't know why she couldn't just let me run off on my own and do what I wanted. "Why should I care?" she said. "You're just like him. I can't keep doing this, Adam."

I looked back over my shoulder as we climbed up a gravel slope to the rails and said, "If it's too much trouble, maybe we should call it quits."

She was making me feel like everything was my fault. Enough people had made me feel that way lately, I wasn't about to let Gracie make me feel that way too. She had a choice. She didn't have to come along. And if she did, I figured she should blame herself for any trouble she got into.

When I said that she stopped walking and her mouth dropped open. "I can't believe you," she said. "Adam McCormick, you are such an ass."

"I don't need anyone making me feel worse," I told her.

"I wouldn't be here if I wanted to make you feel worse,"

she said. "You don't get that, do you?" I kept walking. A few minutes later Gracie said, "I'm sorry. It's just...I don't know what I'm going to tell them this time."

"Tell them something crazy," I said. "Tell them something so crazy they have to believe it."

"What are you talking about?"

"I don't know. What would make them happy? Maybe tell them you went to church to talk to the minister. No, wait! I know! Tell them you went to his grave. To say good-bye to him."

"Adam, they would freak out if I told them something like that."

"Maybe," I said. "But maybe they'd think it was a good thing too. They think you've been acting strange because of finding him, so if you told them you were telling him good-bye, maybe that'd sound good to them."

"It's better than anything I can come up with, I guess," said Gracie.

When we got close to her road, we stopped and I said, "When will I see you again?"

Gracie shook her head. "After getting home so late today, I don't know. But I'll come to your place now that I know where it is. I'll come as soon as it's safe again."

I gave her the flashlight so she could see the rest of the way. She tried to give it back, but I said, "It's not that hard for me to see in the dark. Really."

She said I was going to kill myself trying to get back, but I insisted until she took the light and ran. And then I stood there and watched the beam swing in the dark until she turned onto her road and the light winked off in the distance.

I hadn't been lying actually. It *was* getting easier for me to see in the dark. That first night in the woods, finding my way to Sugar Creek had been hard, but after that I'd begun to notice the shadows moving under the moonlight, and when Gracie came back and we forgot time together, I'd seen them clear as day, wandering among the sunflowers we'd grown in the dark of the Amish logging camp. So as I turned and made my way back down the tracks and into the woods, I found my way without too much trouble. I tripped only two times and I avoided any shadows, even though one held his hand out and waved like he was calling me to come to him. I kept my head forward, my eyes ahead, until I found Sugar Creek's surface rippled with moonlight and followed its flow to the covered bridge and back to the logging camp. Home again.

The next day I looked through the stuff Gracie had brought, but I didn't want anything. It looked good, but I didn't have much of an appetite and also I kept thinking about how it all came from Mr. Highsmith's shining kitchen and that bothered me, and the more I thought about him, the less hungry I got. So I just went down to the creek when I wanted water, and whenever I did feel like eating something, I'd pull out the box of saltine crackers Gracie had packed and nibble a few of those before I felt full again. I compromised by eating the crackers, but they seemed trivial enough to compromise.

Compromising for crackers probably seems stupid, but I've been told before how stupid I am, so that's nothing new. Gracie and my family thought I was clueless, and so did people like Mr. Highsmith who said it behind my back instead of to my face, so probably a lot of other people thought so too. I bet there was probably even an Adam McCormick Is Clueless group that met monthly just to talk about how clueless I was sometimes. But the truth is, I'm not so clueless. I knew the reason why I wasn't hungry anymore and didn't need food that much was because I was dying. My sense of smell and taste couldn't be working properly if I was able to eat those hamburgers from the school Dumpster and think they were fine. They weren't fine even when they were semi-fresh under the heat lamps of the cafeteria. I knew that, but a kid does what he has to do. It doesn't make him stupid.

My real problem was I didn't have good reaction time. I didn't know how to make myself look graceful when confused. I didn't know how to pretend like nothing was the matter or how to seem at ease even though everything we did seemed so scripted. People traded words that meant nothing for more words that meant nothing, and you had to do it if you wanted to be considered a member of the group. *How are you doing? I'm fine, and you? Beautiful weather today, isn't it? Good morning, good afternoon, hello, see you again, be good, behave yourself, have fun! Take care! You all come back now, hear?*

Click, squeak, click-click.

It's hard to believe these words mean much of anything. They're just another part of the sham. People say this stuff automatically, and how can words mean anything if you don't think about saying them, if you don't feel them as you say them? And for some reason people think these are the most important words in the world. If you say them, you're normal. It's funny how people are so shocked when they find out their neighbor is a serial killer. With the standards of normality being whether you say good morning or comment on the weather, why are they so surprised? Maybe the shock is part of the act too. Maybe they just don't want to draw attention to their own weirdness. If it's someone else, it's not you.

So I'd compromise on taking Mr. Highsmith's crackers, but I'd never take these sorts of words unless I felt them for real, and they're the hardest ones to feel when no one in the world can feel them with you. That's not stupid. That's just having principles.

Gracie came back a few days later with more food, even though I hadn't eaten much of what she'd brought the first time. She stayed only a couple of hours and went straight home after we sat around and talked for a bit because her parents were totally on her back because of her recent strange behavior, which really just amounted to them not liking it one bit that she made decisions and did things that had nothing to do with them. Sometimes parents are more selfish than little kids and they justify it by saying they're concerned for you. They probably even believe it themselves when they say stuff like that because it sounds good.

Gracie came back a couple of days after that, though, and then after a while she was coming back every afternoon because a week had passed and she hadn't stolen their car or disappeared in a while, so they were beginning to trust her again. The saying goodbye to Jamie at his grave lie had worked. Gracie said their marriage counselor told them it was a good sign, so they felt they could ease up on her a little and worry about themselves again.

We spent our afternoons huddled on my cot. Gracie brought blankets and a pillow to make it a bit more comfortable. She didn't understand how I could stand the cold. She was always shivering. When she said that, I looked around and realized all the leaves had fallen and that we were halfway through December. I'd been gone for nearly a month and somehow no one had found me.

The days passed like this and even though I was totally bored in some ways—wanting my computer back so I could play *Nevermorrow,* or wanting to be able to use the school track so I could go for a decent run—I was also pretty calm for once. I didn't miss my family and I definitely didn't miss school and all the idiots like Matt Hardin. Between the hours of boredom and calmness, though, I still couldn't help but think of Jamie and wonder where he was, what had become of him, how he could side with that crazy girl who murdered her parents. Even though I was on my way to dying, I didn't understand the dead that well yet.

I took my notebook out of my backpack and wrote:

14. For everything you understand about the dead, something else is always unknowable.

One day I sat on my cot with my back against the wall, my arms folded behind my head, and tried to have a conversation with Charlotte. She was eating something she'd caught in her web, but she listened carefully as she sucked. "Charlotte," I said, "if you were in my position, what would you do?" She only shrugged and kept on sucking, though. I had a feeling she wouldn't have ever got into my position in the first place. She sat in her web and let others get tangled up in it. *Too bad, so sad. Now you're my dinner. That's the way the food chain goes, pal, deal with it.* I wished I had her ability to accept the unfairness of reality so easily.

As I sat there talking with Charlotte, a strange fog began to pour into camp, drifting into the shack, pooling around my feet. I perked up, wondering if Gracie had been caught going home the previous day and now the SWAT team had come back to gas me out of the shack into their waiting arms. But when I stood and looked out the door, I couldn't hear or see anyone. So I went down the path to the covered bridge and crossed over, walking along Sugar Creek in the shroud of fog. Then suddenly I heard voices and saw two silhouettes coming toward me in the white mist from the opposite direction. *Fuck,* I thought. *Someone knows I'm here.*

I ran behind an old brush pile as quick as I could. The brush was all wet black and covered with huge shelves of white fungus. Kneeling down, I peered through the branches to watch as they came by. And when I saw who it was, when I saw them together still, my mouth parted and my breath steamed in the fog, a thicker white, drifting through the sticks and branches into the brush like smoke, as if the brush were kindling and in the center a fire was building.

It was him. And her. Together. Jamie and Frances. They came walking by, him holding her hand while he talked to her in that low, soft voice he used whenever I got upset or scared and he tried to make me feel better. I couldn't hear exactly what he was saying, but I wanted to run out and push him down and beat the shit out of him like I did my brother in our driveway. Who was she that he'd abandon me after we said we'd never leave each other?

"It'll be okay," he was saying as they walked in front of me, his thigh at my eye level. He was still wearing my clothes too. "There's nothing you can do now," he said. "You have to. Or else you'll be like them." He stopped walking when he said that and turned his head from side to side, as if he sensed me. Then he said, "You don't want to end up like them, do you?" and I knew he hadn't spotted me.

Frances sniffed. She wiped at her face with one of her dirty paws and said, "I know. You're right. I just—I'm scared, that's all."

"Me too. I can't believe he did that. I'm sorry, Frances. I'm so sorry."

She shrugged and said, "I told you, Jamie. The living are so ignorant. It's not your fault. You didn't have much choice either."

They kept on walking then, hand in hand along the bank of the creek. I followed, moving out from behind the brush pile, sneaking from tree to tree. *Ice, rock, air, breathe,* I thought. *Don't let them see you.* If he turned and saw me, I didn't know what I'd do. Maybe I'd rush him like I'd thought at first, or maybe I'd rush *to* him, hoping he'd want me by his side again.

I stayed behind enough to watch them walk along Sugar Creek until they came to the old covered bridge, and it was then that I realized how dark it had become. The only light was the moon sitting in the branches of trees above me like a white egg in a nest.

Shadows had come out too. They lingered near the entrance of the bridge, moving back and forth, mumbling, shaking their heads sadly. One sat on a tree stump and sobbed to herself. Another muttered, "How much longer? A day? A week? A month?" One leaned against the arch of the bridge entrance and smoked a cigarette for a while before finally flicking it into the creek and going inside, disappearing into the fog that filled the corridor.

I stood behind my tree and watched Jamie take Frances

to the bridge, where he bent down and gave her a kiss on the cheek. I saw him squeeze her hand. Her fingers trailed across his for a moment, but when she moved toward the entrance finally, she stopped to look back only once before going in.

The fog devoured her as she entered. And when I couldn't see her any longer, Jamie turned in my direction.

I pressed myself against the tree, trying to make myself a part of the bark and the moss. I closed my eyes. *You don't see me, you don't see me.* I said a prayer to darkness right then, I said, "Make him not see me," and when I opened my eyes he walked right by without noticing me.

I waited a while, not wanting him to know I'd been there, and soon I couldn't see him walking along the moonlight-rippled water. He'd gone far enough ahead that I could start back to the logging camp without worrying he'd find me.

I didn't know what I'd just seen, but I knew it felt weird and wrong. It was like that word people say all the time, but don't really mean it. Goodbye. Lots of people use it without thinking about it. It's just one of those click-squeak words that mean nothing most of the time. I didn't want to say it unless I was mad, but even though he'd told me to leave the Wilkinson farm I somehow wasn't angry with him. Not really. I'd left the farm when he said to, but I never did say that word. I couldn't.

I was thinking maybe I should catch up and apologize for being a jerk and burning down the Wilkinson house. I mean, when I thought about it that was a pretty bad thing to do. Not for the reasons most people would think, though. I didn't care what the living thought about me burning down an abandoned farmhouse that hadn't been lived in for decades and decades. I felt bad because the house belonged to Frances. It wasn't mine to burn. I should've known better. If she wanted to kill her parents every morning, who was I to stop her?

Maybe it wasn't too late. I could still say I was sorry. So I took my hands out of my pockets and lifted my head up and started running in the direction I'd last seen Jamie go, and even though it was a foggy dark and shadows patrolled the woods like storm troopers, I didn't fall, not even once.

Instead, I ran into something. Or someone. It was hard to tell at first because I slammed right into someone way bigger than me and I knew it wasn't a tree because it was soft and squishy. And sticky. When I picked myself up from the ground, I still had to look up to meet its hollow eye sockets and dark, vein-filled face. I opened my mouth to say something, but nothing came out. Not even the scream I felt in my stomach.

"Help me," it said at first. And then when I didn't move and just kept looking up at it with my mouth open and my eyes probably bugging out like crazy, it said, "Just a word. Something you can spare a fellow. Please."

Then I heard another voice in the distance, calling my name over and over. "Adam!" she called. It was Gracie. I saw the light around her before I saw her body burn through the fog. She glowed like one of those angels from the illuminated manuscripts Mrs. Motes once showed us pictures of in English class. I wanted to tell her to stop yelling because we weren't in our woods anymore. I'd realized that finally. And if *I* wasn't ready to be in dead space, Gracie definitely wasn't. But as she came toward me and said, "There you are!" and walked right up to him, I realized she wasn't able to see the man with no skin. She only saw me.

I put my finger to my lips and shook my head, trying to make her understand. But she gave me a weird look, furrowing her brows, cocking her head to the side. She stopped talking, but the man with no skin had lost interest in me. He looked at her now, rustling as he turned in her direction. He held his hand out for her, and when his bloody fingers brushed across her cheek, Gracie started to shiver. Then her face twisted and she screamed.

I ran over and got between them, held her arms to calm her down a little while she said, "Fuck, fuck, fuck! What the fuck was *that*?" Her legs buckled and we dropped to the ground and when I looked back up he was reaching down for us.

"Gracie," I said, "I love you," and he stood straight up and sighed. "Ahhhhhhh," he hissed, as if he'd drunk something cold in the heat of summer. A thin layer of skin began to grow over his body, but I still saw his insides beneath it. When I looked back up at his face, a few tufts of black hair grew out of his head like buds unfurling, and his eyes were back as well, roaming in their sockets.

"More, please," he said. "Just a little something. You can spare something, sonny. Something sweet and nice."

He reached down and I hugged Gracie tight while she sobbed and said, "Adam, what's wrong? What's happening?" I closed my eyes, not wanting to feel him pull out any more of the things he wanted. A moment passed, though, and I didn't feel anything other than Gracie's heart beating hard against mine. Then I heard another voice I knew, like I knew Gracie's and my own.

"Stop," he said. "They're mine. You can't have them."

I looked up and there he was, standing between us and the man who had made a new skin out of the words I'd tried to give Gracie, my *I love you*. He'd taken those words, and now he narrowed his new eyes at Jamie, as if he were an insect buzzing around him. "There are no claims in these woods," he said.

"You already took something that doesn't belong to you. Leave," Jamie told him.

"I could take more," the man said, lowering his head like a bull.

"You barely have enough skin to keep yourself together," Jamie said. "Don't make this difficult."

The man glowered down at me and Gracie huddled together on the ground in a heap. He took a big breath, sniffed and coughed, but finally he took a few steps and shuffled away, muttering to himself like any other shadow.

Jamie looked down at us now too. He held his hand out and said, "Come on. Let's get you guys out of here."

We followed him along the creek for a long time, away from the covered bridge, going in the direction of the old railroad tracks toward home. And when I saw those tracks and thought about home again and everything that was waiting there for me, I opened my mouth and said, "That's not where I live now."

"What do you mean?" he said.

"I live in the woods now."

"Oh, that," he said. "I knew that. But we have to go this way to get out. Then we can go back again."

"What the hell is happening?" Gracie said, trudging along behind us. "Adam, where were we a minute ago?"

"You were in dead space," Jamie answered.

"I didn't ask you," said Gracie.

"I don't know," I said. "Jamie knows more than I do."

"Everyone knows more than you do, McCormick," Gracie muttered. When I looked back, I saw she was walking with her head down, watching her feet go one in front of the other.

"What's the matter, Gracie?" Jamie asked.

"What's the matter?" Gracie said. "What's the matter is I told you I didn't want to see you anymore, but here you are anyway. That's what's the matter." She looked at me and shook her head as if I'd somehow betrayed her.

When we reached the tracks, we walked toward Fisher Corinth Road for a while, where Gracie lived just around the bend in the rails. As we walked down the tracks, the fog and dark began to lift, and I could see that it was still just late afternoon. As we came closer to her road I thought that Gracie would just keep going, would just head home after what happened, but instead she turned around with us and walked back down the tracks again and into the woods.

I said, "I should have known walking this way and then walking back might get us out."

"But you need to go a different direction on the way back," said Jamie.

I looked up, surprised to hear him say that. "That's what my grandma always said you have to do," I said. "Where did you hear that?"

"You pick things up along the way," he said.

Gracie said, "Along the way to where?"

"Along the way to dying," I answered.

We were silent after that. Jamie led us back to the covered bridge by a route I didn't know, and when we finally got to the shack, we all sat down on the screechy cot and looked at the floor for a while. Gracie sighed. She was exhausted, I could tell.

"Nice place," Jamie said, standing up to look around. Gracie snorted. "Did I say something funny?" he asked.

"Nice place?" said Gracie. "Well, I suppose it *is* a step up from the Wilkinson farm."

"Let's not talk about that," I said.

"Okay," said Jamie. He looked back at me, his voice low and sweet. "There are better things to talk about anyway," he said, which made Gracie snort even harder.

"Like what?" she said. "Like the fact that you're dead and still insist on hanging around?"

"Stop it, Gracie," I said. I didn't say it in a mean way, but she still made a face like I'd just slapped her.

"Me?" she said. "Adam, this is all a mess. It's all ruined. Can't you see that?"

"It's not ruined," I said. "We can fix it. Together."

Gracie furrowed her brows again, like she had when I'd tried to shush her in dead space. "Adam, this can't be fixed. It'd be great if it could, but it can't. I'm worried about you. Please."

She didn't say anything more. Just that. *Please.* Please what? What did she want me to do? What *she* did? Abandon him? I couldn't look Jamie in the eye and tell him to go, not even after he'd done it to me at the Wilkinson farm.

"Fuck," said Gracie, "it's already getting dark. My parents are going to kill me. I have to go."

The cot screeched as she stood up. After she stepped down out of the shack, she looked back and said, "I'll be back tomorrow. Okay, Adam?"

"Okay," I said. "Be careful going home."

"Bye, Gracie," Jamie said after she'd already started walking away. She didn't turn around, though, just lifted her hand in the air and waved.

After she left, Jamie and I stayed up talking. He told me I'd misunderstood, that he'd been angry but not so much that he never wanted to see me again. When he'd asked me to leave the Wilkinson farm, it was because he didn't want any more trouble between me and Frances. It hadn't been because he sided with her. I told him I'd seen them in the woods, how I'd hidden from them while they were at the covered bridge. "What were you two doing there?" I asked. But he only shook his head. "Is she still mad at me?" I asked. But he only shook his head again.

"I don't think so," he said. "She's probably fine now. I hope so."

We lay on the cot together, on the pillows and under the blankets Gracie had brought. They weren't much use to us now, but we used them anyway, pretending maybe they were still something we needed.

Jamie wanted to talk about old times. About school. When he said it, he looked wistful and happy, his stupid grin sliding up one side of his face. "Do something for me?" he said, and I nodded. "I'm going to tell you a story," he said, "then you tell me one, okay?"

"Sure," I said. "What kind of story?"

"A story about me," he said. "Something you remember. Like this," he said, and he started to tell me the story of the time he went to the track meet when I won first place and would go on to run in the state championship, how everyone on the team had lifted me up on their shoulders and I'd laughed and smiled. He'd never seen me look as happy as I had when I'd burst across that finish line. I asked him how he could remember that race and he said, "I was there. I used to watch you run."

"You did? I don't remember you there. When did you watch me?"

"I started coming when we had computer lab together."

"You never said anything."

"I didn't want to bother you. You always had people around you at those things."

"You wouldn't have bothered me," I said. I put my arm around his shoulder and he turned his face to me and smiled.

"I always liked watching you run," he said. "You had this way about you. It was like reading a poem. You could run that way, like a line in a poem runs."

I didn't know what to say, so I hugged him. No one had ever talked about me like that before. It made me feel more important than when I'd actually won that race. I imagined him at my track meets sitting on the hill beside the track, leaning back on his elbows watching me run and thinking I looked like a line in a poem. He'd been in my life then, in the background waiting for me to notice. And I'd noticed. I just hadn't said anything. Then it was too late to say anything.

So I said something now. "Thank you," I whispered into his ear as we lay on the cot, and as I said those words I knew they were mine, that I'd said them for the first time in my life and meant them. My collection was growing. The man with no skin had taken love from me, but I still had *ad infinitum,* sunflower, and now thank you. Maybe I could find love again, I thought. I'd just have to look around hard enough.

"Now you," he said. "Tell me a story."

So I told him about how I'd been running last spring after my grandma died and how I'd run past his house and saw him in the window of his bedroom, the room above the kitchen. How I hadn't waved and he hadn't either, but as I ran past we looked at each other and I didn't turn away until I was so far past his house I had to turn around almost completely and run backward to see his window and him inside it still watching me.

"I remember that," he said, putting his face against my chest. "Tell me again," he said. "Tell me as much as you can remember. What did I look like? What was I wearing? Did I look happy or sad?" So I told him again, trying to remember everything, and as I talked he held on to me and I smelled that hair burning smell and felt his body warming against mine. When I finished, he sighed long and loud and looked up, his cheeks pink, his eyes sparkling. "I liked that story," he said. "Do you remember any others?"

I looked up at Charlotte in her web. She was watching with her many eyes as if she were sizing us up.

"I remember some more," I told him.

"Good," he said. "Don't forget them. Someone has to remember. Someone has to be the rememberer."

I slept that night, just a little. It was peaceful sleep, which I hadn't had in a while, but when I woke up in the morning and sat up rubbing my eyes in the light, all that peace was gone. Someone stood in the door of my shack with one foot on my floor and one arm bent to lean on his knee. A man in a uniform. A cop. He nodded at me and said, "You might as well get your things and come along quietly. There's nowhere for you to run now. Okay?"

When he moved aside, I saw another cop waiting outside, hands planted on his hips. Mr. Highsmith stood beside him, staring in at me with a scowl on his face. And in front of Mr. Highsmith was Gracie, bundled up in a winter army jacket. When I looked at her, she looked away, unable to face me. *Traitor.* How could she give me away? That was even worse than Jamie telling me to leave the Wilkinson farm.

"Come on," the cop told me. "Don't give us any trouble, kid. Just let me bring you down to the station and everything will be all right."

Let Me Bring You Down

THE COPS LED ME OUT OF THE WOODS, ONE ON each side of me, while Mr. Highsmith and Gracie walked ahead, leading the way. Mr. Highsmith kept his arm around Gracie's shoulder the whole time, like she'd been some sort of victim, but when we came to the road and then to his house where the cop car was waiting, he told Gracie she had to go with them, same as me. She looked up at him, eyes wide, shocked. "What?" he said. "You think you're not in trouble, young lady? You're what they call an accomplice."

"Daddy!" she said. I rolled my eyes—didn't she get it? He was totally trying to scare her. He probably figured a trip to the police station and some firm questioning would make sure his little girl didn't hang around any trash in the future.

He nodded to the cops, and despite Gracie's protests, they put her and me in the backseat together.

We didn't look at each other even though we felt the nearness of our bodies. Instead we looked out our separate windows as the car passed woods and dairies and pastures and the fields I'd known since I was a kid. It was a bleak December, everything brown, black and gray. Brown fields, gray clouds, black birds flocking in both of those places.

Gracie said, "Adam?" but I didn't answer. I couldn't. I was too angry right then. Everything I'd done, every step I'd taken to run as fast and as far away as possible had been useless. God's finger was totally closing in.

It was as we were driving to the police station that it happened again. *Pop!* I flew out of my body. The police car kept going, though, and I tumbled head over heels backward and upward until I was in the sky with those crows I'd seen. I was floating like a kite to heaven. It had been a while since this had happened, but when I found myself high enough to mingle with the clouds I wasn't afraid. I'd been to death and back. I only worried about losing the body that hurtled away from me in the police car to the police station, where it would most likely be given a sentence to go to a juvenile detention center and then sent home afterward, where it would walk and talk and take showers and return to school to take tests and get good grades and continue to grow in death, its fingernails curling in on themselves, a saint, a saint of a body, better than I could ever be, a son anyone could be proud of, doing everything he's supposed to, a son who would wheel his mother around and feed her broth by her bedside, who would rub her feet until she felt them, who would say please and thank you to the paralyzer, the woman who should be thankful the body kept its own counsel, who said nothing of himself. *Nothing*. Not a thing.

For a moment I thought I should just let them have the body, to be rid of it, to be free to float above the lights of earthly cities. Goodbye! Glad to have been inside you! But then a strange sense of duty rose up from the center of my being and I thought, *Don't give him up*. They couldn't have *me* because I was floating free, high above them all, but why should I let them have the body? It was mine in this world, so I flew after it. Faster than the speed of light, I flew at the speed of thought and made it back just as the cops pulled into the station. *Pop!* I went back in, shrugging it on like a winter coat, just in time to hear Gracie whisper, "He caught me coming to see you. I didn't mean to. I can't lie anymore, Adam."

"You did what you had to do." I shrugged.

I could tell she wasn't satisfied with that answer and wanted me to be a big forgiver and tell her everything was fine, not to worry, but that was a bit much for me right then as I was being taken out of a police car and into a station where for the next two hours I would be questioned about a million things that had nothing to do with me and a few things that had everything to do with me. Mostly they wanted to find out why I'd run away and why I'd stolen the five hundred dollars they found in my backpack from Mr. Highsmith. But I wasn't talking. So they called my parents.

I'd seen Gracie sitting with an officer in a glassed-in office for a while, and then, while I waited with a cup of cocoa for my parents to show, she came out of the office shrugging her coat on, and Mr. Highsmith came around a corner where he must have been waiting the whole time to pick her up. I stood up and said, "Gracie," but didn't know what to say after that. It was hard with phones ringing and cops talking their I-know-what's-going-on-in-the-world talk all around me, and Mr. Highsmith staring at me. I couldn't say what I wanted, but I hoped the look I gave her would say what I meant. That I was sorry, that I did love her, even if the man with no skin took it when I said it. That this wasn't the end of our story.

I once saw a movie about two friends who were majorly tight. I mean, they were actually more than friends. They were friends but also lovers and they loved each other more than anyone else in the world. But it was like the whole world conspired against them and in the end there's this scene where they're being split apart by their parents. The friends keep reaching out for each other, kicking and screaming and crying, "You'll never keep us apart! Never!" I'd imagined if my and Gracie's parents ever tried to separate us, that's how we'd be, screaming our heads off as our parents tugged and pulled.

What I found when this happened, though, what I found when Mr. Highsmith looked at me with a stare that would melt polar ice caps, what I found when he said, "Stay the hell away from my daughter, McCormick," through gritted teeth, was that Gracie didn't say anything. Nothing at all. For a moment she looked at me and shook her head. Then she wiped her glistening eyes and walked out of the station with her father, without a word for me. Not even that one people say all the time. Goodbye.

A few moments after they turned the corner, my family came around the same one. I saw my father first, his head swiveling back and forth until he saw me and glared. Then my mother's feet came around the corner behind him, then her wheels, then my mother herself with tear-streaked cheeks, wearing a Christmas green sweater buttoned up to her neck. I almost ran to her, I almost shouted, "I'm home! I love you!" Because I did love her and I wanted her to love me back even though it was difficult, I knew. I wanted to fall at her knees and hold her lifeless legs in my arms and put my head on her lap while she patted my head with her hands, her good hands that still had life in them, to have this reunion that would somehow make all of the dead parts of me all better. I wanted to say, "I was just kidding!"

and have her forgive me on the spot like the Highsmiths always did with Gracie. I took a fast step toward her, almost breaking into a run, but stopped before I took a second one.

Behind my mother, her hands resting on my mother's chair like the jointed legs of a spider, came the paralyzer. And seeing that hand, following it up to the arm, up to the head and shoulders, seeing the face of Lucy Hall, seeing the pink tip of her tongue slip out to lick her lips, seeing those lips slide into a grin when she looked at me, seeing how she was still a part of my family after all this time made my moment of hope shrivel to nothing.

Just like that, I no longer wanted reconciliation. Right then I realized I had limits. I would have to negotiate for my demands. But for my family negotiations only happened in movies about terrorists taking hostages. I'd taken myself hostage, but I knew they still wouldn't listen. It would be their way or no way. I'd failed to make a way out of no way like I'd planned.

The cop who had been watching me from his desk said, "Looks like you've got some people who want to see you. Better go on over, son."

I looked at him and tried to glare like my father glared. I wanted to say I wasn't his son. But I was outnumbered here more than I was at home even, so I rolled my eyes and nodded like he was majorly stupid and went over to them, not really sure how to go about saying hello.

But it turns out that didn't matter. As soon as I came to my mother, she held her arms out wanting a hug without saying a word, so I bent down and put my arms around her. I felt tears on her cheeks, but didn't say anything. We just kept hugging and I was going to do it then, I was going to tell her how I was sorry and loved her and hoped she still loved me anyway, but right at the moment when I looked up at her, his hand grabbed my shoulder and spun me around to face him. My father was staring straight at me for the first time in ages, his finger pointing in my face as he started in on me in front of everyone.

"Listen here, boy," he said, his voice filled with a tremor. "You've had your fun. You've caused enough trouble. Now you're back and this is how it's going to be. I'm in charge now, hear? And you're gonna grow up real fast or find yourself in a heap of trouble. Got it? Do you *got* it?"

"John," said the cop who told me to go over to them. "What do you want? The kid to run off again?"

My mother covered her face with her hands.

"Fine!" my dad shouted to everyone. "Man can't discipline his own child these days? See if I care!"

I could tell that he didn't. I could see him for the first time in my life. I could see how much he hated me, how he was no longer afraid to show it. I'd given him enough reasons to justify his feelings and now he could say what he wanted. He could tell me I was a waste and how he wished I'd never been born, and everyone else would understand.

I narrowed my eyes, staring back to let him know I understood him better than he thought. To let him know he might have me in his power now, but not forever. *I'm working on that wish,* I wanted to tell him. *I'm working on unlearning the life you gave me.*

We drove home in the van, my father and Lucy up front, my mother and I in the back. No one spoke. We just listened to a country music station on the radio.

As we pulled into our drive, I waited for someone to say

something, to do something extreme like I'd done that night my father pulled me out of Jamie's grave, but no one said a thing. Not when we climbed out of the van and unloaded my mother, not when we trudged through the garage door into the kitchen. We were doomed to repeat ourselves, to be in a constant state of returning. I wondered if it was possible to ever really change. Could we ever break ourselves open and be different people than the ones who hurled beer bottles and called each other names?

Mr. Highsmith was right, and I knew it even when his voice had come running up the stairs of his house to find me. We were trash. I was no good. Take one look at me. Take one look at my family. The evidence was stacked against us. I could run all I wanted, but I couldn't outrun the truth.

Lucy pushed my mother over to the table in the dining room, then came back to the kitchen side to turn on the stove. Andy wandered out of his room and stood in a corner, yawning through a drugged-out haze. He smiled to see me returned, proven wrong, just like my mother had been.

Lucy handed out mugs of coffee and we all stood in the kitchen with our eyes glazed, as if we were a cult preparing to drink cyanide. Everyone but me drank their coffee in big gulps, then set the mugs in the sink before going off to do whatever they planned on doing next. Watching TV, hunting, smoking another joint out in the back field.

No one said anything about where I'd been for the past month. I stood alone in the kitchen with my unsipped coffee, wondering why no one was talking. Because right then, even if it meant getting yelled at, I wanted to hear their voices.

It was useless, though. My family didn't have enough words. They hadn't collected enough or they had stopped collecting at some point, and this was what we had to work with, this void.

When I finally put my mug in the sink and wandered back to my bedroom, I found Lucy folding her clothes on my bed. "What are you doing in here?" I said, and Lucy looked at me.

"I moved in a few days ago," she said. "I'm divorcing Doug. He was upset because I was never home and he thought I spent too much time with your family."

"You do," I said. I didn't move from the doorway.

"Well, that's gratitude," said Lucy, stacking a folded towel on another. "And after all I've done for your mother. Now your poor father's gone and lost his job and it's all because of you. Not to mention that social worker who's been sniffing around since you disappeared. She'll be back, so get ready to do some fast-talking. Do you know the grief you're causing? You're a very selfish boy. Do you know that?"

"You shouldn't have tried helping," I said. "You should have stayed with your husband, or at least not here."

My words came out without me having to think about them. They came out without sounding angry or upset. I just said what I felt and it started to make sense, even to myself. I felt bad that my dad had lost his job, but he'd lost jobs before and most likely it wasn't because I'd run off. I'd heard things. Things like what Mr. Highsmith had said about what kind of worker he was. Taking long breaks. Being found far from whatever task had been set for him. He was a good worker when he wanted. It was the wanting my dad wasn't good at.

Maybe we had that in common.

"You don't understand, Adam," said Lucy. "You'll see

what I've gone through after you've grown up and gone through some of the things I've seen."

"I'm not a child," I said. "I've seen things. Things you can't even imagine."

"What have you seen, Adam?" said Lucy, her voice so soft and full of syrup I could see she was thinking I might know something that could damage her. Her shadow was huge and black against the wall behind her, bigger than when I'd left. It crossed its arms and waited for my answer.

I said nothing, though. I turned and walked away.

I tried sleeping on the couch that night, but as it had for so many of the nights since I'd climbed into Jamie's grave, sleep rejected me. I was getting used to rejection, but I was still tired. Looking at the Christmas tree's winking lights, its shiny tinsel and satin bulbs, didn't mesmerize me like it had when I was little, so I lay on the couch, picked up the remote and flipped on the TV, hoping to find something that would exhaust me.

Immediately the Weather Channel came on, its blue screen washing through the living room like a wave of ocean. I thought of the past few weeks and closed my eyes, wishing myself away again. Sure it had sucked in some ways, living in closets and abandoned Amish loggers' shacks, but it hadn't been this black hole in the center of my family that vacuumed everything good into it, leaving only shells of what we were supposed to look like moving around in this world. Out there, outside of this house, I was me at a higher volume. Here you had to turn yourself down or else off completely.

I spent the next few hours channel surfing, not really seeing the shows. I was thinking about Jamie. I had faith he'd return at any moment, even though he'd been gone when the police had taken me that morning, and that thought kept me hoping I wouldn't be alone forever. Gracie had turned out to be someone who shifted loyalties when it was convenient, but I still had him. He followed me when I didn't think he was with me. He'd saved me when I needed saving. Now all I had to do was wait for him to find me again.

I watched the hands of the clock sweep through the night and finally fell asleep around six that morning. An hour later, though, I was woken up by my father.

My father's hands were rough from working construction. They were huge mitts that could swallow a baseball or cover a face almost completely. The skin of his palms felt like the skin on the bottoms of my feet: thick and sandpapery. My feet got that way from all the running I did and my father's hands got that way from the heavy things he made them lift, from the rough surfaces he had to hold steady. Carpenter's hands, he called them. Full of splinters. Once he came home with a fingernail blackened from being hit by a hammer. The nail filled up with blood and fell off a day later, and then my father's finger had no cover for a while. The nail grew back eventually, but during the in-between time, I asked him if it hurt to not have the nail protecting him. "Nah," he said. "These hands are used to pain. They don't feel anything."

Here they were, those numb devices, lifting me up from the couch. He slipped one under each of my armpits and hauled me up like a kitten. "Shit, shower and shave!" he hollered. Spit flew out of his mouth, but I didn't feel it as it

landed on me. "You're not going to do whatever you want,"
he said. "I'm in charge now. Not your useless mother!"

Lucy and Andy came thumping into the living room.
"John? What on earth?" said Lucy.

"He's going to school," said my father, making it a point
to not look away from me. "He's not going to stay home
and sleep all day."

"Dad," said Andy. "It's Christmas break."

My dad looked at Andy. His eyes were filled with rage,
but they drained into embarrassment quickly. "Fuck," he
whispered, still holding me up. "Jesus," he said, before he
threw me back on the couch like a piece of trash.

"What's going on out there?" My mother's voice came
from the bedroom.

"Nothing," Lucy hollered over her shoulder. She folded
her arms across her chest and said, "Well. Now that we're all
up, I guess I should make breakfast."

Half an hour later, we all sat around the dinner table for
the first time in I didn't know how long, eating scrambled
eggs and sausage, pancakes and bananas. I couldn't taste
anything, but I kept forking food into my mouth to make
them happy.

I hated the forced mechanics of our movements, not
just at the dinner table where the only sound was our forks
clinking, but the mechanical movement of our lives. The
way everyone always said and did the same thing and pretended they didn't notice the seasons changing or the way
other people changed. Why the Weather Channel all the
time? Why settle for the wheelchair without trying therapy? Why a joint every day after school, right on schedule?

Why did a dead boy come watch me run, but none of you bothered?

I was thinking these things, looking down at my plate, when Lucy's shadow said, "That's the way life is. Get used to it."

I looked up to find her shadow spread out against the wall in front of me, but Lucy herself was on the kitchen side of the room preparing more pancakes. I looked back and forth between them. A thin tendril of darkness ran across the floor from Lucy to her shadow. It looked like, at any moment, her shadow could pull out a pair of scissors and snip the cord.

My father herded us into the van later that day and we went to the cemetery to brush off my grandparents' headstones, to put Christmas wreaths on their graves. I thought of the Mexican cemeteries Gracie had told me about and wondered how Mexican cemeteries looked in winter. Probably it was sunny all year round there; if that were true it probably helped make everyone want to keep things colorful and festive.

We had trouble pushing my mother's wheelchair through the snow, so Andy and I picked the chair up and carried her to the graves as if we were Egyptian slaves and my mother our Cleopatra on a litter. She laughed and her hand fluttered near her heart. She looked down at us, smiling to be held up in the December air with snowflakes drifting around her. "Be careful," she chided. "Don't hurt yourselves." It was too late for that, I wanted to tell her. We'd been hurt. We'd all been wounded, and the blood still seeped out.

After we cleared the headstones and replaced the flowers with wreaths, we backed off as usual to let my mom have some private time with her parents. Correction: we all backed off except Lucy. She stayed beside my mom with her hand on her shoulder. Me, my father and Andy stood side by side, my father between us. Their breath steamed as it left their mouths, but mine remained invisible. My breath was as cold on the inside as it was outside. I was the walking dead, slouching through their lives. I didn't understand the secret of how to keep going like everyone else. I could keep running, but only on the outside. On the inside, I was a corpse waiting for the body to catch up.

Afterward we went to town for lunch. My dad parked the van next to the curb in the town square, and we walked across the park together. The ground was covered with snow and people were out last-minute shopping because Christmas was only three days away. We went to the Wildwood Café and sat at a table instead of a booth so my mom could sit on the end in her wheelchair.

The Wildwood Café was my father's favorite diner. In the summer the place was crowded with flies and smelled of grease and burned potatoes. In the autumn they served hot apple cider. In the winter they made cocoa and chili with venison instead of ground beef. In the spring the café shut down for a month while the owners, the Wintersons, vacationed in Florida. While they were gone, the chalkboard in the front window always said, "Back in a jiff! Happy Easter!" in soft pastel colors.

We ordered lunch and sat around like a real family, and I looked from the corners of my eyes to find everyone getting an eyeful of the McCormick family, together again, with a cameo appearance by Lucy Hall and the runaway son, the fuckup who was once a good runner and got decent grades. *Pathetic,* they all thought. Their shadows said what their faces wouldn't.

My dad kept nodding and smiling at these people, these fakes who didn't have much good to say about us behind our backs. I didn't understand why he wanted the approval of people who thought badly of us even when they had shit going on in their own lives. Mr. Winterson and his pornography collection hidden from his wife in the shed behind their barn. Alice Chapman and her lover in the next town over. What would her husband think if he knew she was cheating on him with the man who sold him his new tractor? And then Reverend Mann and his thing for boys around my age. Both his shadow and those of some of the guys at school had things to say about that, but no one but people like me ever heard them.

My father had never been good at listening to live people, let alone shadows, so he didn't notice we weren't as bad as anyone else. He thought his family had gotten out of control and now he had to put us in line again, as if that had ever been the case. He wanted to show off. *Look! Here they are! I've got them all rounded up!*

I wanted to laugh in his face. How could he sit there and eat his goddamn chili and think these other people would let him make things better? They liked it when they saw a person down. Everyone likes seeing someone down—it makes them forget their own fuckups. Help someone who needs it? No way. Keep them there, is the way people think. But my father hadn't figured that out.

I kept these thoughts to myself. It wouldn't help to tell anyone how I felt. Life in the McCormick family was non-negotiable. So I ate my toasted cheese and my tomato soup, trying to imagine the buttery toast on my tongue, the crumbly bread and the warm, soft cheese. But no matter how I concentrated, I couldn't taste or feel a thing. I ate because I was supposed to.

The next morning, I woke to the sound of a car crunching over the gravel of our drive. I rubbed the sleep out of my eyes and went to the picture window. Past the branches and tinsel of the Christmas tree I could see a black woman getting out of her car carrying a briefcase. She wore a dark skirt to her knees, a white blouse with frills down the center, and a dark buttoned-up jacket. She looked official, which should have been my first clue she'd bring trouble. And after taking a deep breath and standing up straighter than she already had been, she marched up to our front door and knocked.

I didn't answer. I kept peeking out between the branches of the Christmas tree and, after a while, she knocked again. There was movement in the back bedroom and a moment later my father came out in his underwear, asking, "Why don't you answer the goddamn door?"

"It's a black woman with a suit on," I told him.

"Fuck," he said. "It's the social worker."

"Let's ignore her," I said. "She'll go away."

She knocked again, hard and quickly.

"Lucy!" my father yelled.

"What?" Lucy called from my bedroom.

"Can you answer the door while I get dressed?"

Lucy came into the living room in her nightgown and we all stood around looking at each other like stupid people. "Who is it?" Lucy asked.

"The social worker," I said.

My father said, "Keep her busy until I can get some clothes on and get Linda dressed."

He turned the corner and I realized that this was the first time I'd seen him almost naked since I could remember. Then I realized Lucy had seen him almost naked too. It made me feel weird. Like maybe this was the beginning of a new set of signs to look for.

The social worker knocked once more and Lucy opened the door asking the woman to excuse her for not getting to the door sooner. We'd all been sleeping, you see, she explained. But the social worker was unfazed.

I heard her voice before I saw her. "I'm sorry to have disturbed you folks," she said. "I'm from Social Services. I spoke with you on the phone last week? The police called to say Adam McCormick's been found. I just need to ask you some questions, Mrs. McCormick."

"Oh bless you," said Lucy, her cheeks flushing. "I'm not Mrs. McCormick. I'm just a friend. My name's Lucy Hall."

She brought the social worker into the living room and said, "Right here's our little missing person. Say hello, Adam."

I was still in my T-shirt and sweatpants, not really the sort of armor I'd prefer to be wearing to take on this lady, but I knew I had to get her off our backs in order to make it up to everyone. So I said, "Hello, ma'am," like a good boy, and she smiled. Her teeth were huge and white.

"Good to finally meet you, Adam," she said in a buttery soft voice that made me want to trust her. But I knew better. People who sound like her always get picked to talk to troublemakers, but really they're just as bad as the rest.

My father wheeled my mother into the living room, both of them looking dragged-out-of-bed tired. My father's beard had started to grow in, even though he'd shaved the night before. My mother offered her hand to the social worker and said, "Please. Won't you sit down?" The woman sat, and then she told everyone she'd need a little time alone with me.

I spent the next hour with her, answering questions. Why had I run away? Did I feel threatened by a family member? What had I encountered while I was gone? Could I explain my actions so she could understand my feelings? Why did I choose to stay in Gracie Highsmith's closet, of all places? Why did I burn down the Wilkinson farm?

Goddamn it. Gracie had told them more than I'd thought. How can someone so smart get scared so easily? I mean, there's no difference between them and us. They're just older. You can't let them intimidate you.

I answered as evasively as possible. I told her I was just having a bad time and not to take it out on my parents. I told her I might need medication. I told her I felt threatened, but not by my family (although this wasn't true). I told her I'd stayed in Gracie's closet because she let me. I mean, that was a really dumb question. When she asked about the Wilkinson farm, I said, "I don't know what you're talking about," and she looked up from her notebook and gave me a look.

"You had nothing to do with that incident?"

"I didn't know it had burned down until you told me."

"Mmm-hmm," she said. She looked down again and began to write something in her notebook.

When she asked about Gracie, I said, "She told me to stay there. I only planned on running away for a couple of days, you know, just to be on my own for a bit, but she convinced me to stay in her closet."

"Is that right?" said the social worker. She'd told me her name, but I'd already forgotten. I didn't want to know her. To me she would always be the social worker. Formality is best with these sorts of people.

"That's right," I said. I could have spared Gracie, but after the way she'd walked away from me without a word, after finding out she'd told them everything, I felt justified. Why should she get off just because she was from a good family?

When she asked why I'd taken Mr. Highsmith's money, I said, "Gracie told me to take it. She wanted to take a train to California and told me where I'd find the money while she and her parents were visiting her uncle and aunt in Youngstown."

"California?" the social worker said, looking doubtful.

"She told me to pick a place I've never been," I said, "so I picked California. That's where my aunt Beth lives."

"I see," said the social worker, scribbling furiously on her notepad.

Finally the social worker stopped recording the session and brought my family back in. She thanked us for our time and said she'd be in contact, and that possibly I'd have to go to court.

"Court?" said my mother, looking bewildered.

"Court?" I said, getting mad.

"Yes," said the social worker. "It's standard procedure with runaways and delinquents. Which is what your son is, I'm afraid. You'll have to have a session with a juvenile court judge."

"That is so lame," I said, but Lucy hushed me.

"What could happen to him?" my mother wanted to know.

"He could be sentenced to juvenile hall, or possibly placed in a foster home."

"A foster home?!" my mother cried.

"Yes, ma'am," said the social worker. "I'm afraid so."

After we closed the door on her, my mother burst into tears. "Oh God," she moaned. "Where did I go wrong?"

My father said, "Don't cry, Linda." But my mom kept on crying. He couldn't stop her, which I guess must have made him feel out of control, because he shouted, "Stop it! Stop your goddamn crying already!" and my mother wheeled back to her bedroom, the tears still coming.

My father turned to me and his face was filled with the same rage he'd woken me with the other morning. In an instant I saw his hand go up, but I couldn't move out of the way. It came down fast, the back of his hand against my mouth, and then I was on the ground looking up at him.

"This is all your fault! If you ever try to pull a stunt like this again, you better hope the cops find you before I do!"

I stayed on the floor. If I moved, he'd hit me again, so I lay there and looked up at him and said, "I'm sorry, Daddy, I didn't mean it," which made him run right out of the room. I knew a few of his weaknesses. I knew which words could hurt him.

Afterward I touched my fingers to my lips, not feeling any pain, and came back with blood. I held my fingers in the air and looked at the red wetting my fingertips and thought, *There. There it is.*

Me.

Christmas Eve came and we all tried not to look at one another or talk most of the day in fear that if we did we'd start brawling. By the time we exchanged presents, it felt al-most like things were getting a little back to normal. A cheery glow filled the living room. The whiskey-flavored coffee Lucy made probably helped.

My mom gave me a new pair of running shoes and my father gave me one of his old hunting rifles. *Just what I need,* I thought. *A gun.* I tried to be thankful, like when I'd thanked Jamie, because now with my dad out of work, money was tight. I kissed my mother and patted my father's shoulder from a distance, then opened the present my aunt Beth had sent me from California. She hadn't come this year. After all the trouble I'd caused, she thought maybe it would be better if she visited for Easter.

Her gift was in a small box wrapped in gold foil, and when I opened it, I found a silver necklace with a charm of winged running shoes on it, and a note as well.

> Dear Adam,
> No matter what, remember you're a runner. No one can take that away from you.
>
> Love,
> Aunt Beth

I know it was a good gift and all, but I wanted to tell Aunt Beth she was a little idealistic and perhaps not as clued in to the situation I found myself in at that moment as she thought. My mother couldn't run. My mother couldn't even walk anymore. I had no guarantee no one could take my ability to run away from me either. Still I put the neck-lace on and showed it to everyone. "That's beautiful," said my mother, holding it in the palm of her hand while I leaned toward her. "Oh, Beth always knows just the right thing to get."

My father grunted and said my aunt Beth was a hippie freak and my mother said, "I don't care what you think, John. My sister is better than ten of you stacked up together."

Lucy sat next to my father on the couch and laughed.

"Oh, not you too, Lucy!" said my mother.

"I'm sorry, Linda. But *really.* Your sister should have never left Ohio. I tell you, the West Coast is different. All sorts of crazy people. It'll change a person. It will definitely change a person."

"They're no different from us," I said, fondling the shoes on my necklace.

"And how would you know?" said my father. "You don't know nothing about nothing. You're just a smart-ass kid."

My mother said, "John, it's Christmas."

"Not for another three hours," said Andy.

I said, "You know what she means, idiot."

"Fuck off, fag," said Andy.

"Fuck you," I said back.

"Don't even start," said my father.

Andy and I stared each other down for a while, but we eventually got over it. By the end of the night, I even gave him his lighter back, it being Christmas and all.

"I wondered where that had gone!" he said. "Little thief." He lightly punched my shoulder. "You don't even smoke."

"I used it to burn down Fuck You Frances's house."

He said, "Who?"

I said, "Fuck You Frances."

"You mean Grandpa?"

"No idiot," I said. "Fuck You Frances. Frances Wilkinson? The Wilkinson farm?"

"Oh yeah," he said, grinning as if he were proud of me. "The Wilkinson farm. Everyone figured that was you."

"Yeah," I said, "but don't tell anyone. I told the social worker it wasn't me."

"No problem," said Andy, which gave me this really odd family feeling. Andy would keep his mouth shut for me? Maybe things could be different. With the way things were going, with how everyone was on their best behavior to make things work, I kind of hoped the past month was just me having gone temporarily insane, and that everyone would understand like Andy and forget about it.

Then Andy said, "Give me the gun and we'll call it even."

Of course there had to be a catch. What was I thinking?

I didn't know why my brother could treat me like I was just some stranger, but I didn't understand lots of things. I was beginning to get comfortable with not knowing, though. When something happens often enough, you kind of get numb to it, and then you don't feel it anymore. Like my father's hands.

I stayed the night on the couch again, watching the Christmas tree twinkle. Usually my mother made us turn the lights off before bed, but on Christmas she let them stay on all night. I was watching the blinking patterns of lights when I felt his breath cold on my shoulder. And when I turned, I found him kneeling by the arm of the couch where I rested my head.

When I looked up, he brushed hair out of my eyes.

"Welcome home," I said.

"Are you all right?"

"I guess so," I said, shrugging a little. "But Gracie—"

"She doesn't understand," he said, coming around to sit by me. "She's selfish, that's all. Don't worry. I love you."

He slid down and pressed the length of his body against mine, but what he said reminded me of something else. "Hold on," I said, and ran down to the basement, and searched the laundry basket until I found the pair of jeans that held Gracie's heart-shaped rose quartz.

"What are you looking for?" Jamie asked.

I slipped my hand into the pocket and found the heart where I'd left it. Only it wasn't the same as the last time I'd checked. It didn't beat. It didn't feel soft or warm. It was cold still stone again, and when I brought it out, I found a crack running down the center.

A moment later, while I held the heart in the palm of my hand, it split in two.

I tried not to look at it. It wasn't a real heart, I told myself. It was just a stone. It must have gotten busted when I was sleeping in the woods, or when we accidentally wandered into dead space. Somehow. When you live rough, things get broken. I slipped the pieces into my pocket and went back upstairs.

"That was hers, wasn't it?" Jamie said.

I nodded.

"She gave it to you, didn't she?"

"I took it," I said. "Then she gave it to me."

"That's okay," he said. "You can go without one of those anyway."

"I know."

"I know you know," he said, and that grin slid up one side of his face. Still that lopsided smile. It made me not so sad, and I smiled back.

"That's better. I hate to see you sad," he said. "You deserve better. You deserve to be loved."

I said, "That's what she said."

"She was selfish, that's all."

"I miss her."

"Don't worry," he said. "Where we're going, you won't have to think about it. I've got a plan. They think they've got us, but they haven't."

"They'll just catch us again."

"No way," he said. "This time it's just us. Just listen to me and we'll be fine."

"But I've caused enough problems."

"Things won't get better if we stay here," he said.

"I know," I said. "I trust you." I needed someone to trust really bad.

"Then it's settled." He sat next to me on the couch. He put his arms around me and pushed me down so that I lay on my back with him on top of me. The lights from the Christmas tree played over his waxy skin. He studied my face while I touched the gash near his temple, touched the jellyish blob of blood filling it. It was just another part of him, this damage. It didn't make me shudder.

"Merry Christmas, Adam," he whispered, placing his cheek against mine, the tree lights twinkling over the crown of his head.

"Merry Christmas, Jamie," I said.

In the Valley

DEAD SPACE. WE NEEDED SOME. BUT LUCY WAS in my bedroom and my parents were in theirs and my brother in his, so it was the hall closet we'd have to go through. No one ever went in the hall closet. It's where we put all the things we no longer wanted. My father's old hunting jackets and my mother's old coats with fake fur collars, Andy's high school jacket with the school symbol on it—a rocket shooting into the night sky—boots with holes in them and my old baseball glove and bat from when I was a little kid and thought playing baseball would make my dad happy. If you put something in the hall closet, it never ever came out. Closets are where dead things go. The things we use every day have shelf lives, just like people.

Jamie opened the door and we pushed through the coats, hangers clacking together as we squeezed in. "Shh," I said. "Be quiet or they'll hear." But Jamie only made a face and shrugged.

"Even if they heard," he said, "by the time they got here, we'd be gone."

He took my hand and pulled me in deeper. Then the clothes were behind us and the dark of dead space before us. I reached back to close the door and take one last look at the tree lights twinkling on their timer, off and on, off and on, in a sort of chorus of colors. I almost said goodbye to everything like I did when I'd tried leaving before, but since I'd been found and brought back again, I figured goodbye might not be the word I needed this time either.

I shut the door and turned to Jamie. "Don't worry, Adam," he said, like he could read my mind. "It's me and you this time. Things will be different. Trust me."

A cold wind swirled around us then. I could smell the moonlight on the snow as it fell over the frostbitten field we stood in. Silhouettes of trees were stitched along the purple horizon and, beyond that wall of shadow, wolves were howling. Their voices gathered above the trees like sheaves of wheat bound together. I couldn't see any wolves, but I could feel them watching as we ran toward their woods, waiting for us to enter.

Which we did, the branches of trees smacking our arms and faces as we rushed through, taking the pathless way that Jamie knew. It was best, he said, to stay off the path in this place. Not as many chances to run across one of the ladies who kneeled under trees, combing chunks of hair out of their own heads with their fingers, moaning. Not as many chances to stumble across men with no skin, their muscles bunched and bleeding, walking around like biology models of the human body. The first time Jamie brought me here, I wasn't able to see anything, but now I could. Now I saw everything.

Even so, Jamie held on to my hand to guide me to where we were going. I followed, looking down at my feet as they moved through the dead leaves that littered the forest floor, powdered with snowflake patterns that had frozen along the webs of their veins. I was thinking I was far along on my way to dying because of being able to see in dead space finally, but then I realized I'd smelled the moonlight on the snow and felt the cold seep through my clothes as we ran, making me shiver. "Jamie," I said, whispering so I didn't call attention to us. "Something's wrong. I'm feeling."

He didn't stop running, though. He just nodded and then—*whoosh*—we left the woods, the branches of trees whipping back together behind us. Then we were climbing a steep hill to where the railroad tracks rested above us on the hilltop.

As we climbed, the grass slowly vanished and a blanket of gravel crunched beneath us. I glanced down at my shoes again. They were cracked, worn-out; they should have been tossed out already. But they'd brought me this far. I couldn't abandon them. I'd keep them till they fell right off my feet. I'd keep them till they had no life left in them.

At the top of the hill, we stopped and I bent at my waist, bracing my hands against my thighs like I did after running a race, feeling the air cut down my throat like a razor. It hurt but it felt good too, to feel a little human. And that's when I saw the steam leaving Jamie's mouth for the first time. *He's alive,* I thought.

"Are we out now?" I asked.

Jamie shook his head. "Still in." He pointed a little ways down the tracks and said, "Over there's where I was born."

I stood up again and looked to where he was pointing. I saw the yellow police banners flapping in the wind first, then the hole they surrounded. The hole they'd buried him in. The hole we'd gotten into together.

The wind broke through my jean jacket, and I wrapped my arms around myself, teeth chattering. "That's where I was born too," I said. But Jamie shook his head.

"You haven't been born yet," he said. His face was sad, his mouth turned down in a grimace. "I came out on this side. You haven't."

"Then what am I?"

He put his hands on my shoulders and said, "I'm glad you came, Adam. You don't know what this means to me." He made it sound like we were going to war together, or into outer space to destroy a meteor before it crashed into earth. When I didn't say anything, he smiled that lopsided smile and I saw that, even though he seemed more alive here, he was changing. Brown rot grew between his teeth, and his eyes were sinking deeper into their sockets. His skin had a waxy sheen to it, as if someone had filled him with embalming fluid, and there was something in his eyes too. A distance grew in him like a far horizon.

He turned and started walking in the direction opposite the hole and I followed behind, still holding my arms over my chest. I asked where we were going, but he only said, "You'll see," and kept walking. I started to watch my feet move beneath me again. Pebbles and slats, pebbles and slats. *Ice, rock, air, breathe,* I thought. No entry.

As we walked I kept thinking about Gracie, about how things had ended between us without any discussion. Without any words. The way she just looked at me and left with her father. No turn of her head, no see you later. It was like all of a sudden she didn't know me. When I thought about her, it felt like broken glass was piled in my stomach, cutting me. Sometimes, though, it felt more like a wolf clawing at my insides, trying to get out. At any moment it would push through my throat, pry my jaws open and come through my mouth howling, ready to destroy everything in its path.

At one point the tracks split in two directions, curving away from each other. One line led to the old covered bridge over Sugar Creek, the other continued into the dark before us. Some shadows were going inside the entrance to the bridge, like bees slipping into a honeycomb. Others lingered outside still. "What is this place?" I asked as we passed, but it wasn't until we were well beyond it that Jamie answered.

"The crossing."

"To where?"

"I don't know." He shrugged. "I just know it's where you're supposed to go. You know. Afterward."

"Why don't you?" I asked.

"Why don't you go to school?" was his answer.

"Okay." I nodded. "Fair enough. But why here?"

"I don't know. A lot of the others come here too. It's where I brought Frances."

"Frances?"

He nodded. "After you burned down her house, she had nowhere to live in the world. So she needed to come here and cross."

"But she's *dead*," I said. "She didn't need a place to live anyway."

"Come on, Adam," he said. "Death isn't just a body thing. You know that."

"How was she?" I asked, even though I'd watched him bring her to the place. I wanted to hear what he'd say, to see if he'd try to spare me the details of what I'd done to her.

"She was furious," he said.

"But she went through?"

He nodded.

"Do you think she's okay now?"

"I don't know," he said, shaking his head, his eyes shifting down to look at the railroad ties we were walking. "I hope so."

We didn't talk much after that, just kept making our way down the tracks. We seemed to be moving without direction, but Jamie insisted he knew where we were going, so eventually I stopped asking and eventually we stopped talking altogether.

It was hard to keep track of time here. Night never faded, the stars never brightened or darkened, day never came. There was a short period where the color of the sky lightened to a lighter shade of purple, but other than that, years could pass and I'd never be able to tell the difference.

But then suddenly, after we'd walked for what seemed no more than an hour, banks and corporate buildings began to rise out of the darkness in the distance, blinking their names in bright red letters. And as we got closer, I recognized a few. "Hey," I said, "this is Youngstown, isn't it?"

Jamie nodded.

"But we've barely been walking an hour. It took Gracie that long to get here by car."

"Time is different here," he said. "You know that, Adam."

He pointed to one of the taller buildings in the distance with red letters spelling out Home Savings on one of its walls. That was where we were headed. I said the word home to myself a few times, but I still didn't trust it, so I left it behind in the tracks I'd walked while saying it.

Youngstown. It didn't seem big enough or far enough

away to make me feel safe, but I reminded myself it was better than where I was leaving.

The tracks led into the downtown through a valley that was full of rusty old mills and factories and we followed them until we came out of dead space. Under the cover of real night, we entered the city and lights began to spread in all directions like a sea of strange, glowing pearls.

The valley itself was a wasteland. Vacant factories with smashed-up windows. Black scars on the ground where steel mills had been demolished by their owners years ago. Yellow-brown weeds and thorny bushes. Leftover machine parts. Rotting car frames and engines. Rusty metal workings. Toilets covered in strange stains. Broken forty ounce beer bottles. Couches with springs curling out of the stuffing. And far too many stones to look at and be reminded of Gracie.

The dead were here too, trudging through the thin layer of snow that had fallen. They wandered the rubble of the mills, leaving no footprints as they went. They lingered in doorways, smoking cigarettes, nodding as we passed. Most were men wearing grease-stained jumpsuits; others were young women wearing long tweed skirts, carrying folders pressed to their chests.

A whistle shrieked once, twice, a third time, and the dead lifted their heads in its direction. A moment later they poured from the abandoned factories, and others materialized to take their places and begin their shift. The mills had closed years and years ago, but the dead still came here, even though it was clear that what they wanted didn't want them.

"My grandpa used to work in these mills," I told Jamie. And then I started wondering if my grandpa was here among the others. I didn't know him like I knew my grandma. He was rough around the edges with not much good to say about people, so when he was alive I'd kept my distance. When he was in the hospital with cancer the year before my grandma came to live with us and you could hear his moans in the hallway, I only went in once to say I loved him before it was too late, like my mom had said I should do. Whenever my grandma talked about him, she'd say, "The mills broke his back when they were open, and when they closed they broke his spirit." He seemed so heartless when I knew him that I often wished I'd known him before the mills had closed, when it was just his back they'd broken.

If it hadn't been for my grandma, I wouldn't have known even that much about my grandpa, which is still not a lot but better than nothing. My grandma was who told me most things about the world. After she died, I felt like I might not ever learn anything real again. I told myself I had to at least remember everything she'd already told me. Like how she used to worry away at how her life would end. She was keen on dying with nothing left undone here. If you died without being okay about it, she said you'd get stuck in this place trying to sort things out. "Not for me!" she'd shout, grinning, her wrinkles folding over one another. "I'll have all my ducks in a row!" If my grandma were here walking into the wreckage of this city with me, she'd say, "All sorts of ducks out of place. What were they thinking?"

I really missed her.

"This way," said Jamie, his voice sounding far away. I looked around and found him climbing a set of concrete steps built into a wall of the valley. He ran up them, hitting the iron rails on both sides of the steps with a piece of pipe.

Bing! Bing! Bing! Metal on metal echoed through the valley. But the dead paid no attention. They had their own work to finish.

I ran to catch him, racing up the steps until I reached the top where I found him squatting down on his haunches, twirling the pipe on his fingers like a baton. "There were a lot of dead people down there," I said. "I thought we were out of dead space."

"Well, we are, sort of," he said, dropping the pipe, standing up. "The world is thin here. You can come and go more easily."

A wind picked up as we started walking into town. Snow swirled around us and, as we passed under the flickering cones of streetlights downtown, the flakes looked like tiny galaxies spinning beneath them.

We turned up Hazel Street, leaning forward against the steep incline. Pillars of steam rose from manhole covers and whenever snowflakes fell into the columns of steam, they melted in midair. A cathedral made of brown, grainy stone loomed above us, its bell tower still lit even this late. We pushed toward it until we were at the top of the street facing down a stone statue of some guy wearing robes near the cathedral's front doors. He held one hand up as if he were in class, waiting to be called on; in his other he held a book, probably the Bible. He must have been some sort of saint. I didn't know. My mom couldn't tell saint from stranger either, but whenever she'd get into a car, she'd cross herself like she was Catholic, something she inherited from my grandma without realizing.

We kept to the shadows the cathedral cast over the road, and walked up Elm Street only a little ways before Jamie stopped to say, "This is it. Home for the holidays."

I looked around but couldn't tell where he meant for us to stay. No building on the street seemed livable. But I'd lived in a closet and a lean-to in the woods already. If I had to, I could handle pretty much anything.

There was an old church that looked like it'd been burned up a long time ago, and a building across from it that seemed connected to the cathedral. Up ahead, at the next intersection, I could see a few newer buildings that were probably part of the university. Where was he talking about? Did he mean we'd stay right here in the street like homeless people? Like that kid I'd seen when Gracie and I had driven through the downtown. The one with my face. We were only a couple blocks away from that corner. I only had to run down the hill we'd just climbed and take a right on Commerce and there he'd probably still be, sitting on his haunches against the playhouse. I wished I'd never seen him. Thinking of him just reminded me of everything I'd been doing and if I'd learned one thing since I'd started running away from God's finger, it was that the person who could frustrate your most well-laid plans because they knew all about you was yourself.

Jamie pointed to the old burned-up church. I hated churches, even abandoned ones. I figured God might still be living in them, and the last thing I wanted was to run away from one home to live in one run by some other distant dictator.

This church looked like one of the big Victorian houses Gracie and I had passed on our way into Youngstown. Smoke stained the outer walls, and there were cross-topped turrets on both front corners. There was a bell tower in the center of the roof between the turrets too. Some of the slats covering the tower sides had been broken out. The front doors were locked with chains, the windows covered with plywood. Except for in the smashed-up tower, the place was sealed tight so no one could get in.

I turned to Jamie but before I could even say a word, he said, "There's always a way in for us. Don't worry."

We went around back, skulking like thieves, and at a basement window Jamie knelt down to remove the plywood covering. He didn't struggle, just slipped it out of the frame like it was nothing. Someone must have pried it off and left it sitting in the frame to look like it was still covered, which made me think other people might stay here from time to time. Before I could say anything, though, Jamie slipped through on his stomach, feetfirst. Something splashed when he landed, and a moment later his face loomed in the window. "Come on," he said. "Quick. Before anyone sees."

He placed a wooden crate under the window so I could step down without landing in the water that covered that corner of the floor. A bare bulb lit the basement from the center of the ceiling, and a worktable stood beneath it, tools scattered over the top like surgical instruments. I thought of mad scientists and insane asylums deep in the center of strange forests, bolts of lightning cracking open the sky. Not at the Wilkinson farm, not in the Amish logging camp, not even when I was lost in dead space and a man with no skin stole my words for Gracie had I felt this spooked. "It looks like maybe people are already using this place," I said, hoping Jamie would change his mind, but it was no good.

"Look," he said. "There's even a generator down here."

A large piece of machinery stood in one corner of the basement, taking up half the wall. It had buttons and switches and wires coming out of it, which Jamie flipped randomly until a flush of air came through unseen vents and light seeped through the spaces between the floorboards in the ceiling. He looked at me over his shoulder with his lopsided grin and said, "Come on. Let's explore."

We ran up the stairs and turned a corner into the front entrance area, then went through what used to be a set of double doors into the chapel, which was nothing but a husk of what it must have once been. The floorboards had all been stripped, the walls stained black with smoke, the stained glass broken. There was an organ up on the altar, but when Jamie played his fingers over the keys, no sound came out. Just keys clicking. It had lost all of its notes. Lightbulbs in metal cages hung from the rafters on yellow cords and underneath them a bunch of sawhorses stood next to each other. There were no pews and no paintings of Jesus. There were no signs of life anywhere at all.

Then a noise came from above us. Maybe I was wrong. Something was alive in here after all. It thumped around above us once, twice, a third time. Then fell silent. Jamie and I looked at each other, then up at the ceiling, as if it would have answers for us.

"Probably just the wind," said Jamie. "You know, coming through the broken shutters in the tower."

"Probably," I said, hoping if we agreed with each other it would be true. But when the thumping sound started up again, I decided to investigate.

There was a small door at the back of the room, next to the altar. I opened it and, sure enough, there were stairs in there that creaked the next moment as I started up them. There were no lights, so the way up was dark. I brushed aside webs and sneezed out dust as I breathed it. Then I lifted my foot to search for the next step, but I'd reached the top. A moment later my eyes adjusted and I could see the outline of the bell tower take shape in the moonlight coming through the broken shutters.

It was just a little octagon-shaped room big enough for a bell and a person to ring it. Wind came through the broken shutters, and snow rode in on the current. A sliver of moon hung in the sky outside, silver on the dark. There was nothing else in the room except the bell hook and its pulley. The bell itself was gone, probably ringing in some other church tower. I looked around to see what could have made the noise we'd heard, but I found nothing. That made me even more spooked than I'd felt just being in the church to begin with, and suddenly I got a *get-out* feeling. The same feeling I'd felt when I saw God's finger coming. I started to back up, slow and quiet, but before I could turn and go back downstairs, the thumping came again.

A crow was hurling itself against the ceiling, fluttering blindly in the rafters over and over until it finally dropped to the floor in front of me, where it shook off the fall and picked itself up to hop onto a windowpane. The wind blew snow around its sleek black feathers and the crow opened its wings as if to fly off, then had a change of heart and folded them back under. Tipping back and forth on the ledge, it turned its beady black eyes on me and cawed, then flashed its wings open like a fan and flew straight at me. I ducked just in time to hear it buzz my ear before it circled back around to fly against the wind, out the window, into the night.

A single feather floated back on the wind and landed at my feet. I bent to pick it up. "One for sorrow," I said softly to myself, hoping another crow would appear.

But there had been just the one. Just that one.

I stood in the tower thinking of the picture of me and Jamie that I'd buried, thinking of the heart-shaped quartz I'd stolen from Gracie. Bad things come in threes. Jamie's murder, my mother's accident, and then we'd gotten in his hole together. Here was the result of my actions: a single black feather.

While I stood there, wishing and wishing that time could go backward, Jamie shouted, "Find anything?" from down the stairs.

When I looked, I couldn't see him at the bottom—darkness came between us—but I still shook my head and called back, "Nothing," knowing he was there.

I dropped that word like a wishless penny, *nothing,* then slipped the feather in my front pocket with the broken pieces of Gracie's heart and followed it down the stairs.

We stretched out on the altar with my backpack and a bag of potting soil from the basement for pillows. We didn't have blankets, but we couldn't feel the cold anyway, and it wasn't like Jamie could sleep. Even I could only get an hour or two each night, waking almost as soon as I drifted, unable to fall back even if I wanted. But we still found ourselves in familiar positions, nibbling on candy bars I'd smuggled from my mother's kitchen, making up makeshift beds as if we were able to sleep like normal boys.

Another thing to put down in my notebook:

15. When you're dead, you do the same things you did when you were living, so you can sometimes believe you're still alive.

Only a few weeks had passed since we'd separated at the Wilkinson farm, but Jamie made it seem like it had been forever. "I missed you so much," he said, shaking his head and looking down into his lap as if he were embarrassed to admit it. "It was like you'd died and left the world. I didn't know what I was going to do."

"I'm sorry," I said. "But really, where could I have gone that you wouldn't have been able to find me?"

He shrugged, turning his head toward his shoulder to avoid my eyes. "Things happen," he said. "Things you don't have any control over. You might have died and crossed over for all I knew."

"*You* didn't do that," I said. I thought I was pointing out something significant, locating a flaw in his fears, but instead he winced as if I'd said something painful.

"Yeah," he said, sighing. "I didn't do that." Talking about himself seemed to bother him, and I let him change the subject. He wanted to talk about me instead. "You're so good," he said. "You're so smart and brave. You ran away from them. You made it."

"I didn't make it," I reminded him. "And I didn't do it alone. Gracie helped."

"Well, *virtually* alone then."

"She was just scared," I said, feeling like I should defend Gracie a little. Even if she wouldn't answer me when I called her name at the police station. Even if she walked away and out of my life without a word.

"Still," said Jamie. "What you did was great. It's like when you're running. Like that day. When was it? Something happened."

"I ran a race."

"You ran a race," he said. "And then you won and they lifted you on their shoulders. It was like that day, running away, winning, wasn't it?"

"A little," I said. "Yeah, it felt a little bit like winning."

I couldn't help but take his compliments and slip them in a private pocket of myself and feel good about the things he told me. Each time he said something nice, I was flattered in a way that was both weird and wonderful. I wanted to hear more and more. *Go on*, I was thinking. *Tell me anything good about me you've noticed.* I couldn't do that, so I swelled with his words when he gave them to me, when he told me I was good.

"Adam?" he said before I fell asleep for a couple of hours.

"Yeah?"

"Thanks for coming."

"Thanks for bringing me," I said.

"No, really. I couldn't have come without you."

"Sure you could have," I said, trying to make him feel better about himself, like he was always doing for me.

But he only smiled lopsidedly, staring across the space between us on the altar, and said goodnight before my eyelids started to flutter and fall.

We wandered the city for the next few days, getting to know its roads and bridges, its dead ends and alleys, its drive-thru liquor stores and fast food chains and abandoned theaters, its scrubby parks with falling down fences and vacant lots and bars. This was a world of cracked concrete and buckling sidewalks, a world where the trees lining the streets rotted and buildings disappeared every day. Jamie said he felt like maybe he could be more alive here. "This is my city," he said. "I feel stronger here. Stronger than when I ever visited home."

He meant his old house. He told me his mother still talked to him every night before going to sleep, calling him to come to her bedside so she could tell him all of the things she'd never said when he was alive. I love you, I miss you, you're such a good boy, I'm sorry, I'm so sorry, why didn't I love you better, can you forgive me, will you give me a sign, just a little one, to let me know you love me still?

It made him angry, but he went to her anyway. "She just feels guilty," he said. "But it's not because of how she feels about me. It's because of what she used to do to me when I was little."

"What did she do?"

"She used to get crazy sometimes. You know. She'd hear voices and sometimes get angry or sometimes crazy mad and come at me out of nowhere. One time she beat my head with a metal spatula until blood came down my face. I can still remember tasting it. I haven't burnt that memory yet."

"A metal spatula?" I said. "Why would she hit you with a metal spatula?"

"She'd been cooking hamburgers and I broke one of her figurines in the living room. She always had a nativity scene up on the shelf, even if it wasn't Christmas. I'd been lying on the floor tossing a basketball at the ceiling, just tossing it up and trying to catch it on my fingertips. I wanted to play a sport like you do. But when I broke the third wise man she came out of the kitchen with the spatula already swinging."

"When did that happen?"

"When I was twelve, I think." He looked at me without

blinking. His blankness made him more beautiful. I wanted that too, but I didn't know how he did it.

"She beat you over the head with a metal spatula when you were twelve?" I said, my voice climbing higher. "That's fucked up. I mean, my dad hits me every now and then but he doesn't like doing it, I can tell, and mostly he pulls his punches and is really just trying to scare us for screwing up at school or something. But I don't get the spatula. What's wrong with her?"

"Something's wrong in her head," he said, tapping his temple with two fingers. "That's all."

We were walking across Veteran's Bridge, which spanned the valley where we'd entered the city. From there I could look down and see the wasteland we'd passed through on Christmas Eve. The dead still wandered down there, picking through rubbish, but from the bridge they weren't as noticeable. They flickered in and out of sight, as if they knew how to slip through the cracks in the air.

For a while we didn't say anything, just kept walking, but the spatula incident kept running through my mind like a scene from a horror movie, so I finally asked what his dad had been like. For me it was his dad who was dead, in the past tense, and it was Jamie who was still alive.

"He was okay, I guess. Not home so often. Mostly he was on the road. He drove an eighteen-wheeler for a company here in Youngstown. I don't think he came home sometimes, even when he had time off. But when he did, my mother always ran around like a crazy person, trying to clean up the messes she'd made over the weeks he'd been gone. She loved him more than she loved me. She told me that once when I was eating breakfast before school and he was coming home that night. I didn't think we were competing, but maybe she did. I don't know. She'd get so sad when he left, she couldn't get out of bed for days."

"She couldn't get out of bed?"

"Well, she could, but only if she made herself. It's like this, you know, what do you call it?" He waved his hand around, looking at it like he didn't recognize it. "You know, this thing that has your fingers?"

"A hand?"

"A hand," he said. "Yeah. It's like this hand is pressing down on her, keeping her on the mattress."

"What hand?" I asked. I wondered if it might be God's hand pressing down on her, the same way he pointed his finger at my family.

"You know," said Jamie, "this huge weight that can't be lifted. That's how she described it. I think it's just in her head, but that doesn't mean it's not real."

"My mom can't get out of bed either," I said. "But that's because of Lucy."

"The accident," Jamie said gravely. He was good about making me feel like I could be sad about it. He understood. Tragedies happen and sometimes you can live in them with the right person. He was that right person for me.

Cars zoomed past as we walked the bridge, filling our ears with the roars of their engines. We walked with our heads down, steady against the wind that pushed through our clothes and past our collars. One thing I realized about Youngstown immediately was how the landscape buckled with hillsides moving like waves toward the Pennsylvania border, and although walking was the only way we could get anywhere, it wasn't the kind of city where you could walk anywhere easily. Maybe back in its heyday you could find anything you wanted within a couple of blocks from your house, but now the place was mostly boarded up store-fronts and abandoned buildings with faded signs in their windows that said, Your homes, your jobs, your dignity. I recognized those words. My grandfather had put one of those signs in his front yard when I was way little and everyone in his mill had gone on strike.

Once in a while we came across a little market with a deli inside, but if you looked at the cans and boxes on the shelves, you found nothing but dust growing over every-thing, as if the cans and boxes had been sitting on the shelves for years, the same cans of soup and boxes of cereal that had been out when all the factories closed.

Most of the shops were run by Arabic people, and every time I saw someone who had moved here from some far-away country, I'd wonder why they'd come. Not to America. I mean, I wondered why they'd come to Youngstown. It couldn't have been for a money-making opportunity. I won-dered how bad things in their home countries had been that they'd up and leave to settle in a city that looked like it had been occupied during a war.

It was at one of these places that I got a little hungry and went to buy a candy bar from a woman who wore a white cloth over her head and didn't speak much English, except to say how much I owed her. That's when I realized I hardly had any money at all. I searched my pockets and came up with barely enough to pay. Other than the crow feather and the pieces of Gracie's heart, my pockets were empty.

I hadn't thought about money when Jamie had me

come with him, and the five hundred I'd taken from Mr. Highsmith had been returned when the police found it in my backpack. *Real smart, McCormick,* I thought. But it wasn't so bad. One thing I had going for me was that I didn't get as hungry as I did before I started on my way to dying, and after eating a candy bar I was usually full for a while. I'd make things work, I told myself. I'd get by somehow.

Jamie talked through the nights with his arms beneath his head, looking up at the soot-blackened ceiling. "This is it," he said a week or so after we'd made the church our home. "Now we'll have some peace." Peace sounded good, and I said as much, because the past couple of months had been getting harder and harder to deal with everyone trying to parent me or be my friend or lover or something else that required me to care about them. No matter what anyone says, don't believe the lie that we're told, that love is the greatest thing on this planet. It isn't. Love only means you have something to lose.

Jamie was concerned with his own plans, though. He wasn't interested in love, just in living. "That's where you come in," he said. "Together, they can't touch us. Alone, they'll make me disappear." He wasn't making any sense, though, and when I asked him to tell me more, he struggled for the words. "You know," he said. "This place will remember me if I have anything to, you know, what's that word? Talking about it?"

"Say about it?"

"Exactly!" he said. "This place will remember me if I have anything to say about it."

When he talked like this, I didn't say anything. I'd just listen and nod.

I fell asleep with him still chattering beside me, and when I woke the next morning I expected to find him still going on about his future, but when I turned over I found only the bag of potting soil he'd been leaning against, the impression his head had made still on the bag.

A moment later, keys rattled in the padlock on the front doors, and muffled voices drifted in from outside as the lock jiggled in its chain. I grabbed my backpack and jumped up, looking around for the nearest place to hide. The bell tower was that place, so up those steps I ran, even though I didn't like going up there, and stood still as a statue in the shadows and dust, straining to hear if they'd heard me as the front doors squealed open and they came in.

It was the church people. Their voices became clear as they entered the front room. One boomed loud, filling the room below, traveling up the stairs to reach me. "What's all this?" it said. "Who's been throwing candy wrappers on the altar? We're trying to *fix* this place, not use it as a waste-basket!"

Mumbles. Then someone said, "Wasn't me, Pastor."

Footsteps came close to the tower door. Then someone pushed it all the way open, making it squeal on its hinges, and a small shadow appeared at the bottom of the stairs. I thought I'd been found and would be hauled home again, this time only days after escaping, but whoever owned that shadow didn't see me standing at the top. Behind the shadow, the pastor said, "Tia, come here and help me clean up this mess. God knows I'm working with a crew of litter-bugs."

But the shadow called Tia said, "Maybe it wasn't them,

Daddy," and the pastor laughed and said if it wasn't members of his own congregation throwing trash around, who was it?

The shadow didn't move. She kept looking up the stairwell in my direction. "I don't know, Daddy," she said. "Maybe we have ourselves a ghost."

The Rule of Doors

SATURDAYS WERE USUALLY WHEN THE REVEREND and his people worked on fixing up the church. They'd come at nine or ten in the morning and work until afternoon, banging and sawing and scraping the whole time. Often when I woke Jamie was already gone, so I started hanging out by myself, usually on the block that separated the church and the university, where the street was deserted on weekends, without students and people who worked in law firms and banks and downtown businesses to walk along its sidewalk laughing and smiling, making jokes or complaining about supervisors and professors. During the week they swung their briefcases with purpose, carrying their packs and bags slung over their shoulders, checking their purses for change as they approached the hot dog vendor who would greet them with a "How's it going?" like good old Marty Chapman always did. Except when it came to me. When *I* passed by the hot dog guy, he'd scowl at me a warning not to approach, and after a while I realized I'd started to look like a street person. After that, when I looked around, I noticed a lot of people with faces determined to look straight ahead as they passed me by.

It wasn't everyone who pretended not to see me,

though. Sometimes there were people who kept their eyes locked with mine and said things like, *Hey, son,* or *Hey, young fella,* or *Hey kid, you okay? You need something?* It was because of their words forcing me to respond that I began to realize I'd been leaving the body without even knowing it. They'd say, "Hey kid," and I'd fall from the sky or outer space where I'd been looking down at everything happening around me instead of out at it all from behind my eyes like we're supposed to.

It was getting to be a regular event, leaving. I'd left my family, I'd left my town, I'd left everything I knew behind me. Now when I slipped out of my flesh, it didn't shock me. I could be flying high above where nothing touched me, and when I looked down I couldn't even tell which of the tiny humans moving around below belonged to me.

It was in this way, swooping through the bell tower like the crow that left me its single feather, that I watched the work being done by the church people on Saturday mornings.

The same ones came every week, along with the preacher, Reverend Taylor, who was a stumpy little black guy built like a barrel. He always wore a long, black wool coat and dress shoes shined to a gleaming polish. From what I could tell, he didn't do any of the actual work. He would just boss around everyone else, going in and out the front doors hollering the whole time, *Do this! Do that! No, not there! There!* And everyone would run around, following his directions.

A few middle-aged black guys and a couple of younger black kids around my age always came to help, and except for when the reverend brought his daughter, none of them looked happy. The reverend's daughter's name was Tia, and everyone said her name like it was holy. Even if the reverend was mad at someone for screwing up, he always said her name smooth as butter, or if Tia herself did something wrong, they'd all say it was nothing and not to worry, Tia, like if you said her name any other way but nicely you might get struck down by God's lightning. She had black hair slicked back in a bun, and skin the color of caramel. She must have got that from her mother, though, because the reverend was way dark. Like the ace of spades, my dad would have said with a grin I never understood. He had lots of weird sayings like that for nonwhite people. I don't know why. It's not like he even knew anyone who wasn't white.

The reverend's eyes were always roaming, assessing the work, surveying his property. You could tell that he didn't even see the fire stains, that the broken stained glass windows and empty bell tower didn't register for him. In his mind it was the same church he still preached in, large and Victorian, with gleaming white walls and a bell hanging in the tower, calling people in to pray. Never mind that it was gutted, the reverend heard the organ playing. Never mind that services had been held in a gym several blocks away for the past year, he saw nothing but crowds of believers filling his church with their voices. I almost saw it too; I almost heard the organ and all those prayers. *Here is the church, here is the steeple,* I thought on one of those Saturday afternoons in winter. *Open the doors and there are the people.*

I was standing beside a fire hydrant painted to look like the university's mascot, a penguin, watching the church people pack up their things and lock the chains on the doors before leaving. Jamie wasn't with me. Like the past few Saturdays, he'd already left by the time I woke. Like my leaving my body, Jamie's disappearances were becoming a regular occurrence. I didn't know where he went, but every day it seemed I was more alone than I thought I'd be when I decided to come with him. It made me wonder why he said he needed me. I mean, things were bad back where I'd come from, and knowing I'd had to leave, I was still glad I'd left with Jamie. But I couldn't understand why we'd come here, why we'd settled in this shadow of a city, why, if he needed me like he said, he was always going away.

When he finally came back later that evening, he said we should go out looking for food. I wasn't really hungry and to tell the truth I couldn't smell much of anything anymore either, but he insisted. He said if I didn't keep eating, I'd get sick and then what would we do? So I said I'd eat, even though it only reminded me of how my mom and dad made me eat after they brought me back home from the police. Being forced. Like my body belonged to them or something.

We went into the Uptown, the part of the south side where the buildings were all two stories of burnt bricks and broken windows, and the houses were all barely able to stand. Even though it was run down worse than other sections of the city I'd seen, you could tell that it used to be well-off, full of life at some point. The streets were packed with ghosts that day, out shopping, returning books to the library, slipping through the rotted, chained-up front doors of the Uptown Theater with its rusty marquee that said, Close, because the d had fallen off who knows how long ago.

Close, I thought, testing it, wondering if it had any meaning for me, whether or not it was a word I should take since it'd been left up on the marquee like that, abandoned. I didn't feel close to anything right then, though. I felt as far away from everything as a person could get.

In so many of those buildings that looked ready to fall over you had your pick of dance clubs, porn stores and strip joints. I'd never been in any of those places because I wasn't old enough, but I'd passed by while drifting through the city with and without Jamie. Usually these were spots where I could hear people's shadows clearer than usual. They were constantly complaining or arguing, picking fights, making pleas for their lives to complete strangers. They made me nervous, like maybe they would ask me to help them, and since I couldn't even help myself that well I tried not to come this way too often.

The houses here were almost all Victorians, some with their stained glass windows still intact. I couldn't help but think of my dad when I looked at them. I'm sure he'd never worked on a Victorian since they haven't been in fashion in forever and ever, but when I thought about how long they'd lasted—were lasting—through their breakdowns, I thought of my father's hands. I heard his voice mix with the voices of the shadows. "Did the closets in that one," he said, and I looked down at my feet as they carried me over the cracked and broken sidewalks.

Heaps of dirty snow piled up against the curbs of Market Street, black from ash and salt spread during winter storms. As we passed the remnants of the Rendezvous Lounge, a drunk with yellow, bloodshot eyes stopped us. "Hey, fellas," he said, his voice like an old recording with static in the background. He put his hand on my shoulder like he was my friend, but I pulled back. "Sorry there," he said. "But can you spare some change, kid?" When I told him I didn't have any, he turned to Jamie and said, "What about your friend?" When he really took a look at Jamie, though, his eyes grew round and wide. He waved his hands crazily, saying, "Ah, fuck. Ain't a haint in this city has any money. Forget it," then pushed his face into his collar and walked the other way.

Jamie seemed slower than usual, like he was tired, even though things like exhaustion usually meant nothing to him. He stopped several times on Market Street as we were going back, our food foray a failure, and looked around as if he didn't know where he was. "Is that a—you know? What is it? That sound?" he said, and I listened to hear what he heard but couldn't name.

"An ambulance?" I said, and he nodded, smiling with relief.

"An ambulance," he said. "Is that what that is?"

I nodded.

"Didn't we go there sometimes?" he said as we passed by a diner we wouldn't have ever had the money to eat at since we'd been staying here. I shook my head. "Really?" he said. "I thought they had really good apple pie."

"Maybe you're thinking of the Wildwood Café," I offered. But, no, it wasn't the Wildwood Café. He was sure it was the diner on that corner.

"Adam?" he asked a little while later, as we walked back through the downtown and up the hill to the church. He stopped suddenly and looked around, saying, "Are you still there?"

"I'm still here," I said. "Jamie? What's the matter?"

"Nothing," he said, turning his face to me finally. "I just didn't see you there for a moment. It's nothing. Sorry."

Back in the church, we sat down on the altar below the

picture of the Last Supper. The reverend had hung it the week before. It was a show of faith, a sign that it wouldn't be just a picture of Christ hanging in this place again, but that soon God Himself would be returning. I looked at this picture some days and wondered why that man ever gave a damn about the world. He looked so alone at that table of people. I could understand that feeling, but what I didn't understand was how he could be surrounded by traitors and still care about everybody. He was called the Prince of Peace, but I think that name is a little wrong. A lot of things are misnamed in this world. Peace might have been what Jesus wanted for people, but I think the proper name would have been if they'd called him the King of Sorrow, because really, every time I saw the guy, he looked so damned sad.

The thing I liked about Jesus was that he wasn't like his father. He didn't send storms or plagues or angels to destroy people's lives or test their loyalty. He just loved everyone. It gave me a little bit of hope to think that a son didn't have to follow in his father's footsteps. Even sitting right beneath his picture, I wasn't afraid of him like I was afraid of God's finger. Jesus didn't seem like the finger-pointing type. I would probably have gotten along with the guy.

We slept in the church; I ate food in the church, stolen from McDonald's and Burger King garbage cans; we sat around and talked in the church, laughed in the church, remembered our families in the church, told each other secrets in the church. I watched Jamie's eyes flicker to life as he burned fistfuls of memories—a birthday cake shaped and decorated like Batman his mom had made him when he was five; the Christmas his dad didn't come home and he and his mom spent the night with an aunt in Bloomfield, a town even smaller and even more in the middle of nowhere than ours, with only a stocking of candy canes as a present; the day at school when he found out he'd got all A's for the first time and then Matt Hardin and his idiot crew stuffed him in a locker. I watched his eyes fade in the church as the warmth of his burnt memories grew cold. Everything we needed to do and everything that wasn't needed we did in the church, avoiding the rest of the world. Eventually I got over my fear that God was in there with us. Besides the crow I'd found in the bell tower the first night, after a few weeks it became clear that Jamie and I were the only ones living there. Or kind of living.

I didn't mind. I'd almost always felt alone anyway. At least this aloneness was more honest, I figured. The two of us being together defined the world; and as long as that existed the world would keep spinning. Even though we lived in a burned-out church in the middle of a city no one knew existed—even though we were kids no one cared about—it was enough, I thought, to have just him keeping me company.

He started to ask me a lot of questions after a while, as if I might know something he didn't. I don't know how long we'd been gone. Weeks definitely, but it felt more like months. Mostly he wanted to talk about the bridge. "Do you think there are only certain kinds of people who cross it?" he asked, but I could only shrug. "Do you think you need to be a good person to get across?" he asked, but again I didn't know. It was like being back in English class with Mrs. Motes, talking about death and *ad infinitum* and other philosophical matters. She didn't treat us like we had no ideas just because we were kids. She didn't pretend like there were two separate worlds, adult world and kid world, or act like we should only think about kid stuff. Which was cool, even if it was difficult, because I don't think adults have any good answers for things like death, so why would we? I still liked that she had asked, though, even if it hadn't prepared me to answer Jamie's questions.

Or my own questions, really. I still didn't know where Jamie had been going to, and I finally decided to find out for myself where he went before I'd wake up most mornings, why he was always leaving. So instead of falling dead asleep toward morning one night, I closed my eyes, pretending. And when I heard his feet on the floor beside me, stepping down from the altar, I opened my eyes a sliver, waiting for him to get a head start, then got up to follow him into the dark.

Outside it was way early and totally quiet in this way that made it feel like no one else but us existed in the world. No cars, no people in the street. It was five in the morning on the clock of the Home Savings building and I was following far enough behind Jamie to keep him in sight. It felt like we'd changed places, as if it were me doing the haunting, following him, almost hoping he'd turn around and see me.

When Jamie didn't take the steps down to the valley of abandoned factories we'd come through that first night, and then again when he walked through the downtown and out of it, toward the east side of the city, I wondered where he could be going. I'd never explored that area of the city, with or without him, and he'd never shown any interest in it, so I'd assumed there was even less to see over there than the parts we stuck to. The roads led down and curved away from the downtown, which I'd thought was the lowest part of the valley, but I could see now there was a bottom to the place that I hadn't discovered yet.

We walked past abandoned strip malls, where the lots were fields of pavement and the parking light poles curled up and out of the cracks, unfolding like night-blooming flowers into three-petaled lamps at their tops. Farther ahead, I watched as Jamie turned down a side street, and when I reached it and turned too, I saw it wasn't a real street at all, but the entrance to a huge, fenced-in parking lot full of semis.

The front gate of the fence was open, its chains sagging to the ground. Jamie stood with his hand on the gate, his fingers curled tight around its links, looking at the trucks and the warehouse at the back of the place.

I stuck to the shadows of trees that grew around the road and fence, taking a step or two forward when Jamie moved from the fence and into the compound. There were lights on in the main building, and I could see a few men in an office in there, frowning and talking a little, probably complaining about having to be at work at such an early hour. Jamie went straight up and looked through the window, his hands pressed against the glass. They didn't notice him. They just burst out laughing at something one of them had said.

Finally one came out of the office, shrugging his arms into a worn-out-looking high school jacket. There was a basketball patch stitched onto one of the arms. He'd probably been a jock who'd thought the rest of his life was already settled until he graduated and found out there were a bunch of guys who'd been thinking the same thing. Jamie followed him from the building to one of the semis, where the guy took a pen out and began marking things down on a clipboard. Jamie reached out to touch the man's broad shoulders and said something I couldn't hear. The guy looked up, turned his head one way then the other, as if he might have heard something, but quickly looked down at his clipboard again.

Jamie moved to stand in front of him then, and placed his hand over the clipboard, looking up at the man's face, saying something softly. I moved closer, but I still couldn't hear.

The man couldn't see Jamie's hand or hear him either. It was obvious by the way he kept checking things off and writing things down. He saw the paper and the words on the paper, not the fifteen-year-old kid standing in front of him talking, and finally he stopped writing and turned to open the door of his cab to climb in. That's when I saw the rocket shooting into the sky stitched on the back of his jacket. And just above it, the name Marks.

I didn't need to see any more. I turned and went out the gate, onto the street, and walked back the way we'd come. I waited for Jamie at the foot of Hazel Street, in the shadow of the cathedral. When I finally saw him coming toward me a while later, his head down, hands in his pockets, the sun starting to edge around the corners of the buildings behind him, I said, "Hey," and he looked up, blinking as if he didn't recognize me.

"Hey," he finally said.

"Was it for him?" I asked. "Did we come here for him?"

Jamie didn't try to pretend he didn't know what I was talking about. "I was hoping he'd be able to hear or see me," he said. "Like you and Gracie. Like my mom could."

I asked why he said could instead of can and he said, "She's stopped listening."

"What do you mean?"

"About a month and a half ago. I used to go to her when she prayed before bed. She always had something to say, usually that she was sorry. She always listened for me and I was able to make her see me this one time. But she can't now. Or she won't. She's stopped trying."

"Why?"

"It's what people do, that's all."

"What?"

"Forgetting."

"And him?"

Jamie shook his head. "No. He couldn't even see me back when—"

He looked away, back toward the direction he'd come from. "You know," he said. "Before. He couldn't see me then. I should have known he wouldn't be able to now."

"I still see you," I said.

He gave me that lopsided smile. "Yeah," he said, "you still see me. Thank you, Adam. If you didn't, I don't know what would happen."

"What do you mean?"

"Just that," he said, and started to walk up the street toward our burned-up church.

We didn't talk about his dad anymore after that. But he kept disappearing, going back there, still trying to get his dad to see him before it was too late.

I watched him. I followed behind and stayed in the shadows, keeping my eyes on him, worried that if I ever stopped seeing him, he might go away for good.

When winter had settled in deep, when icicles had formed on the eaves of the roof and even the church people had skipped two Saturdays in a row to stay warm inside their own homes, he came to me, his skin bluish-gray like one of Gracie's pieces of marble, his eyes sunk deep in his skull, his teeth full of rot. "Adam," he said, his voice barely a whisper. "Adam, I need your help."

I helped him up onto the altar so he could lie down with his head on the bag of potting soil, and asked what I could do. He didn't say anything for a while, and I wasn't sure if he didn't know the words for what he needed or if he was just too weak to say them. "Jamie," I said. "What can I do?"

"I need something," he said. "Just something small. I promise I'll give it back if I can."

"Anything," I said, and he tilted his head to look up at me.

"I need some of your words," he said.

I didn't say anything straight off. I couldn't help but think of the man with no skin who had taken my *I love you* when I tried giving it to Gracie, and I didn't want to think of Jamie like that. So I willed that memory away and nodded. It was the least I could give him.

He told me to lie down beside him, so I laid down. Then he grabbed my hand. "It's a little like dead space," he said, "but you don't have to worry about the men with no skin. Close your eyes," he said, so I closed them. "Imagine a great white light and listen to my voice so you don't get lost."

The longer he talked, the more his words grew far away, but I could still hear them. I imagined the great white light in my mind and suddenly I felt the *pop!* of coming out of the body. I opened my eyes, afraid I'd drift away, but I was still in the room with Jamie, who held my hand like a tether. *My* hand, not the body's. The body lay on the altar like a dead dumb thing, its hand flung out to one side, its fingers curled inward. The body looked like it was sleeping peacefully and I felt a spark of happiness, seeing that. I hadn't felt peace in a while and even though I still didn't feel it, the body looked like it was restful. I felt like maybe I was next in line for peace or something like it.

"How do you feel?" Jamie asked.

I thought about it for a moment. I could feel his hand, his warmth, the texture of his skin, like I'd been able to feel in dead space. I could smell him. He still wore the jeans and old shoes and Cleveland Indians jersey I'd given him months ago. I thought we'd smell awful since we hadn't washed our clothes in who knows how long, but he didn't. He smelled like lilies of the valley and dirt and autumn leaves being burned. I thought his flesh would be cold, but it was warm. I thought his eyes would be sunken in and hollow, but they were blue all the way down. "I can feel you," I said. "I can smell you again. The real you."

He leaned over and kissed me on my mouth and a great white light appeared without me imagining it. It blinded me for a second, and I blinked until I could look straight at it.

It was the moon, I realized. A bright, blinding full moon, falling at me through the dark. It sizzled. It popped with cold heat, pulsing over and over. Then slowly it began to fade away as quickly as it had come into existence.

Moonlight, I was thinking when I came to again. The word, not the thing itself. I set it up alongside sunflower and they looked like they were meant to hold each other up, or else to hold something between them, like they belonged together more than anything else in this world.

I said, "Thank you," because those were the words I felt, that I wanted him to have more than any others.

"In my mouth," he said. "Say them in my mouth."

I put my mouth over his and kissed him. I whispered, "Thank you," into that hot cavern, and he lapped my words up, licked my tongue clean of them, and they were his then. His for the keeping.

Later, after he'd begun to feel a little more like himself again, I said, "Why don't we just stay like this? I like it better."

"Because you aren't dead," he said. "You need to go back in your body, Adam. You can't stay out of it like this forever. You need to stay in it."

I circled it, considering. It wasn't much. Just a sad sack of flesh. Just bones grinding, blood swishing and brains blipping. Machinery. Why was it important? Why couldn't I live like him? Without it?

"I know what you're thinking," said Jamie, putting his hand on my back. "But that's not how it works. If you stay like this, you won't be able to do a lot of things."

"Like what?"

"Like go to school and learn new things, or eat when you feel hungry. Do you see me doing that?"

"No," I said. "But you don't need to."

"Right. And there's a reason. It doesn't do anything for you when you're—"

He looked away, casting glances around the charred church before continuing. "When you're what I am."

I didn't say the word to finish his thought for him. I didn't know if he needed me to remind him or if he just couldn't bear to say it, so I said nothing at all. I slipped back into the body, a little angry with him for making me, back into that heavy overcoat, back to not feeling.

When I was inside again, I opened the body's eyes and said, "I don't go to school anymore."

"This is true," said Jamie, blinking sadly. "This is very true."

Take me. Could you. If. A long time ago. Do you remember when? Shh. Listen. Look at me. Close. Closer. Tell me what you see. What's the word for that? What's the word for me? Can you give it to me?

I gave him what I could. After that first time, whenever he began to weaken and forget himself, he'd ask me to give him more. Sometimes a word. Sometimes a sentence. Something he could live on for a while. Something that could make him warm again. Once I gave him an entire story. I made it up while we lay on the altar side by side, watching the dark gathered under the ceiling. I don't remember the story much. Only that it was about two boys living in a church like we were. But these were normal boys. They ate meals and slept eight hours. They took showers and wore nice clothes and the church wasn't really a church, it just looked like one. Every day they sat on the altar together and prayed that the church would burn down, and then one day a fire actually happened and they died inside it, and what became of them no one knew. In the end, they both lived happily ever after. There were details, but I gave all those to him, hoping they would keep him with me longer. But no matter how many I gave him, he'd eventually begin to fade.

He disappeared for a few hours, sometimes for days. Once he was gone for almost an entire week. And the longer he was gone, the more words he'd ask for when he came back. I wanted to be able to not care about him not being there, but I cared. It was terrible, the way his absence made me feel like my mother going on like a crazy woman whenever my dad went on a binge and didn't come home. I didn't like feeling that way, but it helped me understand her more. It helped me understand how much my father needed her. And even though I still cared about Jamie, after a while I started to wonder why I needed him at all.

But I didn't want to answer that question. I just wanted him to stay.

One day I curled up on the floor of the bell tower, my knees tucked against my chest, my arms wrapped around my legs. He'd been gone for nearly a week, and I wondered what words he'd ask for when he came back this time. I was starting to get protective of them. I'd already given him so many. *Right, wrong, shut up, go away, go ahead, please, please don't, thank you, can you, will you, may, may I, fight, brave, keep, always, danger, faith,* and he'd always need more. I was beginning to not understand a few things myself now. My head resting on the dusty floorboards, my eyes wide open, I waited for him to come back, his eyes pleading before he even spoke. I hadn't slept in days and after three nights without closing them, my eyes were sore from too much seeing.

So in the middle of some week in the middle of some winter month, I got up in the middle of a day and left without knowing where I was going. I couldn't stay there anymore without him, so I walked away hoping wherever I ended up would be an answer, a sign telling me what to do, which direction to run in.

Where I ended up was the north side of the city, going back toward home, toward Liberty, where Gracie had told me all the Jewish people in our part of Ohio lived, where the country roads turned into city streets and the Victorian houses had all been chopped up into apartments for university students, where Wick Park and the building that looked like it belonged in Greece still stood, reminding me of the night Gracie tried to take me to a place I'd never been. How long ago had that been?

I was losing count of days. When I looked, my mental calendar was full of blank squares that I spent my time trying to pretend didn't exist. Something was happening. Something in me was changing like the night my blood changed and death began to run along the twists and turns of my veins and arteries. I couldn't smell, taste or feel anymore, but I could still sense something in me disintegrating. I understood how the buildings and houses falling in on themselves felt, the way their walls buckled, the way their porch roofs sagged with too much weight. When I hung from the jungle gym in the park by my knees that day, looking at the world turned upside down made sense to me.

A man passing by while I hung there stopped and asked if I wanted a ride. "My car's around the corner," he said, scanning the park to see if anyone was watching. I looked at him without speaking, and reached inside his shadow. "Death is coming," I whispered to his shadow, "death is coming," and he ran off, spooked, as if he'd seen a ghost.

My shadow had grown tall and dark without me noticing. It spread out under me as I swung on the jungle gym bars. I tried talking to it, but it wouldn't answer. It had turned its back on me for good. It was giving me the cold shoulder. My shadow had grown to the size of three of me so that when I walked I dragged it like a sack of rocks behind me.

As I started back to the church, believing there'd be no more signs to watch for, I came across a small shop called Dorian Books tucked into the first floor of a building just past the dormitories. Inside I could see all sorts of funky lamps on tables where people could sit and read something from the rows and rows of bookshelves. The lamps lit up the front window and everything inside the place looked warm. I remembered a little bit how that felt right then, warmth, and got the idea that I should go inside and find the book I'd read in Gracie's closet. Maybe it would remind me of then, a time when I was still pretty alone but not so lonely, when Gracie was still just on the other side of that door, sleeping or defending me in a screaming match with her father.

When I opened the door, I heard a dull tinkling noise somewhere. The door had been rigged to jingle a bell when it opened, and a guy came out from behind the counter ready to help me. I was about to tell him I was just looking when I noticed that no words came out when his mouth moved. "I'm sorry," I said. "What did you say?" But he only moved his mouth again without speaking. His hair was salt and pepper and he wore a pair of jeans, a blue button up shirt and black socks, no shoes at all, as if he were in his own home. He wore black-framed glasses and a kind smile, but for the life of me, I couldn't hear him.

Then it hit me.

Gone. Just like that. My hearing had left me.

"Sorry," I said, my voice sounding as if I were underwater. "Sorry," I said again, and backed out the door, as if that were the only word I knew.

I ran from the bookstore as fast as I could, not hearing the wind as it whipped past my ears, not even hearing my own breathing. When I reached the church, though, the reverend and his crew were carrying new pews through the front doors, so I waited by the side of the Catholic church across the street, next to a statue of Mary. I ran my fingers down the stone folds of her gown, looking up into her blank eyes as she stared at the baby she held like he was the most special thing in the world, a miracle child. I whispered to her, "Don't tell him anything. Don't let him find out anything about this world."

When the church people finally left, I slipped inside and sat in one of the new pews to wait for Jamie. He'd come back and then everything would be all right, I told myself. We could take care of each other. We were survivors.

I believed this even though I couldn't hear anymore. Not the winter birds nesting in the bell tower, not the mice that shuffled across the floor at night, not the wind that sung in the eaves, not the branches that scratched at the windows, not the endless sirens of the city. I waited in the new pews, and when another day passed without his return, I could feel something happening. My body felt so heavy that I could barely move, and my mind continually returned to thinking of a way out of this place, a way out of everything, the whole goddamn mess of our lives. If I could move a little, if I could find the right kind of door, I could save us both.

There had to be a door in that church that could open up to a different sort of world, one where death couldn't reach us. But before I could even begin to look, I remembered my father, how he liked to go on telling Andy and I his philosophies on architecture. "There's only one rule when it comes to doors," he said on one of our drives past one of his buildings. "They have to go somewhere."

I moved to the altar, dropped to my knees, and thought about what he'd said. What use was it to look for hope where everything was already dead? Even if I found him, even if he found me looking for him, going through a door to dead space wasn't making a way out of no way. It was making a way into nowhere. And that was a door I'd already taken too many times.

Giving Up the Ghost

I'M NOT SURE HOW LONG I WAITED AT THE ALTAR.
Days passed, the sun rose, the moon glowed, the light in the
broken stained glass window square flared, then reflected
nothing but darkness. I was tired. Not tired in the way of
sleep, but in the way that all I could do was lie on the altar
and not move. I had no will, my spark was fading, but I remained conscious even so.

One day I saw a bird, a cardinal, flitting from branch to
rooftop to branch outside the broken windows. It was like
this little spot of blood hurrying through the white glare of
winter. I liked how it paid the weather no attention and did
what it had to in order to survive. I was watching it move
through the cold outside when it suddenly winked out of
existence. I closed my eyes for a second to rest them, but
when I opened them again the tree I'd seen the cardinal in
had disappeared too. I blinked and the Catholic church opposite no longer existed. Then the street was gone. Blink.
Then the window. *Boom, boom, boom.* All the lights went
out inside me.

I couldn't smell or taste or hear or feel or see. I was like a
fetus floating in a jar of formaldehyde. I stayed like that
for I don't know how long. Now that there was no light to

divide the night—no body to watch decaying in front of me, no bells to be heard ringing the hours, no pains to mark my hunger, no bacon frying to wake up to—now that all of those had gone away, time no longer existed.

It was just me. Just me without the world to define my borders.

Then it happened again:

Pop!

I flew out of the body.

And suddenly I could see and hear and smell and touch and taste again. I had sloughed off that shell that didn't work any longer. There it lay on the church altar, head tilted against a bag of potting soil, dead as dead as dead, its heart useless as the broken heart it kept in its front pocket.

"Oh no," Jamie's voice came from behind me. "Adam. What have you done?"

I turned around to find him standing under the arch of the front entrance, hands at his sides, barely able to hold his own head up. He'd lost all his color. Even his eyes were black as the coal that littered the bed of the old railroad. He stood before me in the clothes I'd given him, only now the Cleveland Indians face on the left side of the jersey was no longer red, but white as Jamie's mushroom rotten body. He might have stepped out of an old black and white photo.

"I think I've died," I said.

He trudged toward me, his feet thumping on the wooden floorboards, lifting his arms as he came to me, like he did that first night, after I got into his hole with him. "No, no, no," he said. "This isn't how it's supposed to happen. You can't die, Adam. You have to live."

"It just happened," I said.

"We can fix it," he said. He put his arm around my

shoulders. "Quick. If you do this now, we can live." I wanted to tell him he was already dead, but before I could say anything he put his mouth on mine.

"Can I?" he whispered into me, his breath flowing inside me. "Can I?"

I felt a tug at my stomach and looked down to find a cord running out of me and into the navel of the body. The cord was shrinking, pulling me back toward the body, but no matter how hard I fought, it was stronger than me. In a moment it pulled me on top of the body, where I looked into my own lifeless, staring eyes. Then it jerked hard and I was inside again, fitting my arms and legs and hands and feet and head into that old coat, wanting to die already because it hurt so much to wear such a heavy thing as flesh.

"Food," he said. "Now. You have to."

He picked me up and pulled me off the altar, walked me down the stairs to the back window in the basement, where he helped me onto the crate he'd put there for me the first night we'd come here. "Stop," I told him when we were in the street, but he held on to my hand and pulled me to the hot dog vendor's cart around the corner. A trash can stood next to it. Jamie picked out a half-eaten hot dog with ketchup and mustard still on it. He pushed it up to my mouth and nearly pried my lips apart before I took it inside me and started chewing.

"Jesus Christ," the hot dog vendor said beside me. "If it's that bad, kid, why don't you go to the fucking shelter?"

I looked at him and blinked.

"Are you on drugs?"

I shook my head.

"What's the matter with you then?"

"I'm dying."

He didn't understand for a moment, but then quickly his face dropped out of its mask of disgust and he started putting together a bratwurst. He handed it over with a can of soda and said, "Don't die, kid. Seriously, get yourself to the shelter. They'll take care of you. Do you need me to take you?"

I shook my head but told him thank you between bites of bratwurst and gulps of soda. They felt like nothing going down my throat, just filler, stuffing for the scarecrow of my body. I swallowed and swallowed, though, stepping farther away from the hot dog stand each time I took another bite or drink.

Finally satisfied, Jamie said, "Don't ever do that again. You have to take care of yourself, Adam. I need you."

I shook my head. "No," I said, and started to walk away. "No?"

I looked over my shoulder and said it again, shaking my head as I said it. *No.* It was a word I hadn't given him. It was a word I'd kept just for me.

I went back to the church, where the new pews gleamed in front of the altar. The church was still a major mess, especially on the outside, but in a few more months, if the church people kept up their caretaking, I figured it'd be back to how it was before the fire. Maybe a little different, but livable.

We sat down on the front pew facing the altar. A large cross had been hung on the back wall. Jesus stretched out on it, his face pressed against his shoulder. We didn't look at each other. We looked at Jesus. Finally, still not looking at him, I asked him why.

"You don't understand, Adam. You're still alive."

I was about to say, "You have a chance if you want it," like I would have said months ago, back when I found him, to give him hope, to try to help him. But when I looked at him— when I looked at his sunken eyes and the split in his flesh near the temple, when I looked at his skin, pale and shrinking—I realized I'd been fooling myself all this time. I thought of Fuck You Frances telling us we had a lot of unjustified optimism. She was jealous, I'd thought then, but she'd been right. What made us think we could make him live again?

Hope. Stupid hope.

"But you found me," he said. "You found me. And if you and Gracie can see me, that means I'm still alive. Don't lie, Adam. Not after everything. Not like her. Don't pretend I'm not here anymore." I slipped my arm around his shoulders and he pressed his face into my chest. "Oh God," he said. "Adam, I'm so sorry."

"I'm not pretending," I told him. "I see you, Jamie. I found you. We found each other. But still."

"What do you mean?" he said, afraid to look up, afraid of what I was saying.

"You have to go," I said. "To the bridge. You have to cross it. Like she did. You can't stay, Jamie. Not like this."

He pressed his face back into my chest and made a sobbing sound. I held on to him, like I held him in the grave, like I held him in my arms when he came to me. He grabbed my arms and shoulders, pinching. He shook his head. "I don't want to," he said. "You don't understand."

"I can't keep you here any longer," I said. "I can't give you what you need."

"But what about *him*?" he said. He spoke into the hollow of my throat, still clutching.

"Who?"

"The one who did it!"

"Who is he?"

"It isn't fair. *He* isn't dead! Why did he do it? Why did he take it from me?"

"Who *is* he?"

Jamie pulled back, wiping at his tearless eyes with the backs of his hands. "I can't remember. It's a haze now."

"You have to remember."

But he only shook his head and looked down at the running shoes I'd given him. "It's too late," he said. "I burned that memory. It was the first one to go."

We were quiet then, and the sounds of the city grew around us: buses chugging through afternoon traffic, trains whistling as they arrived and departed, sirens blaring their emergencies, the wind sighing through the broken church windows. And as the light faded, the city began to grow quiet.

Jamie stood up. "Let's go then," he said.

I took his hand, my fingers curling around his. "Are you sure?" I asked. After he'd said it, I didn't want him to leave. Part of me still wanted to keep him here as long as possible, but that was just as selfish as him taking my words, I realized.

He nodded. "You're right," he said. "It's the only thing I can do."

So I got up and we walked out of the church into the darkening streets of Youngstown, down into the valley where the world was thin, and slipped back into dead space, together.

As we followed the rusty rails of the tracks that wound through the valley back into the woods, the howls of the wolves crept around us. Down below the tracks, in the maze of trees, men with no skin stumbled around in their own personal darkness. It's what would happen to him, I realized, if we didn't get him to the bridge. He'd decay until his skin peeled away and his eyes rolled out of their sockets, and then he'd be trapped here, just like them. He didn't have anything as strong and binding as Frances had to keep him here. I felt bad all of a sudden for burning her house down, for burning the one thing that housed all her memories. Even if they were bad memories, they were hers, and I'd taken them from her.

We came to the bend in the tracks where one set of rails continued toward town, back to my mother and father, and the other curved into the mist where the covered bridge crossed over Sugar Creek. Shadows still lingered near the entrance: a woman wearing an Amish dress and bonnet, an old man wearing a flannel shirt and overalls, a young man in a business suit, carrying his briefcase, still looking at his watch, a little boy or girl in a snowsuit, fur-lined hood pulled down, looking around, crying for its mother.

As we got closer, Jamie's hand tightened around mine. I could feel him shaking. "What do you think is on the other side?" he whispered.

"Home," I said. "Whatever that is. The place we came from."

We sat down on the rails for a while, watching the others mill, their eyes wide and frightened like spooked cattle. There was no way to help them understand time was important. It was eternal twilight here, darkening or lightening only a few degrees every now and then.

We rested our elbows on our knees, our heads on the palms of our hands, but didn't speak. There wasn't much left to say, really. The little kid kept crying for its mother, the guy in the business suit kept looking at his watch. *Dude,* I thought. *Whatever time it was when you got here is all you're going to get.* But you can't reason with the dead that easily.

Jamie was silent as he watched the others. The kid in the snowsuit kept getting louder, though, squinting hard as he shouted, "Mommy!" over and over. I thought of my mom back home in her wheelchair. I wondered if she'd given up looking for me, if she'd given up on me completely.

Jamie stood up then, dusting off the back of the jeans I'd given him, straightening his jersey. He held out his hand. I took it and he pulled me up, saying, "I guess this is what goodbye means."

At the mouth of the bridge, I held him again. He shuddered like I'd shuddered the first night he came to me, so I held him tighter until he no longer shook. "It's okay," I said. "It's all right. I'll see you again. It's not goodbye forever." My voice shook, so I'm not sure if I was convincing, or even if I'd convinced myself, but it was all we had to go on, this idea that everything would be all right in the end, that when he crossed the bridge he'd be going someplace wonderful, or at least where he needed to be going. Who knows? I didn't cross that bridge. I took him there to see him off and promise I'd see him again one day. I whispered it in his ear. "I love you. I'll see you soon. You know how time flies here."

He chuckled and rubbed his face on my shoulder. "I love you too," he said. "Tell Gracie that for me too, okay?"

I nodded and let go of him, and he moved toward the mouth of the bridge. At the last minute he took hold of the little kid's hand. "Come on," he said. "It's this way." The kid stopped screaming and stared up at Jamie like maybe he'd start running, but in the end he nodded and wiped his face with the back of his hand, ready to go where Jamie was going.

At the threshold Jamie looked over his shoulder, and as he entered, as he and the little kid disappeared into that dark mouth, I shouted, "Don't worry! I'll find you again! Don't worry, Jamie!" I lifted one pale, white hand and waved. Then the mist and the dark surrounded him, and he was gone.

After Jamie disappeared, I went back through dead space to the valley, back to the church on Elm Street where I slipped through the basement window and climbed the stairs to the bell tower and sat down, gathering my knees to my chest. I didn't know what to do but feel bad and sad and angry. I kicked the remaining shutters out of the tower windows. I screamed. Like the wolves of dead space, it was a kind of howling. My scream rose over the city, joining my mother's and Gracie's, joining the voices of everyone else who had screamed out their horror. My scream hung over the rooftops, a black cloud spreading.

Out of that cloud several crows came flying. They darted through the air until they landed on the street below to look up with their beady black eyes and consider me. I counted seven. Seven for a secret that would never be told.

It wasn't fair. I wanted to know who had done it to him. I wanted to balance the equation. I imagined my father jumping out of his recliner, making his hands into a gun. *Bam! Bam! Bam!* He would have killed that motherfucker if it had been his boy.

But there was no motherfucker to be found. Whoever had done it would go on, just like everyone.

I fell asleep on the floor of the tower, shaking. By morning I could barely speak. My throat was raw. Sweat covered me. I couldn't pick myself up. I shivered. I looked around for something to keep me warm, but there was nothing. And right then I realized something.

I was cold. I hurt. I could feel things. I could feel *me* again.

I blacked out then, and when I woke who knows how long later, the reverend's daughter's face floated above me. "Be quiet," she whispered. "Or they'll hear you."

So I closed my eyes.

Later, when I woke again, it was night and a blanket had been wrapped around me, tucked tight beneath my weight. A jug of water and a brown plastic bottle of pills were beside my out-flung hand. I looked at the label. It was a prescription for Tia Taylor, the reverend's daughter. Take two every six hours. I opened the bottle and drank some down with water, then fell asleep again.

In the morning she came back, and when she saw my eyelids flicker, she said, "You sure are sick, but not like when I found you." She smiled. Her teeth were big and white, her skin soft and sweet looking. Her face hanging above mine made me think of sunflowers. Sunflowers just reminded me of Gracie, though, and I felt my eyes begin to well, but I held it all in.

"What's the matter?" she said. "Oh Jesus, did I say something?"

I shook my head. "It's nothing," I managed to whisper.

She put her hand on my forehead and said, "I got some food." She helped me sit up in my blankets and I noticed she'd set plywood against the broken windows to break the wind. She opened a thermos and filled a cup with steaming soup, handed it to me. I drank one cup, then another. My stomach clenched and I nearly threw up. "Slow down," she said. "Slow it down, baby. You ain't that well yet."

I took more of her medicine and a few hours later, she helped me downstairs to the altar where it was warmer. She had the heat and lights on. "Daddy won't be back for a few days," she said. "But he *will* be back. So you have to get better right quick."

"I'm trying," I said. "Give me a minute."

She made a bed of blankets on the altar and left me there to rest. I stared up at Jesus on his cross. So sad. So sad about the world. He pressed his face against his shoulder like he couldn't bear to look at things any longer. I can relate, I told him. I didn't want to look at the world either.

She came back the next day, and the day after that, and soon I was able to get up and around on my own. I asked why she would help someone who was squatting in her father's church. "That reminds me," she said. "Tomorrow we'll be working in here. You'll have to leave like you used to. Can you do that?"

I nodded. "How did you know I was here?"

"Well, your candy and hamburger wrappers were the first clue, but it sure didn't help you were always hanging around outside, looking all spacey and weird. You're lucky my daddy didn't notice."

"Why are you helping me?" I asked again.

"I like the way you always looking out at something far away," she said, smiling. "Like my daddy. He always got his eye on God."

"I don't believe in that stuff," I said. "Not how you do."

I didn't want God thinking just because one of His people was helping me that He and I were on good terms.

"That's all right," she said. "It don't matter if you believe in Him. God believes in you."

"Thank you," I said. I remembered those words. Even though I'd given them to Jamie, they rushed to my tongue when I felt them now. I had them again. I knew what they meant.

"What's your name?" she asked.

"Adam."

"Adam," she said. "That's a good name. He's the first man."

I got up early the next day and walked out into a snow-covered city. I wore my yellow hood up over my head, my jean jacket buttoned up as far as it could go. My jeans had holes in the knees, though, so the cold still found me. And a hole had opened in the toe of my left shoe. I could see my dirty sock in there, my big toe twitching. Through the snow-laced trees and plowed parking lots of the college, abandoned on this Saturday morning in winter, I trudged, until I made my way up to the north side of the city.

The street's regulars were out already: the homeless, the nervous wreck people talking to themselves, muttering of their suffering, some asking for cigarettes, some for money so they could stop at the Red and White corner store to buy a forty ouncer and drown their sorrow. It was way cold out, the light yellow-gray, the air fused with diesel and grit. There was an edge to everything, like the world was tired and dirty but still trying.

Snow fell in heavy wet flakes, spiraling, filling the air

with down. I felt like I was in one of those glass globes, a little city inside a bubble of water. Before I could make it to Dorian Books, I was soaked clear through. My teeth chattered. Even through my yellow hoody and the T-shirt underneath, I was freezing. Part of me wished I was still on my way to dying, because then I wouldn't have felt the cold. But I wasn't on my way to dying any longer, and I had to give up that wish because in the end I didn't really want it. I wasn't sure what I was on my way to now, but it wasn't dying. I kept telling myself, *You have to take care of yourself. You have to start wanting.*

So I swung the door of the bookshop open and went in, wanting to find that book I'd read in Gracie's closet. The doorbell jangled, and inside the place smelled like tea and cinnamon. I breathed it all in. I hadn't smelled things for a while and now that I was getting my senses back I was shocked half the time by simple things. The scent of snow, the sound of wings fluttering. My heart would break into a thousand pieces just to feel the wind slip under my collar. If I'd had a rose quartz heart like Gracie's, by then it would have been fine as sand.

There were tons of books everywhere, and I started pulling them down one at a time to read a page or two at some random place, wondering what had happened to the people in these stories to make them do or say or think some of the things they did. Like this one woman had opened all the birdcages in her house and shooed the birds out the window into the winter, even the parrot who always told her he loved her. And this other guy got into a fight with his ex-wife and before he left the house (which she'd gotten in the divorce) he stole her ashtray. And then there was this kid whose father was drunk and told him he and

his little friend looked like sisters, and then the father imagined Bessie Smith, this old blues singer from way back in the
early 1900s, sitting on the bed with the boys, and the father
told them they all looked like they could be sisters. That was
pretty funny, especially since they were boys and white and
Bessie Smith was a black woman, but it was true in this way
I couldn't explain. I just felt it.

I was reading bits and pieces of books when I noticed a
shadow fall over my shadow on the floor. When I looked
up, I saw the guy who'd come out to greet me last time I'd
been in here standing beside me. "That's a great book," he
said. He still didn't wear any shoes, just black socks. He had
on a pair of jeans and a black sweater and square black-
framed glasses. He looked like one of the professor types
that lurked around campus, distinguished, clasping his
hands at his stomach, his voice softly rising and falling as
he spoke about the book I was holding, telling me it was a
good read and how he'd read it back in the day and had
loved it. At first I could only stare as he talked, but after a
while of me not replying, he said, "Are you okay?"

As soon as he said that, I closed my eyes and put the
book back on the shelf. I felt shaky all of a sudden, as if I
might puke. I didn't want to say anything, but that one
question made me think of Jamie, and right then I wanted
to forget he existed. Because if he never was, then I
wouldn't have to feel bad about him not being here now.

I had to get out of there. It was either that or else puking
all over the black and white checkered floor, and then I'd
feel real stupid and real afraid because something had come
out of me in front of this guy and then everything would be
real, would be that much worse if I acknowledged it.

I shook my head, a little unsteady, probably walking like my dad on a hangover day, and went toward the door.

"Whoa, whoa, whoa," the guy said. "You look like you need to sit down and rest a little. You shouldn't be out in this weather dressed like that."

"Why not?"

"Because," he said, "you must be freezing."

I looked down at the floor and nodded. "I am," I said.

He let me sit in a big comfy chair and brought me a cup of tea on a saucer and put milk and sugar on the coffee table in front of me. He sat down on the couch opposite, blowing steam off his cup. I put my face over my cup and the steam misted my cheeks. He said his name was Kurt, and for a moment I thought maybe I should tell him I was Andy—you know, in case he figured out I was a runaway—but in the end I decided to be honest and tell him my own.

"Are you in trouble, Adam?" he asked.

I didn't say anything, just looked down into my cup.

He folded one leg on top of the other and spread his arms across the back of the couch. Then he started talking about his bookstore, which sort of made me feel better because it had nothing to do with me. He said it didn't make him much money, but he didn't care. He wanted to have a bookshop, so he did. He went on about it for a while, and then he talked some more. About himself mostly. He said he'd just turned forty a few months ago and that he lived with his partner, which at first I thought meant like his business partner, but it turned out he meant his boyfriend, who taught in the business college at the university, and how the bookstore probably would be a failure if it weren't for him. When he brought up the university, I said how I didn't like the campus and he wanted to know why. I told him it had all those fresh-faced kids with their clean clothes and their lives ahead of them and how they seemed pretty fucking blind. He laughed at that, but told me not to hold it against them. "I'm glad you're finally talking," he said. "I wondered why you ran out of here so fast the other day."

I shrugged. "No reason," I told him.

He got a little serious then, leaning forward to take his cup off the table between us. "Whatever it is that's not good right now," he said, "it can get better. You know that, right?"

I nodded, but didn't say anything. I was a little uncomfortable talking about me again. I wasn't surprised he could tell something was wrong just by the way I was dressed in torn clothes and how I was probably the dirtiest looking kid he'd seen in a while. I wondered if he'd think things could get better if I told him about the shadows I saw, how they talked and talked and told me things about people that I didn't want to know. It was like those activity books my mom used to get when I was little, the ones full of pictures and the activity was to find a certain number of objects hidden in them. Like, say, how many rabbits are hiding in this picture? So you look and look, and all of a sudden you start finding rabbits hidden *everywhere* in this seemingly innocent scene. They're in the trees, they're in the picnic basket. There are even rabbits in the goddamned food on the plates! And these stupid people in the picture are smiling like idiots because they don't notice the damn things. After you've seen them once, though, you always see them. You can't go back. Whenever you look at that picture afterward, you can't see it without seeing the rabbits that the nice but totally oblivious family eating their picnic won't ever see.

I looked down into my empty cup, speckled with tea leaves, and wanted to cry. My throat started to close as I fought the tears back down and forced them to stay inside.

"Hey, I'm sorry," Kurt said. "I didn't mean to make you uncomfortable."

"It's okay," I said. "I'm fine. Really."

I put my cup of tea on the coffee table and got up to leave. Before I left, though, Kurt said if I came back the next morning he'd buy me breakfast. Food sounded good, so I told him I'd come. I also asked him about that book I'd read in Gracie's closet, but when he went to get me a copy, he couldn't find it. "All sold out," he said.

"Oh well," I said. "No big deal. He was just a whiny rich kid anyway."

"Would you have liked it better if he'd been a whiny poor kid?" he asked, smiling.

"Probably not," I said. "If he was a poor kid—"

I stopped then, and tried to smile. I didn't feel like I could muster a real one, though. It was probably one of those lopsided ones Jamie used to give me. "Probably not," I said again, and went out into the cold.

I went back to the church to find Tia waiting for me. She sat on a pew looking up at the altar, and when I came up from the basement, she smiled and said, "There you are! I thought I'd lost you."

"Where would I have gone?"

"I don't know," she said. "Not like abandoned places are hard to come by round here."

"Yeah," I said. "But ones with heat and electricity are."

She laughed into her hand like maybe she thought the

joke was sinful. I sat down next to her, not sure of what to say. It's not like we knew each other, really. She'd helped me out, but other than that she was just this girl from Youngstown whose father was a minister of a congregation without a home. Well, not *without* a home. I guess their home was this place they were trying to fix up to be someplace livable again.

"This Sunday's visitors' day at my daddy's church," she said. "He's going to preach real good. He always preaches real good when we have visitors. Not that he preaches bad when we don't, but anyway, I was wondering if you'd like to come."

She sat there, face intent, waiting for my answer. To tell the truth I didn't want to, but I felt obligated after all she'd done, and if all she wanted was for me to visit her church, that wasn't so bad, I guess. So I said, "Yeah, sure. I'll come."

"Don't say yeah out of obligation," she said.

For a second I thought she could hear my shadow because she'd read my thoughts, but I guess it was obvious from the way I answered that I wasn't that into the idea. I said, "Why else would I come?"

"For yourself. I ain't never met someone in trouble like you are."

"I don't have any trouble," I said.

"Everyone has trouble," she said. "I have trouble, sure enough, and I'm the damn preacher's daughter. Hell, if my daddy knew half of what I do behind his back, he'd have a heart attack. There ain't no one not got trouble."

"Okay," I said. "But I'm warning you. I'm not so good with God."

"Fair enough. Besides, my daddy's church ain't what you think. It's not like white people's churches. All stuffy. Just give it a shot."

I nodded. I didn't expect anything, but I didn't tell her that. I mean, it's not like I don't believe in God or whatever it is that is life in this place. I'm just not sure anyone can describe what God is so easily. If I had my way, I'd take a bit of every religion and science and philosophy, because then maybe the picture of God would be more complete, like a mosaic. I think mostly people pick just one idea of God, but when they do that they end up looking at this one little speck of something that's really big and amazing. They look at that one speck in the mosaic and say, "That's God," and don't see the rest of the picture around it. But then there are people like my mom and dad, who don't look at the picture at all, which is just as bad. Thinking about that, I figured it couldn't hurt to at least go and look at Tia's tile with her.

I went to visit Kurt the next morning and he had a bag of McDonald's waiting for me. It was greasy and salty and back when I was training for running I would have been like, "No way! That's so unhealthy!" but I ate without thinking anything of it. It'd been a while since I tasted something as precious as grease and salt and cheese and sausage and pancakes with syrup, even if the pancakes did feel like foam in my mouth and the sandwich was a heart attack waiting to happen forty years from now.

We talked some more. I told him a little about Gracie and Jamie and how everything happened over the fall and winter. And while I was telling, it occurred to me I had no idea what month it was, so I asked and he said, "End of March."

"No way," I said.

"Way," he said, totally mocking me, but I laughed. "That's nice to hear," he said. "You have a nice laugh."

I suddenly felt weird. I'd never thought about my laugh before. "I have a nice laugh?" I said.

"Yeah. Very boisterous. Not self-conscious."

"My dad's always yelling at me to wake up," I said. "I guess that's what I am. Not self-conscious. Unconscious."

"Fathers are like that," said Kurt. "They don't know what to say to their kids sometimes. Especially to boys. Especially boys like you."

"Like me?"

"Well, you're not typical."

"You mean how I'm not so good with people," I said.

"Well, sort of. And you're different in other ways too."

"What do you mean?"

"Well, to be completely honest, you've got some problems, Adam. People don't always understand that, but they can sense it. They're afraid it's something they can catch, so they steer clear. You can hardly blame them. And well, you're not typical in lots of other ways too."

I could tell he wanted to say what these other ways were, but I didn't want him to be like everyone else, trying to tell me who I was and how I should think about myself. Everyone seemed to always be doing that to me. So even though I mostly appreciated his conversation and what he was trying to tell me, I told him I understood and didn't need to hear anything else. He said I didn't know what he was going to say, but I told him whatever he was going to say was more about what he thought than what I thought, and he nodded and said that was true. Even the most well-intentioned people don't know what's best for you.

Sometimes you've got to be able to listen to yourself and be okay with no one else understanding.

On Sunday Tia picked me up and we walked to the gymnasium where her father's congregation was meeting until the church was ready. Everyone sat in wooden folding chairs in the middle of a basketball court. It reminded me of meetings in the gym before and after track practice and I felt weird and out of place, like I was visiting a me I'd forgotten.

Everyone was black too, which also made me feel out of place, but definitely not forgotten. We got stares, but Tia didn't seem to mind. She sang and raised her hands like nothing was the matter, even if some of the guys around our age looked like they wanted to vaporize us; even though some of the older women squinted at us suspiciously.

Tia's father stood behind a podium and the choir was off to the side. He wore a suit, not robes like a priest. His voice was loud, echoing through the gymnasium, making him sound holier than usual. He kept telling people what they needed to do, like when he was telling the work crew what to do at the church. Tia would nod her head and shout, "Yes!" or "Hallelujah!" and so did the others. They waved their hands at Reverend Taylor, they shouted, "Praise Him!" and would nod their heads at each other, so excited I thought they might even start high fiving. It was a little strange for me, really. I mean, in church I expected the minister to talk and everyone else to just sit there and listen.

Tia's father said some good things about how we all need to love each other, which is what Jesus said too, so it wasn't like anything new or revolutionary, but he also said some dumb things too, like how we all have to get in close with God and live with him and forget the world. I was like, *How do you forget the world?* It's the most impossible thing. You can't just separate yourself from it like that. If you did, you'd have to live in a church day in and day out. Otherwise the world is all up in your face and you *have* to interact with it. *Get in under God and stay there,* he said. But I thought that was too easy, like sticking your head in the sand like an ostrich, pretending not to see anything. Plus, after I thought about how I'd lived in a church for months and hadn't interacted much with the world, it made me even more suspicious. I'd done what he suggested. I'd lived in a church and forgotten the world, but it only made me more unable to figure out a way to live. I thought a better idea would be if everyone looked hard at the world and tried to figure it out instead of turning our backs and running away from it like it was something to be afraid of.

After the service ended, I told Tia I had to go. She wanted me to meet people, but it didn't look like they wanted to meet a dirty white kid wearing ripped up jeans and nasty running shoes. Even though the poor were people they were supposed to be kind to, according to Jesus, they still looked at me like I was trash. Just like Mr. Highsmith had looked at me.

"Don't pay them any attention," Tia said, squeezing my hand. But I shook my head and told her it was time for me to leave.

Tia walked me to the exit and thanked me for at least coming. "Thanks for taking care of me," I told her. I gave her a quick kiss on the cheek and when I pulled back I thought I saw sunflowers unfurling in her eyes. *Oh God, oh*

God, oh God, I thought. Now I wanted to stay. I could see that possibility in her, a place to run to. She could be my light, I thought, like Gracie had been.

But that wasn't what I needed. Maybe the light some-one else gives you can be enough to keep living, but I wanted to be able to see by my own light, not someone else's. So I kissed Tia's other cheek and hugged her, and pushed my way out the door. Out into the world.

I went back to the abandoned church to grab my back-pack, and to look around the place one last time. I whis-pered goodbye to the empty bell tower, I whispered goodbye to the congregation I'd almost seen with the rev-erend weeks ago. I ran my hands over Jesus hanging on his cross over the altar. I whispered goodbye to him, then left by the window with the crate beneath it in the basement.

I made my way past the university to Dorian Books, but the place was closed. When I peered in the window between cupped hands, there was no sign of Kurt either, so I took a piece of paper out of my backpack and wrote him a note, telling him thank you for everything and that I'd try to stay in touch.

I folded the note and slipped it under the door. Then I walked south, down into the valley again, where the world was thin. This time I didn't step into dead space, even though that would have made the trip quicker. This time I walked down the rails that ran through the living world, heading home.

BLACK SHEEP BOY

IT WAS A LONGER WALK THIS TIME. A DAY, A night, another morning. When I finally found myself in familiar territory, a deer—a buck—crossed from one side of the tracks, stopping to stare as if I were a great evil trespassing on its property. Then, kicking its legs into a trot, it ran down the other side of the hill with its white tail lifted.

The temperature had risen in the past few days, and snow was melting. It lay in heaps near the base of trees and in lowlands where water always collected; it dripped from branches and found its way to streams that ran toward spring. As the sky lightened to gray, doves woke and started morning songs. And after a while, squirrels came out to bark their chitchat.

I felt out of place there. Usually I never thought anything of the woods—I'd always gone into it whenever I wanted—but here I was, thinking maybe it wasn't a place to wander around in any longer. It was like this really happy place in some ways, with a bunch of different creatures all living together in it, sharing daily complaints and victories with each other. And me, I wasn't a part of that. I passed through and just disturbed everything.

And that's when I saw it. The yellow police tape torn

down, strewn around the hole where we'd gotten in together. When I came to the edge, I looked down, afraid of
what I'd find.

We weren't in there anymore, but even so, I felt strange
when I looked in. A mixture of longing and fear welled up
inside me. How can you want something and be afraid of it
at the same time? It had to be the most stupid feeling possible. It had to be the kind of feeling that made people lose
their senses.

Gravel and dirt still lay in piles around the place from
when they'd dug out his body, bordering the hole like a
fringe. Like a frame for nothing. The police tape hadn't kept
anyone out, and nothing had kept Jamie in there either,
and the border of dirt around the hole made my head hurt
when I looked at it. Useless. I want to erase it, to stop pretending.

I didn't have a shovel, so I used my hands to scoop the
dirt and gravel and pour it all back in. It took most of the
morning, handful after handful, but eventually I filled it. I
couldn't get it to be full all the way again, though. I tried,
but it was still a few inches lower in that place than the rest
of the hill. His body being there had changed things. Even
the earth couldn't go back the way it was before his murderer had slipped him in there.

I thought of that man he'd forgotten, the man who'd
taken it away from him. He'd been here too. He'd stood
where I stood, looking down as he shoveled gravel and dirt
over Jamie's naked body. How could he have done it? And
whoever did it was still with us. We had no way to know, and
not knowing, no way to protect ourselves. It made me mad
and sad and I started to cry. I could feel the tears warm on my
cheeks already. I was about to tell myself, "Stop! No crying!"

But I didn't. I cried. I bawled like a baby. I made a fool of myself crying, and when I finished, I wiped my face with the sleeve of my jean jacket and thought about how crying isn't all that foolish. It's just something a person does.

It only took me ten minutes to walk through the woods from that spot, back to the road my family lived on. And when I stepped out of the trees and hopped across the ditch to the asphalt, I landed right next to two fat crows pecking at the rotting body of a possum. They weren't moving for nothing. Just cocked their heads up like they were saying, "Excuse us. We're eating here. Move along, young man. Move along."

Two for joy, I counted. I thought of my grandma and hoped her rhyme and reason were right for once. It'd been right for all the bad stuff, I figured, so why not the good? I decided not to hold my breath, though.

I walked down the road with my backpack slung over my back, and as I walked, the shoelace in my right shoe snapped, just like that, and the tongue flopped with each step that I took. I sighed, wondering if I'd make it home at this rate. Looking up at the sky, I searched out God's finger, and even though I couldn't find it among the clouds, I shouted, "Come on! Give me a fucking break!" It wasn't nice, I know. But I figure God hears worse than that, and at least I was being up front about how I felt. God has to respect someone telling the truth, even if the truth is angry.

And then there it was. The line of trees dropped away from the roadside and my family's house appeared in its little square of cleared land. The ranch house my father had built with his own hands. The crab apple tree and red maple in the front yard, the pine trees poking up over the roof in the back like a ridge of green mountaintops.

It was still early. I hung around in the drive for a while, playing with the tongue of my shoe, scratching any itch I could find, looking at the way the Petersons' farm down the road seemed smaller than the last time I'd seen it. Used to be it'd seemed like a huge house and barn and two towering silos with endless fenced-off pasture. Now it looked like something you'd buy at a toy store. Plastic cows to put in the barn and pasture. A farmer and his wife to stand outside on the front porch. That sort of thing.

Even though the Peterson farm looked smaller, my mom and dad's house seemed like a place where giants lived. I kept taking a step or two forward, then stopping, then going forward again, like I was one of the wrecked people who wandered the streets of Youngstown, talking to themselves, hesitant to go forward or backward, because either way might have something dangerous waiting for them. A cop in one direction, a drug dealer in the other. Both are pretty much the same thing: trouble.

But I made it to the ramp my dad built for my mom's wheelchair. And I made it up that to the front porch. And then I was standing at the door with my hand lifted to knock when it swung open and there stood my brother with his nose wrinkled and one eyebrow cocked like he wasn't sure about something. He looked smaller too.

"Asshole!" he said. "You've come home!"

"Hey, Andy," I said.

"You're in so much trouble," he said. "Everyone's so fucking worried about you. But *I* knew. I knew you were okay and making everyone worried for no reason. You're such a dick, Adam."

"I didn't come back to argue with you," I said. "I just want to come home."

Andy blinked, looking stunned. Probably because I wasn't playing along with his back and forth put-downs like I used to. It was a waste of time, I figured. It was a waste of fucking time bitching at each other for no good reason. Andy shrugged the shock off, though, and said, "Your funeral."

"I'm okay with that."

He looked over his shoulder and shouted, "Mom! Adam's home!"

And from the back bedroom I heard her. I heard her call back, "Andy! Stop! That's not a nice joke!" She wheeled into the living room then, still bitching, but when she turned the corner and saw me standing in the front door, her mouth stopped moving and her hands fluttered in the air, her fingers motioning for me to come to her. "Oh God!" she said. "Oh God, come here! Come here this instant!"

I ran past Andy and knelt in front of her, like a knight returning to his queen. She put her shaking hands on my cheeks and tears rolled down her face and she smiled this sort of crazy smile. First a grin, then all wide open and joyful. I put my arms around her waist and my head on her lap and hugged her. I hugged the bottom half of her. She ran her hands over my messed-up hair and I could feel her tears drop against my face. Then I realized it wasn't her tears, but my own. Again. Twice in the same hour. At this rate I figured I'd be institutionalized.

"Where did you go?" she said. "Where have you been?"

"Running away and dying."

"What are you talking about, baby?"

I looked up, wiping tears away, and said, "I'm sorry, Mommy," and burst out sobbing. My whole face crumpled. I could feel it melt.

"Hush," she said. "It's okay. You're home now. You're home, baby."

"But I've ruined everything!" I sobbed.

She said, "No, you haven't."

"Yes, I have!" I said. "I have!"

She said, "Stop this! You haven't ruined anything," and pulled me to her for another hug.

"But you have a psycho for a son," I said. "How is that not ruining everything?"

She held me at arm's length and gave me a good looking over. "I wouldn't have it any other way," she said. "Besides, I love psychos. Who said I didn't love psychos? Psychos are the easiest people to love."

After hugging for a while longer she said she was going to make us breakfast. French toast and scrambled eggs and bacon. "A big breakfast for my boys," she kept saying. "A big breakfast for my boys."

When we went into the kitchen, everything seemed smaller there too, like the Peterson farm, like Andy. Only this was because everything *was* smaller. Also everything was a little fucked up. All the cupboard doors had about a quarter of their doors sawed off at the top, so my mom could reach down and open them easily, and there was this little plywood ramp that led up to a platform by the stove for my mom to sit at and cook. The ramp and platform took up half the kitchen, and I could tell my father had done all of this. It had the mark of his work. A little shoddy but heartfelt.

Andy started to wander back to his room, saying, "Gonna catch a few more Z's," and my mother looked up from a cupboard with a shocked look.

"You're going to what?"

Andy said, "Catch a few Z's."

"You're going to what?"

Andy came back into the kitchen and sat at the table, his face smoldering. "Nothing," he said.

"That's what I thought," said my mom.

I was thinking, *What the hell's happened here?* But I didn't even have to ask.

"I suppose you're wondering where your father is," my mom said. She dropped butter into the frying pan and it started to sizzle.

"Where?"

"Away," she said. "For now. Sit tight and I'll tell you all about it."

So while she wheeled back and forth from refrigerator to stove to counter, she told me what had happened.

What happened was, they kept on fighting as usual, and my dad kept getting on my mom to do her physical therapy, to stop moping around the house with Lucy, and she kept getting mad at him for telling her what to do, especially since, as she told him, she might not be in her situation if he hadn't been so mean. So she stayed at home and didn't try to get better. Or made it seem like that. It was her revenge, she said.

Then my father got called back to the construction company. He'd only been laid off for a little over a month. I guess they hadn't laid him off because he was a crappy worker, but because they really did have a slow month. So during the daytime he was gone again, and soon Lucy began to wake before my mother and go out for the day, sometimes to Abel's to do her drinking and socializing, sometimes just out driving, looking around at the flat land surrounding her on all sides. "My prison," she told my mother. "This place is my fucking prison."

"The thing is," said my mother, "I'd secretly been going to physical therapy all along." She'd called her doctor and said she wanted to do the therapy, but that she didn't want anyone to know. The doctor asked when would be a good time during the day and my mother said, "Afternoons. He'll be at work and I'll get Lucy to go out and run some errands." So the doctor agreed to help her.

He sent over a van for people who didn't have a way to get to the hospital, and four days a week my mother did her therapy religiously, and after a while she began to get a little feeling in her legs back. "It was just a tingle," she said. "But it was there. I felt it. I almost tried to walk for you all at Christmas, but I was worried I'd fall." She worked hard even after I'd run off again, though, and on the day that she was going to surprise my father, on the day she was going to stand up out of that chair on her own and shuffle out to meet him in the kitchen before he left for work, what she found when she got there was Lucy telling my dad, "Oh John. You're such a hard worker. How do you do it?"

And my dad saying, "What do you mean?"

"You know," said Lucy. "I understand. A person works hard for their family and what do you get in the way of love and respect? Nada. Just nagging and sulking and children who run away. Well, let me tell you, John McCormick," she said. "Let me tell you, you're twice the man my stupid old husband is, and you deserve a kiss." She stood on tiptoe to plant a kiss on my father, wrapping her arms around his waist. Her lips were already puckered, but before she could kiss him, my father pushed her away.

"Lucy," he said. "Thank you. But I'm married."

And right then, right there, witnessing her friend's betrayal, my mother's legs turned to butter beneath her, and she fell.

Both my dad and Lucy looked surprised and embarrassed, and what my mom said as soon as they came to her, their faces hovering above her, was, "Get out. The both of you. Get the hell out."

I didn't understand why she threw my dad out. For once he'd said the right thing, not yelling or calling anyone names. So I asked and my mother said, "I didn't throw him out because of what I saw, Adam. I threw him out because I needed to. I couldn't take his belittling any longer. And I couldn't take the way I was with him myself. He needs to learn how to talk to me. I need to learn how to stand on my own two feet. I can't do that with him around. Not right now at least."

I asked where he was living.

"With a friend from work."

"Will he come home again?"

"I don't know," she said, looking flustered. "Maybe after he knows the right words to use when he talks to me. Maybe after I know how to make myself happy."

She didn't look hopeful about either of those things getting done anytime soon, but she served our plates of French toast and scrambled eggs and bacon and the three of us sat around the table for the first time in I don't know how long. Before I even stuck a fork in those eggs, though, my mother said, "And you, mister—even though I am so thankful you are home, even though I will die if you do this to us one more time—you, sir, are grounded."

I didn't say anything, just nodded, then began eating.

God, how I missed her food! How I missed her and even Andy! And with my father not here like I'd expected, I found that I missed him too.

It seemed like I'd made the right decision, coming home, but before long Andy said what neither my mom or I wanted to think about. "You know the social worker is going to want in on this," he said, and we looked up from our food and sighed, our joy being sucked right out of us.

"We'll deal with it," said my mother. Then she cut away a square of French toast and, midway to her mouth, paused to look at me. "We'll deal with it right this time," she said.

I tried to smile innocently, but that didn't work. I wasn't innocent any longer. She finished eating, and after all of our plates were clean, she said, "You need to take a shower."

I said, "I know that."

She said, "I'm just saying."

I said, "Thanks for the reminder."

She said, "No problem. Now get that hot water running."

I said, "Okay, okay," and hightailed it to the bathroom where I could stand under the stream of hot water until it ran cold against my skin.

Later my mom and dad talked on the phone and after work my dad came over. We didn't hug and cry like my mom and I did, but he sat down next to me on the couch while we talked about how we needed to call Social Services and take care of making sure we did everything they needed so that maybe I wouldn't have to go to a detention center. I mean, I came home on my own this time, and it seemed like instead of bickering and fighting we were all ready to work with each other on something. We were all using the word we. Probably because we were exhausted and ready to put down our shields and swords, because we were ready to be wrong about ourselves and each other for once in our lives.

All of this kind of made me think everything would keep getting better, so when my dad got up to leave, I walked him to the front door. I wanted him to do something, to hug me like my mom did, or even tell me something nice. To look at me and say he was happy I was safe, something like that. It didn't have to be revolutionary. Just something that would make me feel like he wasn't sorry I'd been born. But I didn't get that. Instead he got in his van, and I waited in the doorway and watched as he backed out and left.

I sighed and behind me my mom said, "Adam, don't expect any miracles," and she was right. It was better, I figured, than him not being able to look at me at all, or telling me I didn't understand anything about the world. It was better than him breaking me open. I suppose he could have done that instead of just mainly keeping his mouth shut.

The next day my mom called the social worker and when she came a few days later I was clean and wearing nice clothes, and my mom had sent me to the barber to have my hacked-up hair evened out. I didn't give the social worker a hard time this time. I told the truth, mostly. I mean, I still didn't tell her I burned down the Wilkinson farm. That would have been a ticket straight to the detention center. I felt bad enough about burning it down already, so I cut myself that one break.

The social worker was still sweet as pie, with her silky voice and her smile ready to smooth over anything she said that could come off as slightly offensive. I was able to appreciate that more this time, but it still seemed fake. She recorded everything and thanked us and said she'd be in touch, and that with our cooperation things could go better than if we held them up at every corner. I told her I'd do whatever I had to and she said, "Well, now. Someone's had a change of heart." She smiled when she said it, but I felt bad all of a sudden because she was right.

I'd had a change of heart. I'd lost it. It was in a bunch of different places and pieces and I didn't know what to do with all the pieces but hold them in my hands and look down at them stupidly and feel like a loser. Like I'd lost everything good, or nearly everything.

I still had the pieces of Gracie's rose quartz heart too. I'd taken them out of the pocket of the jeans I'd been wearing all winter, along with the crow feather, before my mom threw the jeans in the trash, proclaiming them done for. Gracie's heart and the crow feather sat on my dresser now, the shiny black feather leaning against the rubble of rose quartz. They were my altar. I kept finding myself standing in front of it, staring, wondering how I'd let things get so fucked up. For Gracie, for Jamie, for my family, for myself. I know not everything was my fault, but it sure felt like it.

Most nights I had trouble sleeping, like I had when Jamie first came to me. But now I couldn't sleep because I couldn't stop my thoughts from racing. What if I'd done this differently? What if Gracie had said such and such a thing at such and such a time? What if Jamie hadn't waited so long to cross the bridge? Regrets. Trying to figure out ways things could have gone better. I'd think about these things for hours, until I fell asleep from sheer exhaustion. And then I'd usually fall into a dreamless black sleep.

But one night, several weeks after I came home, I fell asleep after my regular hours of self-torture and immediately stumbled into a dream that, when I woke, I could actually remember.

In the dream my mom and dad and I were standing outside on the front porch. In this dream our house was a split-level, not the one level ranch my dad built years ago. The change didn't shock us. We'd all come from our separate dreams to meet here. We heard a lot of noise going on inside. Someone was in there, smashing plates and glasses, turning over furniture. On the second floor a window shattered and one of my running trophies landed at our feet. My mother said, "Your brother tells me this house is haunted."

My father said, "It is. It's haunted. I've seen it with my own eyes." He said this matter-of-factly, but when I looked at his eyes, they were afraid, and I could tell he was paralyzed by his own knowledge.

I said, "We have to go see it. Whatever it is. We can't just ignore it."

My father wouldn't go inside, but my mother agreed to come with me, so we opened the front door slowly and snuck in.

Immediately all of the noises got louder. Someone was running back and forth along the hall above us. This someone sounded like they kept falling, getting up again, running and falling, over and over, crashing into things and growling.

Then suddenly it appeared at the top of the staircase, a short, stocky creature made of hairy darkness, its eyes glowing red. Its hair dangled and swayed in its face like tendrils of shadow. It ran down the stairs and, as soon as it reached the first floor, fell on its face. It immediately picked itself up, though, as if the fall and the rise were one motion, the same movement, orchestrated like the creature was part of a strange ballet. It turned and ran into the kitchen and I said, "We have to stop it," so my mother and I followed, hot on its heels.

As we turned the corner to the kitchen, we saw it run toward the garage door, seeking a way out. But it could only jiggle the doorknob like an animal that doesn't understand architecture. It heard us then, and turned around in a crouch, growling. A grin slid up one side of its face, and it ran toward us, sharp teeth bared.

"Throw me at it!" I told my mother, who was frozen with fear in her wheelchair.

"No!" she said. "I won't let you do that!"

"You have to help me!" I said. "Throw me at it, damn it!"

She didn't like the idea of me fighting this creature, but she stood up out of her wheelchair anyway. She stood up and grabbed hold of my arms and began to twirl in a circle like a discus thrower. My body lifted out and away from her, and I remembered her and my dad doing this with me when I was little, holding my hands and twirling me in the air like a doll. She spun and spun, finally releasing me. I flew at the creature, who was running full steam ahead, and when we collided—it grabbing hold of my forearms, me grabbing hold of its shoulders, our faces millimeters apart—it began to curse in a dark language that I only half understood. I didn't need to know much in order to understand it meant to kill me, so I cursed back, my own teeth bared, my own spit flying as we wrestled on the kitchen floor.

I woke up still gnashing my teeth and cursing, fighting

my pillow, and couldn't get back to sleep. It was still with me, I realized. Something dark and strange and deadly still lingered. A man with no skin maybe, or a shadow that had cut the cord to its person. I'd gone into its territory and it had followed me out. I'd never be rid of it, I thought. I'll never be far enough away from that hole, I realized, to feel safe.

After a while I started seeing Dr. Phelps again, who was a decent guy really, but I preferred calling Kurt at the bookstore to telling Dr. Phelps about my problems. He was glad to hear I was okay, and said I could call anytime I wanted to just talk about anything. I liked talking to him because he mostly just said things how they are, like my grandma used to. And he didn't try to comfort me with false hope. He'd tell me I was doing fine and to keep going forward, but he wouldn't lie by saying stuff like, "Everything's going to be all right," like just about everyone else in the world told me. Some things would be all right, I knew. But there were also a lot of things that were fucked for good, gone forever, pieces of me from before all of this started that I'd never get back. And the really desperate thing was that sometimes, oftentimes, I didn't know if the me I was now was better than the me I was then. That was one thing I didn't know if I could ever get over.

I started going back to school again too. Only not to the high school. I had to have lessons with a tutor, and I had to go to summer school to catch up, which majorly sucked. All of that running around I'd done hadn't gotten me any-where once I came back to the land of the living. The good thing, though, was that I'm a good runner—I'd proven that—so I wasn't afraid I wouldn't be able to do the things I had to in order to catch up. I'd "apply myself." I'd be a "model student." In no time flat, I figured I could win back the faith of my teachers.

And that's what happened for the most part. I did summer school and rejoined my class in the fall, even though I still had a couple of courses I was behind in. I'd have to make those up on the side with tutoring and summer school again the following year. I was a part of things again, I guess.

School was the same as I'd left it. A bit cold, a bit distant. I walked the hallways alone mostly. Occasionally someone would attempt to strike up something like a friendship with me, and I'd try my best to do that. It was hard, though. Hard to go back to after having seen what I'd seen, after having lost what I'd lost. Hard to try and talk to a kid from a small town in Ohio who'd never run away from home, or didn't know what sunflowers and moonlight were all about yet. They had time. They had plenty of time. I wanted to tell them to stay a kid for as long as possible, because I didn't feel like one any longer and in most ways it sucked. I was doing fine, like Kurt said, but the world didn't always feel fine to me.

I missed them terribly. I missed them with all of what I guess was left of my heart. It hurt a lot, this pain in my chest, to be back home again, to still hear my mom and dad bitching at each other, calling each other names, only now it was on the phone instead of in the house. It hurt to ride my bike past the remains of the Wilkinson farm. The old falling down barn had been burned down too, this time by the volunteer fire department. So what was left was the family cemetery, the headstones leaning toward one another behind the wrought-iron fence. It hurt to ride past the Highsmith house, with its

For Sale sign out front, to look in the front windows and see the empty room where Gracie and I had once sat on the couch watching soap operas, listening to Jamie's mother go on about her son's death eventually meaning something. It was hard to go past the Marks place and see Mrs. Marks feeding the dogs under the weeping willow trees, alone, her husband returning with greater and greater gaps between visits. It was hard to ride through town square, past the Wildwood Café, and catch the stares of people whose shadows still speculated about my disappearance, about what had happened between my parents, about what part Lucy Hall had played in their separation. John McCormick kept telling everyone he and his wife would be back together one day, but the shadows had bets going. Most of them didn't think the odds were in favor of the McCormick family. Maybe that was true, though. My grandma had seen it coming years ago. Our family had been picked out for sadness. But somehow we were surviving. Just in pieces. And even though the shadows set odds against us, I thought we hadn't done so bad really. After all, we'd survived my running away and dying. After all, we'd survived Lucy Hall. We were strong in some ways. Like those families on soap operas who were always targeted by someone evil, in the end we came together. And for me this was a sign of something promising. I told myself to keep a lookout for more signs. My grandma hadn't told me good things come in threes, but I figured if bad things did, good things had to also.

I went back to spending a lot of time on the computer, playing online games like I used to. I didn't play *Nevermorrow*. Instead I played things like Scrabble and Wordbattle, which was this game where you had to figure out the definition of a word before your opponent did. Lots of people got online in game rooms to kill time or socialize to the best of their abilities, and for me it was easier to do this than try too hard at school and attract a lot of negative attention.

One night I was playing a game of Scrabble with several people, and I was winning until one of them spelled out a word so long it put them above my score and I came in second. The word was sunflower. And then a box popped up with a message from the winner: IgneousGirlinOhio.

so ur alive, huh?

who's this?

who do u think, genius?

I froze up then. My fingers hovered over the keyboard in limbo. And then after a while another message popped up.

arent u going to say anything?

i'm sorry i'm sorry i'm sorry

As I sent the message, my eyes filled up. I hadn't cried in a while. I thought maybe I'd cried out everything, but now I knew I could probably cry forever when I thought of either of them. And here she was, this girl, coming toward me out of the ether of words on a screen, asking me—*me*—if I was going to say anything.

i'm sorry 2. i'm glad I ran into u. we should talk.

where r u?

cleveland heights. my dad moved us here after the whole closet incident.

i turned 16 this summer. i'll get my license after my driving lessons. i'll come up & c u.

i already have my license. i'll come down 2 u.

Like that we kept on talking. Words kept appearing on the screen, and with each one I felt a warmth grow inside me.

I went to bed that night with my head full of words, hers

and mine and his. They buzzed around in me like bees darting in every direction. I couldn't sleep. I was used to not sleeping, but I wasn't used to it being because of feeling something like happiness. And I wasn't used to not sleeping because of too much noise in my head either. Usually it was too much silence, me staring up at the ceiling, the silence an ocean roar.

But strangely enough, as my head started to clear, I realized I'd been hearing a sound all night, in the background of my mind's ramblings. I'd thought it was Andy playing music in the next room, but after I listened hard I realized I was hearing my own heart beating. It was a familiar sound. It was a sound I used to hear as a little kid when I went to sleep. It used to lull me into dreams, into oblivion, into a different world. At some point it had faded. I always wondered what had happened, where it went to. But here it was again, beating, beating, thudding its crazy rhythm. I could hear the blood coursing through me. I could feel it again, my own life pulsing.

Right then I thought, *You can live again.* You can take the steps toward the finish line without too much fear or sadness. And even if you sometimes fell in the process of getting there, it didn't have to mean you were done for. It didn't have to mean you'd fallen from grace, but that maybe you'd had the grace to fall in the first place. That you'd had the grace to get back up again. To go toward it. To cross the finish line without knowing what comes after.

Right then I knew that for the rest of my life I'd have to remember everything. I'd have to remember everything so that, next time I saw him, I could tell him all about it. About this place. About the life that came after.

AD INFINITUM

ACKNOWLEDGMENTS

THIS BOOK WOULDN'T HAVE BEEN WRITTEN IF not for the help of a great many people. My parents, Donald and Joyce Barzak, have helped me to pursue my passion for writing without understanding why I do it, and for that I am eternally grateful. Where they were unable to help, teachers and friends were always there. Patricia Kostraba first encouraged me, and my professors at Youngstown State University gave me the guidance I needed in the beginning. Philip Brady, Michael Finney, Linda Strom and Rebecca Barnhouse took my writing seriously. The Imagination Workshop at Cleveland State University introduced me to writers who gave me direction. Karen Joy Fowler, Jonathan Lethem, Jim Kelly and Mary Rosenblum were all early encouragers. Without them I may not have found my way to the Clarion workshop in 1998. Thank you to Kelly Link and Gavin Grant for friendship and support, and all the books and disco balls sent over the years. Alan Deniro and Kristin Livdahl for taking care of me when no one else knew how. Elad Haber for his fierce loyalty. Mary Rickert for her deep-hearted friendship and understanding. Yoshio Kobayashi for befriending this foreigner. Terri Windling and Midori Snyder, for all their kindness and support. Charlie Finlay for inviting me to the Blue Heaven workshop. Maureen McHugh for telling him to. Chris Schelling, agent extraordinaire. Barbara Gilly, Richard Butner, Christopher Rowe, Gwenda Bond, Scott Westerfeld and Justine Larbelestier, for their very treasured friendship. Matthew Cheney, for reaching out across the ocean. Juliet Ulman, for keeping me honest. Regina Donaldson, for all the hours. Ron Gause, for always trying. And Rick Bowes, who said it was time to write a goodbye letter. So I did.

Thank you all so much.